THE ISLE
OF UNREST

HENRY SETON MERRIMAN

The Isle of Unrest

Henry Seton Merriman

© 1st World Library – Literary Society, 2004
PO Box 2211
Fairfield, IA 52556
www.1stworldlibrary.org
First Edition

LCCN: 2004195309

Softcover ISBN: 1-4218-0140-X
Hardcover ISBN: 1-4218-0040-3
eBook ISBN: 1-4218-0240-6

Purchase *"The Isle of Unrest"*
as a traditional bound book at:
www.1stWorldLibrary.org/purchase.asp?ISBN=1-4218-0140-X

1st World Library Literary Society is a nonprofit
organization dedicated to promoting literacy by:

- Creating a free internet library accessible from any
computer worldwide.
- Hosting writing competitions and offering book
publishing scholarships.

Readers interested in supporting literacy
through sponsorship, donations or
membership please contact:
literacy@1stworldlibrary.org
Check us out at: www.1stworldlibrary.ORG
and start downloading free ebooks today.

The Isle of Unrest
contributed by Tim, Ed & Rodney
in support of
1st World Library Literary Society

TO LUCASTA

GOING TO THE WARS

Tell me not, sweet, I am unkind
That from the nunnery
Of thy chaste breast, and quiet mind,
To war and arms I fly.

True: a new mistress now I chase,
The first foe in the field;
And with a stronger faith embrace
A sword, a horse, a shield.

Yet this inconstancy is such
As you too shall adore;
I could not love thee, dear, so much
Lov'd I not honour more.

RICHARD LOVELACE.

CONTENTS

CHAPTER I.

THE MOVING FINGER.

"The Moving Finger writes; and, having writ,
Moves on: nor all thy piety nor wit
Shall lure it back to cancel half a line,
Nor all thy tears wash out a word of it."

The afternoon sun was lowering towards a heavy bank of clouds hanging still and sullen over the Mediterranean. A mistral was blowing. The last yellow rays shone fiercely upon the towering coast of Corsica, and the windows of the village of Olmeta glittered like gold.

There are two Olmetas in Corsica, both in the north, both on the west coast, both perched high like an eagle's nest, both looking down upon those lashed waters of the Mediterranean, which are not the waters that poets sing of, for they are as often white as they are blue; they are seldom glassy except in the height of summer and sailors tell that they are as treacherous as any waters of the earth. Neither aneroid nor weather-wisdom may, as a matter of fact, tell when a mistral will arise, how it will blow, how veer, how drop and rise, and drop again. For it will blow one day beneath a cloudless sky, lashing the whole sea white like milk, and blow harder to-morrow under racing clouds.

The great chestnut trees in and around Olmeta groaned and strained in the grip of their lifelong foe. The small door, the tiny windows, of every house were rigorously closed. The whole place had a wind-swept air despite the heavy foliage. Even the roads, and notably the broad "Place," had been swept clean and dustless. And in the middle of the "Place," between the fountain and the church steps, a man lay dead upon his face.

It is as well to state here, once for all, that we are dealing with Olmeta-di-Tuda, and not that other Olmeta - the virtuous, di Capocorso, in fact, which would shudder at the thought of a dead man lying on its "Place," before the windows of the very Mairie, under the shadow of the church. For Cap Corse is the good boy of Corsica, where men think sorrowfully of the wilder communes to the south, and raise their eyebrows at the very mention of Corte and Sartene - where, at all events, the women have for husbands, men - and not degenerate Pisan vine-snippers.

It was not so long ago either. For the man might have been alive to-day, though he would have been old and bent no doubt; for he was a thick-set man, and must have been strong. He had, indeed, carried his lead up from the road that runs by the Guadelle river. Was he not to be traced all the way up the short cut through the olive terraces by one bloody footprint at regular intervals? You could track his passage across the "Place," towards the fountain of which he had fallen short like a poisoned rat that tries to reach water and fails.

He lay quite alone, still grasping the gun which he had

Henry Seton Merriman

never laid aside since boyhood. No one went to him; no one had attempted to help him. He lay as he had fallen, with a thin stream of blood running slowly from one trouser-leg. For this was Corsican work - that is to say, dirty work - from behind a rock, in the back, at close range, without warning or mercy, as honest men would be ashamed to shoot the merest beast of the forest. It was as likely as not a charge of buck-shot low down in the body, leaving the rest to hemorrhage or gangrene.

All Olmeta knew of it, and every man took care that it should be no business of his. Several had approached, pipe in mouth, and looked at the dead man without comment; but all had gone away again, idly, indifferently. For in this the most beautiful of the islands, human life is held cheaper than in any land of Europe.

Some one, it was understood, had gone to tell the gendarmes down at St. Florent. There was no need to send and tell his wife - half a dozen women were racing through the olive groves to get the first taste of that. Perhaps some one had gone towards Oletta to meet the Abbé Susini, whose business in a measure this must be.

The sun suddenly dipped behind the heavy bank of clouds and the mountains darkened. Although it lies in the very centre of the Mediterranean, Corsica is a gloomy land, and the summits of her high mountains are more often covered than clear. It is a land of silence and brooding quiet. The women are seldom gay; the men, in their heavy clothes of dark corduroy, have little to say for themselves. Some of them were standing now in the shadow of the great trees, smoking their pipes in silence, and looking with a studied indifference at nothing. Each was prepared to swear before a jury at the Bastia assizes that he knew nothing of the "accident," as it is here called, to Pietro Andrei, and had not seen him crawl up to Olmeta to die. Indeed, Pietro Andrei's death seemed to be nobody's business, though we are told that not so much as a sparrow may fall unheeded.

The Abbé Susini was coming now - a little fiery man, with the walk of one who was slightly bow-legged, though his cassock naturally concealed this defect. He was small and not too broad, with a narrow face and clean, straight features - something of the Spaniard, something of the Greek, nothing Italian, nothing French. In a word, this was a Corsican, which is to say that he was different from any other European race, and would, as sure as there is corn in Egypt, be overbearing, masterful, impossible. He was, of course, clean shaven, as brown as old oak, with little flashing black eyes. His cassock was a good one, and his hat, though dusty, shapely and new. But his whole bearing threw, as it were, into the observer's face the suggestion that the habit does not make the priest.

He came forward without undue haste, and displayed little surprise and no horror.

"Quite like old times," he said to himself, remembering the days of Louis Philippe. He knelt down beside the dead man, and perhaps the attitude reminded him of his calling; for he fell to praying, and made the gesture of the cross over Andrei's head. Then suddenly he leapt to his feet, and shook his lean fist out towards the valley and St. Florent, as if he knew whence this trouble came.

"Provided they would keep their work in their own commune," he cried, "instead of bringing disgrace on a parish that has not had the gendarmes this - this - "

"Three days," added one of the bystanders, who had drawn near. And he said it with a certain pride, as of one well pleased to belong to a virtuous community.

But the priest was not listening. He had already turned aside in his quick, jerky way; for he was a comparatively young man. He was looking through the olives towards the south.

"It is the women," he said, and his face suddenly hardened. He was impulsive, it appeared - quick to feel for others, fiery in his anger, hasty in his judgment.

From the direction in which he and the bystanders looked, came the hum of many voices, and the high, incessant shrieks of one who seemed demented. Presently a confused procession appeared from the direction of the south, hurrying through the narrow street now called the Rue Carnot. It was headed by a woman, who led a little child, running and stumbling as he ran. At her heels a number of women hurried, confusedly shouting, moaning, and wailing. The men stood waiting for them in dead silence - a characteristic scene. The leading woman seemed to be superior to her neighbours, for she wore a black silk handkerchief on her head instead of a white or coloured cotton. It is almost a mantilla, and marks as clear a social distinction in Corsica as does that head-dress in Spain. She dragged at the child, and scarce turned her head when he fell and scrambled as best he could to his feet. He laughed and crowed with delight, remembering last year's carnival with that startling, photographic memory of early childhood which never forgets.

At every few steps the woman gave a shriek as if she were suffering some intermittent agony which caught her at regular intervals. At the sight of the crowd she gave a quick cry of despair, and ran forward, leaving her child sprawling on the road. She knelt by the dead man's side with shriek after shriek, and seemed to lose all control over herself, for she gave way to those strange gestures of despair of which many read in novels and a few in the Scriptures, and which come by instinct to those who have no reading at all. She dragged the handkerchief from her head, and threw it over her face. She beat her breast. She beat the very ground with her clenched hands. Her little boy, having gathered his belongings together and dusted his cotton frock, now came forward, and stood watching her with his fingers at his mouth. He took it to be a game which he did not understand; as indeed it was - the game of life.

The priest scratched his chin with his forefinger, which was probably a habit with him when puzzled, and stood looking down out of the corner of his eyes at the ground.

It was he, however, who moved first, and, stooping, loosed the clenched fingers round the gun. It was a double-barrelled gun, at full cock, and every man in the little crowd assembled carried one like it. To this day, if one meets a man, even in the streets of Corte or Ajaccio, who carries no gun, it may be presumed that it is only because he pins greater faith on a revolver.

Neither hammer had fallen, and the abbé gave a little nod. It was, it seemed, the usual thing to make quite

Henry Seton Merriman

sure before shooting, so that there might be no unnecessary waste of powder or risk of reprisal. The woman looked at the gun, too, and knew the meaning of the raised hammers.

She leapt to her feet, and looked round at the sullen faces.

"And some of you know who did it," she said; "and you will help the murderer when he goes to the macquis, and take him food, and tell him when the gendarmes are hunting him."

She waved her hand fiercely towards the mountains, which loomed, range behind range, dark and forbidding to the south, towards Calvi and Corte. But the men only shrugged their shoulders; for the forest and the mountain brushwood were no longer the refuge they used to be in this the last year of the iron rule of Napoleon III, who, whether he possessed or not the Corsican blood that his foes deny him, knew, at all events, how to rule Corsica better than any man before or since.

"No, no," said the priest, soothingly. "Those days are gone. He will be taken, and justice will be done."

But he spoke without conviction, almost as if he had no faith in this vaunted regeneration of a people whose history is a story of endless strife - as if he could see with a prophetic eye thirty years into the future, down to the present day, when the last state of that land is worse than the first.

"Justice!" cried the woman. "There is no justice in Corsica! What had Pietro done that he should lie there?

Only his duty - only that for which he was paid. He was the Perucca's agent, and because he made the idlers pay their rent, they threatened him. Because he put up fences, they raised their guns to him. Because he stopped their thieving and their lawlessness, they shoot him. He drove their cattle from the fields because they were Perucca's fields, and he was paid to watch his master's interests. But Perucca they dare not touch, because his clan is large, and would hunt the murderer down. If he was caught, the Peruccas would make sure of the jury - ay! And of the judge at Bastia - but Pietro is not of Corsica; he has no friends and no clan, so justice is not for him."

She knelt down again as she spoke and laid her hand on her dead husband's back, but she made no attempt to move him. For although Pietro Andrei was an Italian, his wife was Corsican - a woman of Bonifacio, that grim town on a rock so often besieged and never yet taken by a fair fight. She had been brought up in, as it were, an atmosphere of conventional lawlessness, and knew that it is well not to touch a dead man till the gendarmes have seen him, but to send a child or an old woman to the gendarmerie, and then to stand aloof and know nothing; and feign stupidity; so that the officials, when they arrive, may find the whole village at work in the fields or sitting in their homes, while the dead, who can tell no tales, has suddenly few friends and no enemies.

Then Andrei's widow rose slowly to her feet. Her face was composed now and set. She arranged the black silk handkerchief on her head, and set her dress in order. She was suddenly calm and quiet. "But see," she said, looking round into eyes that failed to meet her own, "in this country each man must execute his own justice. It has always been so, and it will be so, so long as there are any Corsicans left. And if there is no man left, then the women must do it."

She tied her apron tighter, as if about to undertake some hard domestic duty, and brushed the dust from her black dress.

"Come here," she said, turning to the child, and lapsing into the soft dialect of the south and east - "come here, thou child of Pietro Andrei."

The child came forward. He was probably two years old, and understood nothing that was passing.

"See here, you of Olmeta," she said composedly; and, stooping down, she dipped her finger in the pool of blood that had collected in the dust. "See here - and here."

As she spoke she hastily smeared the blood over the child's face and dragged him away from the priest, who had stepped forward.

"No, no," he protested. "Those times are past."

"Past!" said the woman, with a flash of fury. "All the country knows that your own mother did it to you at Sartene, where you come from."

The abbé made no answer, but, taking the child by the arm, dragged him gently away from his mother. With his other hand he sought in his pocket for a handkerchief. But he was a lone man, without a housekeeper, and the handkerchief was missing. The child looked from one to the other, laughing uncertainly, with his grimly decorated face.

Then the priest stooped, and with the skirt of his cassock wiped the child's face.

"There," he said to the woman, "take him home, for I hear the gendarmes coming."

Indeed, the trotting of horses and the clank of the long swinging sabres could be heard on the road below the village, and one by one the onlookers dropped away, leaving the Abbé Susini alone at the foot of the church steps.

Henry Seton Merriman

CHAPTER II.

CHEZ CLÉMENT.

"Comme on est heureux quand on sait ce qu'on veut!"

It was the dinner hour at the Hotel Clément at Bastia; and the event was of greater importance than the outward appearance of the house would seem to promise. For there is no promise at all about the house on the left-hand side of Bastia's one street, the Boulevard du Palais, which bears, as its only sign, a battered lamp with the word "Clément" printed across it. The ground floor is merely a rope and hemp warehouse. A small Corsican donkey, no bigger than a Newfoundland dog, lives in the basement, and passes many of his waking hours in what may be termed the entrance hall of the hotel, appearing to consider himself in some sort a concierge. The upper floors of the huge Genoese house are let out in large or small apartments to mysterious families, of which the younger members are always to be met carrying jugs carefully up and down the greasy, common staircase.

The first floor is the Hotel Clément, or, to be more correct, one is "chez Clément" on the first floor.

"You stay with Clément," will be the natural remark of

any on board the Marseilles or Leghorn steamer, on being told that the traveller disembarks at Bastia.

"We shall meet to-night chez Clément," the officers say to each other on leaving the parade ground at four o'clock.

"Déjeuner chez Clément," is the usual ending to a notice of a marriage, or a first communion, in the *Petit Bastiais*, that greatest of all foolscap-size journals.

It is comforting to reflect, in these times of hurried changes, that the traveller to Bastia may still find himself chez Clément - may still have to kick at the closed door of the first-floor flat, and find that door opened by Clément himself, always affable, always gentlemanly, with the same crumbs strewed carelessly down the same waistcoat, or, if it is evening time, in his spotless cook's dress. One may be sure of the same grave welcome, and the easy transition from grave to gay, the smiling, grand manner of conducting the guest to one of those vague and darksome bedrooms, where the jug and the basin never match, where the floor is of red tiles, with a piece of uncertain carpet sliding hither and thither, with the shutters always shut, and the mustiness of the middle ages hanging heavy in the air. For Bastia has not changed, and never will. And it is not only to be fervently hoped, but seems likely, that Clément will never grow old, and never die, but continue to live and demonstrate the startling fact that one may be born and live all one's life in a remote, forgotten town, and still be a man of the world.

The soup had been served precisely at six, and the four artillery officers were already seated at the square table near the fireplace, which was and is still exclusively

Henry Seton Merriman

the artillery table. The other *habitués* were in their places at one or other of the half-dozen tables that fill the room - two gentlemen from the Prefecture, a civil engineer of the projected railway to Corte, a commercial traveller of the old school, and, at the corner table, farthest from the door, Colonel Gilbert of the Engineers. A clever man this, who had seen service in the Crimea, and had invariably distinguished himself whenever the opportunity occurred; but he was one of those who await, and do not seek opportunities. Perhaps he had enemies, or, what is worse, no friends; for at the age of forty he found himself appointed to Bastia, one of the waste places of the War Office, where an inferior man would have done better.

Colonel Gilbert was a handsome man, with a fair moustache, a high forehead, surmounted by thin, receding, smooth hair, and good-natured, idle eyes. He lunched and dined chez Clément always, and was frankly, good naturedly bored at Bastia. He hated Corsica, had no sympathy with the Corsican, and was a Northern Frenchman to the tips of his long white fingers.

"Your Bastia, my good Clément," he said to the host, who invariably came to the dining-room with the roast and solicited the opinion of each guest upon the dinner in a few tactful, easy words - "your Bastia is a sad place."

This evening Colonel Gilbert was in a less talkative mood than usual, and exchanged only a nod with his artillery colleagues as he passed to his own small table. He opened his newspaper, and became interested in it at once. It was several days old, and had come by way of Nice and Ajaccio from Paris. All France was at this time eager for news, and every Frenchman studied the journal of his choice with that uneasiness which seems to foreshadow in men's hearts the approach of any great event. For this was the spring of 1870, when France, under the hitherto iron rule of her adventurer emperor, suddenly began to plunge and rear, while the nations stood around her wondering who should receive the first kick. The emperor was ill; the cheaper journals were already talking of his funeral. He was uneasy and restless, turning those dull eyes hither and thither over Europe - a man of inscrutable face and deep hidden plans - perhaps the greatest adventurer who ever sat a throne. Condemned by a French Court of Peers in 1840 to imprisonment for life, he went to Ham with the quiet question, "But how long does perpetuity last in France?" And eight years later he was absolute master of the country.

Corsica in particular was watching events, for Corsica was cowed. She had come under the rule of this despot, and for the first time in her history had found her master. Instead of being numbered by hundreds, as they were before and are again now at the end of the century, the outlaws hiding in the mountains scarce exceeded a score. The elections were conducted more honestly than had ever been before, and the Continental newspapers spoke hopefully of the dawn of civilization showing itself among a people who have ever been lawless, have ever loved war better than peace.

"But it is a false dawn," said the Abbé Susini of Olmeta, himself an insatiable reader of newspapers, a keen and ardent politician. Like the majority of Corsicans, he was a staunch Bonapartist, and held that the founder of that marvellous dynasty was the greatest man to walk this earth since the days of direct Divine inspiration.

It was only because Napoleon III was a Bonaparte that Corsica endured his tyranny; perhaps, indeed, tyranny and an iron rule suited better than equity or tolerance a people descended from the most ancient of the fighting races, speaking a tongue wherein occur expressions of hate and strife that are Tuscan, Sicilian, Greek, Spanish, and Arabic.

Now that the emperor's hand was losing its grip on the helm, there were many in Corsica keenly alive to the fact that any disturbance in France would probably lead to anarchy in the turbulent island. There were even some who saw a hidden motive in the appointment of Colonel Gilbert as engineer officer to a fortified place that had no need of his services.

Gilbert himself probably knew that his appointment had been made in pursuance of the emperor's policy of road and rail. For Corsica was to be opened up by a railway, and would have none of it. And though to-day the railway from Bastia to Ajaccio is at last open, the station at Corte remains a fortified place with a loopholed wall around it.

But Colonel Gilbert kept his own counsel. He sat, indeed, on the board of the struggling railway - a gift of the French Government to a department which has never paid its way, has always been an open wound. But he never spoke there, and listened to the fierce speeches of the local members with his idle, easy smile. He seemed to stand aloof from his new neighbours and their insular interests. He was, it appeared, a cultured man, and perhaps found none in this wild island who could understand his thoughts. His attitude towards his surroundings was, in a word, the usual indifferent attitude of the Frenchman in exile, reading only French newspapers, fixing his attention only on France, and awaiting with such patience as he could command the moment to return thither.

"Any news?" asked one of the artillery officers - a sub-lieutenant recently attached to his battery, a penniless possessor of an historic name, who perhaps had dreams of carving his way through to the front again.

The colonel shrugged his shoulders.

"You may have the papers afterwards," he said; for it was not wise to discuss any news in a public place at that time. "See you at the Réunion, no doubt."

And he did not speak again except to Clément, who came round to take the opinion of each guest upon the fare provided.

"Passable," said the colonel - "passable, my good Clément. But do you know, I could send you to prison for providing this excellent leveret at this time of year. Are there no game laws, my friend?"

But Clement only laughed and spread out his hands, for Corsica chooses to ignore the game laws. And the colonel, having finished his coffee, buckled on his sword, and went out into the twilight streets of what was once the capital of Corsica. Bastia, indeed, has, like the majority of men and women, its history written on its face. On the high land above the old port stands the citadel, just as the Genoese merchant-adventurers planned it five hundred years ago. Beneath the citadel, and clustered round the port, is the little old Genoese town, no bigger than a village, which served for two hundred and fifty years as capital to an island in constant war, against which it had always to defend itself.

It would seem that some hundred years ago, just before the island became nominally a French possession, Bastia, for some reason or another, took it into its municipal head to grow, and it ran as it were all down the hill to that which is now the new harbour. It built two broad streets of tall Genoese houses, of which one somehow missed fire, and became a slum, while the other, with its great houses but half inhabited, is to-day the Boulevard du Palais, where fashionable Bastia promenades itself - when it is too windy, as it almost always is, to walk on the Place St. Nicholas - where all the shops are, and where the modern European necessities of daily life are not to be bought for love or money.

There are, however, two excellent knife-shops in the Boulevard du Palais, where every description of stiletto may be purchased, where, indeed, the enterprising may buy a knife which will not only go shrewdly into a foe, but come right out on the other side - in front, that is to say, for no true Corsican is so foolish as to stab anywhere but in the back - and, protruding thus, will display some pleasing legend, such as "Vendetta," or "I serve my master," or "Viva Corsica," roughly engraved on the long blade. There is a macaroni warehouse. There are two of those mysterious Mediterranean provision warehouses, with some ancient dried sausages hanging in the window, and either doorpost flanked by a tub of sardines, highly, and yet, it would seem, insufficiently, cured.

There is a tiny book-shop displaying a choice of religious pamphlets and a fly-blown copy of a treatise on viniculture. And finally, an ironmonger will sell you anything but a bath, while he thrives on a lively trade in percussion-caps and gunpowder.

Colonel Gilbert did not pause to look at these bewildering shop-windows, for the simple reason that he knew every article there displayed.

He was, it will be remembered, a leisurely Frenchman, than whom there are few human beings of a more easily aroused attention. Any small street incident sufficed to make him pause. He had the air of one waiting for a train, who knows that it will not come for hours yet. He strolled down the boulevard, smoking a cigarette, and presently turned to the right, emerging with head raised to meet the sea-breeze upon that deserted promenade, the Place St. Nicholas.

Here he paused, and stood with his head slightly inclined to one side - an attitude usually considered to be indicative of the artistic temperament, and admired the prospect. The "Place" was deserted, and in the middle the great statue of Napoleon stood staring blankly across the sea towards Elba. There is, whether the artist intended it or not, a look of stony amazement on this marble face as it gazes at the island of Elba lying pink and hazy a few miles across that rippled sea; for on this side of Corsica there is more peace than in the open waters of the Gulf of Lyons.

"Surely," that look seems to say, "the world could never expect that puny island to hold me."

Colonel Gilbert stood and looked dreamily across the

Henry Seton Merriman

sea. It was plain to the most incompetent observer that the statue represented one class of men - those who make their opportunities; while Gilbert, with his high and slightly receding forehead, his lazy eyes and good-natured mouth, was a fair type of that other class which may take advantage of opportunities that offer themselves. The majority of men have not even the pluck to do that, which makes it easy for mediocre people to get on in this world.

Colonel Gilbert turned on his heel and walked slowly back to the Reunion des Officiers - the military club which stands on the Place St. Nicholas immediately behind the statue of Napoleon - a not too lively place of entertainment, with a billiard-room, a reading-room, and half a dozen iron tables and chairs on the pavement in front of the house. Here the colonel seated himself, called for a liqueur, and sat watching a clear moon rise from the sea beyond the Islet of Capraja.

It was the month of February, and the southern spring was already in the air. The twilight is short in these latitudes, and it was now nearly night. In Corsica, as in Spain, the coolest hour is between sunset and nightfall. With complete darkness there comes a warm air from the ground. This was now beginning to make itself felt; but Gilbert had not only the pavement, but the whole Place St. Nicholas to himself. There are two reasons why Corsicans do not walk abroad at night - the risk of a chill and the risk of meeting one's enemy.

Colonel Gilbert gave no thought to these matters, but sat with crossed legs and one spurred heel thrown out, contentedly waiting as if for that train which he must assuredly catch, or for that opportunity, perhaps, which was so long in coming that he no longer seemed to look for it. And while he sat there a man came clanking from the town - a tired man, with heavy feet and the iron heels of the labourer. He passed Colonel Gilbert, and then, seeming to have recognized him by the light of the moon, paused, and came back.

"Monsieur le colonel," he said, without raising his hand to his hat, as a Frenchman would have done.

"Yes," replied the colonel's pleasant voice, with no ring of recognition in it.

"It is Mattei - the driver of the St. Florent diligence," explained the man, who, indeed, carried his badge of office, a long whip.

"Of course; but I recognized you almost at once," said the colonel, with that friendliness which is so noticeable in the Republic to-day.

"You have seen me on the road often enough," said the man, "and I have seen you, Monsieur le Colonel, riding over to the Casa Perucca."

"Of course."

"You know Perucca's agent, Pietro Andrei?"

"Yes."

"He was shot in the back on the Olmeta road this afternoon."

Colonel Gilbert gave a slight start.

"Is that so?" he said at length, quietly, after a pause.

"Yes," said the diligence-driver; and without further comment he walked on, keeping well in the middle of the road, as it is wise to do when one has enemies.

CHAPTER III.

A BY-PATH.

"L'intrigue c'est tromper son homme; L'habileté c'est faire qu'il se trompe lui-même."

For an idle-minded man, Colonel Gilbert was early astir the next morning, and rode out of the town soon after sunrise, following the Vescovato road, and chatting pleasantly enough with the workers already on foot and in saddle on their way to the great plain of Biguglia, where men may labour all day, though, if they spend so much as one night there, must surely die. For the eastern coast of Corsica consists of a series of level plains where malarial fever is as rife as in any African swamp, and the traveller may ride through a fertile land where eucalyptus and palm grow amid the vineyards, and yet no human being may live after sunset. The labourer goes forth to his work in the morning accompanied by his dog, carrying the ubiquitous double-barrelled gun at full cock, and returns in the evening to his mountain village, where, at all events, he may breathe God's air without fear.

The colonel turned to the right a few miles out, following the road which leads straight to that mountain wall which divides all Corsica into the "near" and the "far" side - into two peoples, speaking a different dialect, following slightly different customs, and only finding themselves united in the presence of a common foe. The road mounts steadily, and this February morning had broken grey and cloudy, so that the colonel found himself in the mists that hang over these mountains during the spring months, long before he reached the narrow entrance to the grim and soundless Lancone Defile. The heavy clouds had nestled down the mountains, covering them like a huge thickness of wet cotton-wool. The road, which is little more than a mule-path, is cut in the face of the rock, and, far below, the river runs musically down to Lake Biguglia. The colonel rode alone, though he could perceive another traveller on the winding road in front of him - a peasant in dark clothes, with a huge felt hat, astride on a little active Corsican horse - sure of foot, quick and nervous, as fiery as the men of this strange land.

The defile is narrow, and the sun rarely warms the river that runs through the depths where the foot of man can never have trodden since God fashioned this earth. Colonel Gilbert, it would appear, was accustomed to solitude. Perhaps he had known it so well during his sojourn in this island of silence and loneliness, that he had fallen a victim to its dangerous charms, and being indolent by nature, had discovered that it is less trouble to be alone than to cultivate the society of man. The Lancone Defile has to this day an evil name. It is not wise to pass through it alone, for some have entered one end never to emerge at the other. Colonel Gilbert pressed his heavy charger, and gained rapidly on the horseman in front of him. When he was within two hundred yards of him, at the highest part of the pass and through the narrow defile, he sought in the inner pocket of his tunic - for in those days French officers possessed no other clothes than their uniform - and produced a letter. He examined it, crumpled it between his fingers, and rubbed it across his dusty knee so that it looked old and travel-stained at once. Then, with the letter in his hand, he put spurs to his horse and galloped after the horseman in front of him. The man turned almost at once in his saddle, as if care rode behind him there.

"Hi! mon ami," cried the colonel, holding the letter high above his head. "You have, I imagine, dropped this letter?" he added, as he approached the other, who now awaited him.

"Where? No; but I have dropped no letter. Where was it? On the road?"

"Down there," answered the colonel, pointing back with his whip, and handing over the letter with a final air as if it were no affair of his.

"Perucca," read the man, slowly, in the manner of one having small dealings with pens and paper, "Mattei Perucca - at Olmeta."

"Ah," said the colonel, lighting a cigarette. He had apparently not troubled to read the address on the envelope.

In such a thinly populated country as Corsica, faces are of higher import than in crowded cities, where types are mingled and individuality soon fades. The colonel had already recognized this man as of Olmeta - one of those, perhaps, who had stood smoking on the "Place" there when Pietro Andrei crawled towards the fountain and failed to reach it.

"I am going to Olmeta," said the man, "and you also, perhaps."

"No; I am exercising my horse, as you see. I shall turn to the left at the cross-roads, and go towards Murato. I may come round by Olmeta later - if I lose my way."

The man smiled grimly. In Corsica men rarely laugh.

"You will not do that. You know this country too well for that. You are the officer connected with the railway. I have seen you looking through your instruments at the earth, in the mountains, in the rocks, and down in the plains - everywhere."

"It is my work," answered the colonel, tapping with his whip the gold lace on his sleeve. "One must do what one is ordered."

The other shrugged his shoulders, not seeming to think that necessary. They rode on in silence, which was only broken from time to time by the colonel, who asked harmless questions as to the names of the mountain summits now appearing through the riven clouds, or the course of the rivers, or the ownership of the wild and rocky land. At the cross-roads they parted.

"I am returning to Olmeta," said the peasant, as they neared the sign-post, "and will send that letter up to the Casa Perucca by one of my children. I wonder" - he paused, and, taking the letter from his jacket pocket, turned it curiously in his hand - "I wonder what is in it?"

The colonel shrugged his shoulders and turned his horse's head. It was, it appeared, no business of his to inquire what the letter contained, or to care whether it be delivered or not. Indeed, he appeared to have forgotten all about it.

"Good day, my friend - good day," he said absent-mindedly.

And an hour later he rode up to the Casa Perucca, having approached that ancient house by a winding path from the valley below, instead of by the high-road from the Col San Stefano to Olmeta, which runs past its very gate. The Casa Perucca is rather singularly situated, and commands one of the most wonderful views in this wild land of unrivalled prospects. The high-road curves round the lower slope of the mountains as round the base of a sugar-loaf, and is cut at times out of the sheer rock, while a little lower it is begirt by huge trees. It forms as it were a cornice, perched three thousand feet above the valley, over which it commands a view of mountain and bay and inlet, but never a house, never a church, and the farthest point is beyond Calvi, thirty miles away. There is but one spur - a vast buttress of fertile land thrown against the mountain, as a buttress may be thrown against a church tower.

The Casa Perucca is built upon this spur of land, and the Perucca estate - that is to say, the land attached to the Casa (for property is held in small tenures in Corsica) - is all that lies outside the road. In the middle ages the position would have been unrivalled, for it could be attacked from one side only, and doubtless the Genoese Bank of St. George must have had bitter reckonings with some dead and forgotten rebel, who had his stronghold where the Casa now stands. The present house is Italian in appearance - a long, low, verandahed house, built in two parts, as if it had at one time been two houses, and only connected later by a round tower, now painted a darker colour than the adjacent buildings. There are occasional country houses like it to be found in Tuscany, notably on the heights behind Fiesole.

The wall defining the peninsula is ten feet high, and is built actually on the roadside, so that the Casa Perucca, with its great wooden gate, turns a very cold shoulder upon its poor neighbours. It is, as a matter of fact, the best house north of Calvi, and the site of it one of the oldest. Its only rival is the Chateau de Vasselot, which stands deserted down in the valley a few miles to the south, nearer to the sea, and farther out of the world, for no high-road passes near it.

Beneath the Casa Perucca, on the northern slope of the shoulder, the ground falls away rapidly in a series of stony chutes, and to the south and west there are evidences of the land having once been laid out in terraces in the distant days when Corsicans were content to till the most fertile soil in Europe - always excepting the Island of Majorca - but now in the wane of the third empire, when every Corsican of any worth had found employment in France, there were none to grow vines or cultivate the olive. There is a short cut up from the valley from the mouldering Chateau de Vasselot, which is practicable for a trained horse. And Colonel Gilbert must have known this, for he had described a circle in the wooded valley in order to gain it. He must also have been to the Casa Perucca many times before, for he rang the bell suspended outside the door built in the thickness of the southern wall, where a horseman would not have expected to gain admittance. This door was, however, constructed without steps on its inner side, for Corsica has this in common with Spain, that no man walks where he can ride, so that steps are rarely built where a gradual slope will prove more convenient.

There was something suggestive of a siege in the way in which the door was cautiously opened, and a man-servant peeped forth.

"Ah!" he said, with relief, "it is the Colonel Gilbert. Yes; monsieur may see him, but no one else. Ah! But he is furious, I can tell you. He is in the verandah - like a wild beast. I will take monsieur's horse."

Colonel Gilbert went through the palms and bamboos and orange-trees alone, towards the house; and there, walking up and down, and stopping every moment to glance towards the door, of which the bell still sounded, he perceived a large, stout man, clad in light tweed, wearing an old straw hat and carrying a thick stick.

"Ah!" cried Perucca, "so you have heard the news. And you have come, I hope, to apologize for your miserable France. It is thus that you govern Corsica, with a Civil Service made up of a parcel of old women and young counter-jumpers! I have no patience with your prefectures and your young men with flowing neck-ties and kid gloves. Are we a girls' school to be governed thus? And you - such great soldiers! Yes, I will admit that the French are great soldiers, but you do not know how to rule Corsica. A tight hand, colonel. Holy name of thunder!" And he stamped his foot with a decisiveness that made the verandah tremble.

The colonel laughed pleasantly.

"They want some men of your type," he said.

"Ah!" cried Perucca, "I would rule them, for they are cowards; they are afraid of me. Do you know, they had the impertinence to send one of their threatening letters to poor Andrei before they shot him. They sent him a sheet of paper with a cross drawn on it. Then I knew he was done for. They do not send that *pour rire*."

He stopped short, and gave a jerk of the head. There was somewhere in his fierce old heart a cord that vibrated to the touch of these rude mountain customs; for the man was a Corsican of long descent and pure blood. Of such the fighting nations have made good soldiers in the past, and even Rome could not make them slaves.

"Or you could do it," went on Perucca, with a shrewd nod, looking at him beneath shaggy brows. "The velvet glove - eh? That would surprise them, for they have never felt the touch of one. You, with your laugh and idle ways, and behind them the perception - the perception of the devil - or a woman."

The colonel had drawn forward a basket chair, and was leaning back in it with crossed legs, and one foot swinging.

"I? Heaven forbid! No, my friend; I require too little. It is only the discontented who get on in the world. But, mind you, I would not mind trying on a small scale. I have often thought I should like to buy a little property on this side of the island, and cultivate it as they do up in Cap Corse. It would be an amusement for my exile, and one could perhaps make the butter for one's bread - green Chartreuse instead of yellow - eh?"

He paused, and seeing that the other made no reply, continued in the same careless strain.

"If you or one of the other proprietors on this side of the mountains would sell - perhaps."

But Perucca shook his head resolutely.

"No; we should not do that. You, who have had to do with the railway, must know that. We will let our land go to rack and ruin, we will starve it and not cultivate it, we will let the terraces fall away after the rains, we will live miserably on the finest soil in Europe - we may starve, but we won't sell."

Gilbert did not seem to be listening very intently. He was watching the young bamboos now bursting into their feathery new green, as they waved to and fro against the blue sky. His head was slightly inclined to one side, his eyes were contemplative.

"It is a pity," he said, after a pause, "that Andrei did not have a better knowledge of the insular character. He need not have been in Olmeta churchyard now."

"It is a pity," rapped out Perucca, with an emphatic stick on the wooden floor, "that Andrei was so gentle with them. He drove the cattle off the land. I should have driven them into my own sheds, and told the owners to come and take them. He was too easy-going, too mild in his manners. Look at me - they don't send me their threatening letters. You do not find any crosses chalked on my door - eh?"

And indeed, as he stood there, with his square shoulders, his erect bearing and fiery, dark eyes, Mattei Perucca seemed worthy of the name of his untamed ancestors, and was not a man to be trifled with.

"Eh - what?" he asked of the servant who had approached timorously, bearing a letter on a tray. "For me? Something about Andrei, from those fools of gendarmes, no doubt."

And he tore open the envelope which Colonel Gilbert had handed to the peasant a couple of hours earlier in the Lancone Defile. He fixed his eye-glasses upon his nose, clumsily, with one hand, and then unfolded the letter. It was merely a sheet of blank paper, with a cross drawn upon it.

His face suddenly blazed red with anger. His eyes glared at the paper through the glasses placed crookedly upon his nose.

"Holy name!" he cried. "Look at this - this to *me*! The dogs!"

The colonel looked at the paper with a shrug of the shoulders.

"You will have to sell," he suggested lightly; and glancing up at Perucca's face, saw something there that made him leap to his feet. "Hulloa! Here," he said quickly - "sit down."

And as he forced Perucca into the chair, his hands were already at the old man's collar. And in five minutes, in the presence of Colonel Gilbert and two old servants, Mattei Perucca died.

CHAPTER IV.

A TOSS-UP.

"One can be but what one is born."

If any one had asked the Count Lory de Vasselot who and what he was, he would probably have answered that he was a member of the English Jockey Club. For he held that that distinction conferred greater honour upon him than the accident of his birth, which enabled him to claim for grandfather the first Count de Vasselot, one of Murat's aides-de-camp, a brilliant, dashing cavalry officer, a boyhood's friend of the great Napoleon. Lory de Vasselot was, moreover, a cavalry officer himself, but had not taken part in any of the enterprises of an emperor who held that to govern Frenchmen it is necessary to provide them with a war every four years.

"Bon Dieu!" he told his friends, "I did not sleep for two nights after I was elected to that great club."

Lory de Vasselot, moreover, did his best to live up to his position. He never, for instance, had his clothes made in Paris. His very gloves came from a little shop in Newmarket, where only the seamiest and clumsiest of hand-coverings are provided, and horn buttons are a *sine qua non.*

To desire to be mistaken for an Englishman is a sure sign that you belong to the very best Parisian set, and Lory de Vasselot's position was an enviable one, for so long as he kept his hat on and stood quite still and did not speak, he might easily have been some one connected with the British turf. It must, of course, be understood that the similitude of de Vasselot's desire was only an outward one. We all think that every other nation would fain be English, but as all other countries have a like pitying contempt for us, there is perhaps no harm done. And it is to be presumed that if some candid friend were to tell de Vasselot that the moment he uncovered his hair, or opened his lips, or made a single movement, he was hopelessly and unmistakably French from top to toe, he would not have been sorely distressed.

It will be remembered that the Third Napoleon - the last of that strange dynasty - raised himself to the Imperial throne - made himself, indeed, the most powerful monarch in Europe - by statecraft, and not by power of sword. With the magic of his name he touched the heart of the most impetuous people in the world, and upon the uncertain, and, as it is whispered, not always honest suffrage of the plebiscite, climbed to the unstable height of despotism. For years he ruled France with a sort of careless cynicism, and it was only when his health failed that his hand began to relax its grip. In the scramble for place and power, the grandson of the first Count de Vasselot might easily have gained a prize, but Lory seemed to have no ambition in that direction. Perhaps he had no taste for ministry or bureau, nor cared to cultivate the subtle knowledge of court and cabinet, which meant so much at this time.

His tastes were rather those of the camp; and, failing war, he had turned his thoughts to sport. He had hunted in England and fished in Norway. In the winter of 1869, he went to Africa for big game, and, returning in the early weeks of March, found France and his dear Paris gayer, more insouciant, more brilliant than ever.

For the empire had never seemed more secure than it did at this moment, had never stood higher in the eyes of the world, had never boasted so lavish a court. Paris was at her best, and Lory de Vasselot exclaimed aloud, after the manner of his countrymen, at the sight of the young buds and spring flowers around the Lac in the Bois de Boulogne, as he rode there this fresh morning.

He had only arrived in Paris the night before, and, dining at the Cercle Militaire, had accepted the loan of a horse.

"One will at all events see one's friends in the wood," he said. But riding there in an ultra-English suit of cords at the fashionable hour, he found that he had somehow missed the fashion. The alleys, which had been popular a year ago, were now deserted; for there is nothing so fickle as social taste, and the riders were all at the other side of the Route de Longchamps.

Lory turned his horse's head in that direction, and was riding leisurely, when he heard an authoritative voice apparently directed towards himself. He was in one of the narrow *allées*, "reserved for cavaliers," and, turning, perceived that the soft sandy gravel had prevented his hearing the approach of other riders - a man and a woman. And the woman's horse was beyond control. It was a little, fiery Arab, leaping high in the air at each stride, and timing a nasty forward jerk of the head at the worst moment for its rider's comfort.

There was no time to do anything but touch his own trained charger with the spur and gallop ahead. He turned in his saddle. The Arab was gaining on him, and gradually leaving behind the heavy horse and weighty rider who were giving chase. The woman, with a set white face, was jerking at the bridle with her left hand in an odd, mechanical, feeble way, while with her right, she held to the pommel of her saddle. But she was swaying forward in an unmistakable manner. She was only half conscious, and in a moment must fall.

Lory glanced behind her, and saw a stout built man, with a fair moustache and a sunburnt face, riding his great horse in the stirrups like a jockey, his face alight with that sudden excitement which sometimes blazes in light blue eyes. He made a quick gesture, which said as plainly as words - "You must act, and quickly; I can do nothing."

And the three thundered on. The rides in the Bois de Boulogne are all bordered on either side by thick trees. If Lory de Vasselot pulled across, he would send the maddened Arab into the forest, where the first low branch must of a necessity batter in its rider's head. He rode on, gradually edging across to what in France is the wrong side of the road.

"Hold on, madame; hold on," he said, in a quick low voice.

But the woman did not seem to hear him. She had dropped the bridle now, and the Arab had thrown it forward over its head.

Then Lory gradually reined in. The woman was reeling in the saddle as the Arab thundered alongside. The wind blew back the long habit, and showed her foot to be firmly in the stirrup.

"Stirrup, madame!" shouted Lory, as if she were miles away. "Mon Dieu, your stirrup!"

But she only looked ahead with glazed eyes.

Then, edging nearer with a delicate spur, de Vasselot shook off his own right stirrup, and, leaning down, lifted the fainting woman with his right arm clean out of the saddle. He rested her weight upon his thigh, and, feeling cautiously with his foot, found her stirrup and kicked it free. He pulled up slowly, and, drawing aside, allowed the lady's companion to pass him at a steady gallop after the Arab.

The lady was now in a dead faint, her dark red hair hanging like a rope across de Vasselot's arm. She was, fortunately, not a big woman; for it was no easy position to find one's self in, on the top, thus, of a large horse with a senseless burden and no help in sight. He managed, however, to dismount, and rather breathlessly carried the lady to the shade of the trees, where he laid her with her head on a mound of rising turf, and, lifting aside her hair, saw her face for the first time.

"Ah! That dear baroness!" he exclaimed; and, turning, he found himself bowing rather stiffly to the gentleman, who had now returned, leading the runaway horse. He was not, it may be mentioned, the baron.

While the two men were thus regarding each other in a

polite silence, the baroness opened a pair of remarkably bright brown eyes, at first with wonder, and then with understanding, and finally with wonder again when they lighted on de Vasselot.

"Lory!" she cried. "But where have you fallen from?"

"It must have been from heaven, baroness," he replied, "for I assuredly came at the right moment."

He stood looking down at her - a lithe, neat, rather small-made man. Then he turned to attend to his horse. The baroness was already busy with her hair. She rose to her feet and smoothed her habit.

"Ah, good!" she laughed. "There is no harm done. But you saved my life, my dear Lory. One cannot have two opinions as to that. If it were not that the colonel is watching us, I should embrace you. But I have not introduced you. This is Colonel Gilbert - my dear and good cousin, Lory de Vasselot. The colonel is from Bastia, by the way, and the Count de Vasselot pretends to be a Corsican. I mention it because it is only friendly to tell you that you have something more than the weather and my gratitude in common."

She laughed as she spoke; then became suddenly grave, and sat down again with her hand to her eyes.

"And I am going to faint," she added, with ghastly lips that tried to smile, "and nobody but you two men,"

"It is the reaction," said Colonel Gilbert, in his soothing way. But he exchanged a quick glance with de Vasselot. "It will pass, baroness."

"It is well to remember at such a moment that one is a sportswoman," suggested de Vasselot.

"And that one has de Vasselot blood in one's veins, you mean. You may as well say it." She rose as she spoke, and looked from one to the other with a brave laugh. "Bring me that horse," she said.

De Vasselot conveyed by one inimitable gesture that he admired her spirit, but refused to obey her. Colonel Gilbert smiled contemplatively, He was of a different school - of that school of Frenchmen which owes its existence to Napoleon III. - impassive, almost taciturn - more British than the typical Briton. De Vasselot, on the contrary, was quick and vivacious. His fine-cut face and dark eyes expressed a hundred things that his tongue had no time to put into words. He was hard and brown and sunburnt, which at once made him manly despite his slight frame.

"Ah," he cried, with a gay laugh, "that is better. But seriously, you know, you should have a patent stirrup - "

He broke off, described the patent stirrup in three gestures, how it opened and released the foot. He showed the rider falling, the horse galloping away, the released lady-rider rising to her feet and satisfying herself that no bones were broken - all in three more gestures.

"Voila!" he said; "I shall send you one."

"And you as poor - as poor," said the baroness, whose husband was of the new nobility, which is based, as all the world knows, on solid manufacture. "My friend, you cannot afford it."

"I cannot afford to lose *you*" he said, with a sudden gravity, and with eyes which, to the uninitiated, would undoubtedly have conveyed the impression that she was the whole world to him. "Besides," he added, as an after-thought, "it is only sixteen francs."

The baroness threw up her gay brown eyes.

"Just Heaven," she exclaimed, "what it is to be able to inspire such affection - to be valued at sixteen francs!"

Then - for she was as quick and changeable as himself - she turned, and touched his arm with her thickly-gloved hand.

"Seriously, my cousin, I cannot thank you, and you, Colonel Gilbert, for your promptness and your skill. And as to my stupid husband, you know, he has no words; when I tell him, he will only grunt behind his great moustache, and he will never thank you, and will never forget. Never! Remember that." And with a wave of the riding-whip, which was attached to her wrist, she described eternity.

De Vasselot turned with a deprecatory shrug of the shoulders, and busied himself with the girths of his saddle. At the touch and the sight of the buckles, his eyes became grave and earnest. And it is not only Frenchmen who cherish this cult of the horse, making false gods of saddle and bridle, and a sacred temple of the harness-room. Very seriously de Vasselot shifted the side-saddle from the Arab to his own large and gentle horse - a wise old charger with a Roman nose, who never wasted his mettle in park tricks, but served honestly the Government that paid his forage.

The Baroness de Mélide watched the transaction in respectful silence, for she too took *le sport* very seriously, and had attended a course of lectures at a riding-school on the art of keeping and using harness. Her colour was now returning - that brilliant, delicate colour which so often accompanies dark red hair - and she gave a little sigh of resignation.

Colonel Gilbert looked at her, but said nothing. He seemed to admire her, in the same contemplative way that he had admired the moon rising behind the island of Capraja from the Place St. Nicholas in Bastia.

De Vasselot noted the sigh, and glanced sharply at her over the shoulder of the big charger.

"Of what are you thinking?" he said.

"Of the millennium, mon ami"

"The millennium?"

"Yes," she answered, gathering the bridle; "when women shall perhaps be allowed to be natural. Our mothers played at being afraid - we play at being courageous."

As she spoke she placed a neat foot in Colonel Gilbert's hand, who lifted her without effort to the saddle. De Vasselot mounted the Arab, and they rode slowly homewards by way of the Avenue de Long-champs, through the Porte Dauphine, and up that which is now the Avenue du Bois de Boulogne, which was quiet enough at this time of day. The baroness was

Henry Seton Merriman

inclined to be silent. She had been more shaken than she cared to confess to two soldiers. Colonel Gilbert probably saw this, for he began to make conversation with de Vasselot.

"You do not come to Corsica," he said.

"I have never been there - shall never go there," answered de Vasselot. "Tell me - is it not a terrible place? The end of the world, I am told. My mother" - he broke off with a gesture of the utmost despair. "She is dead!" he interpolated - "always told me that it was the most terrible place in the world. At my father's death, more than thirty years ago, she quitted Corsica, and came to live in Paris, where I was born, and where, if God is good, I shall die."

"My cousin, you talk too much of death," put in the baroness, seriously.

"As between soldiers, baroness," replied de Vasselot, gaily. "It is our trade. You know the island well, colonel?"

"No, I cannot say that. But I know the Chateau de Vasselot."

"Now, that is interesting; and I who scarcely know the address! Near Calvi, is it not? A waste of rocks, and behind each rock at least one bandit - so my dear mother assured me."

"It might be cultivated," answered Colonel Gilbert, indifferently. "It might be made to yield a small return. I have often thought so. I have even thought of whiling away my exile by attempting some such scheme. I once contemplated buying a piece of land on that coast to try. Perhaps you would sell?"

"Sell!" laughed de Vasselot. "No; I am not such a scoundrel as that. I would toss you for it, my dear colonel; I would toss you for it, if you like."

And as they turned out of the avenue into one of the palatial streets that run towards the Avenue Victor Hugo, he made the gesture of throwing a coin into the air.

CHAPTER V.

IN THE RUE DU CHERCHE-MIDI.

"Il ne faut jamais se laisser trop voir, même à ceux qui nous aiment."

It was not very definitely known what Mademoiselle Brun taught in the School of Our Lady of the Sacred Heart in the Rue du Cherche-Midi in Paris. For it is to be feared that Mademoiselle Brun knew nothing except the world; and it is precisely that form of knowledge which is least cultivated in a convent school.

"She has had a romance," whispered her bright-eyed charges, and lapsed into suppressed giggles at the mere mention of such a word in connection with a little woman dressed in rusty black, with thin grey hair, a thin grey face, and a yellow neck.

It would seem, however, that there is a point where even a mother-superior must come down, as it were, into the market-place and meet the world. That point is where the convent purse rattles thinly and the mother-superior must face hunger. It had, in fact, been intimated to the conductors of the School of the Sisterhood of the Sacred Heart by the ladies of the quarter of St. Germain, that the convent teaching taught too little of one world and too much of another. And the mother-superior, being a sensible woman, agreed to engage a certain number of teachers from the outer world. Mademoiselle Brun was vaguely entitled an instructress, while Mademoiselle Denise Lange bore the proud title of mathematical mistress.

Mademoiselle Brun, with her compressed mouth, her wrinkled face, and her cold hazel eyes, accepted the situation, as we have to accept most situations in this world, merely because there is no choice.

"What can you teach?" asked the soft-eyed mother-superior.

"Anything," replied Mademoiselle Brun, with a direct gaze, which somehow cowed the nun.

"She has had a romance," whispered some wag of fourteen, when Mademoiselle Brun first appeared in the schoolroom; and that became the accepted legend regarding her.

"What are you saying of me?" she asked one day, when her rather sudden appearance caused silence at a moment when silence was not compulsory.

"That you once had a romance, mademoiselle," answered some daring girl.

"Ah!"

And perhaps the dusky wrinkles lapsed into gentler lines, for some one had the audacity to touch mademoiselle's hand with a birdlike tap of one finger.

"And you must tell it to us."

For there were no nuns present, and mademoiselle was suspected of having a fine contempt for the most stringent of the convent laws.

"No."

"But why not, mademoiselle?"

"Because the real romances are never told," replied Mademoiselle Brun.

But that was only her way, perhaps, of concealing the fact that there was nothing to tell. She spoke in a low voice, for her class shared the long schoolroom this afternoon with the mathematical class. The room did not lend itself to description, for it had bare walls and two long windows looking down disconsolately upon a courtyard, where a grey cat sunned herself in the daytime and bewailed her lot at night. Who, indeed, would be a convent cat?

At the far end of the long room Mademoiselle Denise Lange was superintending, with an earnest face, the studies of five young ladies. It was only necessary to look at the respective heads of the pupils to conclude that these young persons were engaged in mathematical problems, for there is nothing so discomposing to the hair as arithmetic. Mademoiselle Lange herself seemed no more capable of steering a course through a double equation than her pupils, for she was young and pretty, with laughing lips and fair hair, now somewhat ruffled by her calculations. When, however, she looked up, it might have been perceived that her glance was clear and penetrating.

There was no more popular person in the Convent of the Sacred Heart than Denise Lange, and in no walk of life is personal attractiveness so much appreciated as in a girls' school. It is only later in life that *ces demoiselles* begin to find that their neighbour's beauty is but skin-deep. The nuns - "fond fools," Mademoiselle Brun called them - concluded that because Denise was pretty she must be good. The girls loved Denise with a wild and exceedingly ephemeral affection, because she was little more than a girl herself, and was, like themselves, liable to moments of deep arithmetical despondency. Mademoiselle Brun admitted that she was fond of Denise because she was her second cousin, and that was all.

When worldly mammas, essentially of the second empire, who perhaps had doubts respecting a purely conventional education, made inquiries on this subject, the mother-superior, feeling very wicked and worldly, usually made mention of the mathematical mistress, Denise Lange, daughter of the great and good general who was killed at Solferino. And no other word of identification was needed. For some keen-witted artist had painted a great salon picture of, not a young paladin, but a fat old soldier, eighteen stone, on his huge charger, with shaking red cheeks and blazing eyes, standing in his stirrups, bursting out of his tight tunic, and roaring to his *enfants* to follow him to their death.

It was after the battle of Solferino that Mademoiselle Brun had come into Denise Lange's life, taking her from her convent school to live in a dull little apartment in the Rue des Saints Pères, educating her, dressing her, caring for her with a grim affection which never wasted itself in words. How she pinched and

Henry Seton Merriman

saved, and taught herself that she might teach others; how she triumphantly made both ends meet, - are secrets which, like Mademoiselle Brun's romance, she would not tell. For French women are not only cleverer and more capable than French men, but they are cleverer and more capable than any other women in the world. History, moreover, will prove this; for nearly all the great women that the world has seen have been produced by France.

Denise and Mademoiselle Brun still lived in the dull little apartment in the Rue des Saints Pères - that narrow street which runs southward from the Quai Voltaire to the Boulevard St. Germain, where the cheap frame-makers, the artists' colourmen, and the dealers in old prints have their shops. To the convent school, the old woman and the young girl, walking daily through the streets to their work, brought with them that breath of worldliness which the advance of civilization seemed to render desirable to the curriculum of a girls' school.

"It must be heavenly, mademoiselle, to walk in the streets quite alone," said one of Mademoiselle Brun's pupils to her one day.

"It is," was the reply; "especially near the gutter."

But this afternoon there was no conversation, for the literature class knew that Mademoiselle Brun was in a contrary humour.

"She is looking at that dear Denise with discontented eyes. She is in a shocking temper," had been the whispered warning from mouth to mouth.

And in truth Mademoiselle Brun constantly glanced down the length of the schoolroom to where Denise was sitting. But a seeing eye could well perceive that it was not with Denise, but with the schoolroom, that the little old woman was discontented. Perhaps she had at times a cruel thought that the Rue des Saints Pères, emphasized as it were by the Rue du Cherche-Midi, was hardly gay for a young life. Perhaps the soft touch of spring that was in the March air stirred up restless longings in the soul of this little grey town-mouse.

And while she was watching Denise, the cross-grained old nun who acted as concierge to this quiet house came into the room, and handed Denise a long blue envelope.

"It is addressed in a man's handwriting," she said warningly.

"Then let us by all means send for the tongs," answered Denise, taking the letter with a mock air of alarm.

But she looked at it curiously, and glanced towards Mademoiselle Brun before she opened it. It was, perhaps, characteristic of the little old schoolmistress to show no interest whatever. And yet to her it probably seemed an age before Denise came towards her, carrying the letter in her outstretched hand.

"At first," said the girl, "I thought it was a joke - a trick of one of the girls. But it is serious enough. It is a romance inside a blue envelope - that is all."

She gave a joyous laugh, and threw the letter down on Mademoiselle Brun's knees.

"It is my father's cousin, Mattei Perucca, who has died suddenly, and has left me an estate in Corsica," she continued, impatiently opening the letter, which Mademoiselle Brun fingered with pessimistic distrust. "See here! that is the address of my estate in Corsica, where I shall invite you to stay with me - I, who stand before you in my old black alpaca, and would borrow a hairpin if you can spare it."

Her hands were busy with her hair as she spoke; and she seemed to touch life and its entanglements as lightly. Mademoiselle Brun, however, read the letter very gravely. For she was a wise old Frenchwoman, who knew that it is only bad news which may safely be accepted as true.

The letter, which was accompanied by an enclosure, was from a Marseilles solicitor, and began by inquiring as to the identity of Mademoiselle Denise Lange, instructress at the convent school in the Rue du Cherche-Midi, with the daughter of the late General Lange, who met his death on the field of Solferino. It then proceeded to explain that Denise Lange had inherited the property known as the Perucca property, in the commune of Calvi, in the Island of Corsica. Followed a schedule of the said property, which included the historic château, known as the Casa Perucca. The solicitor concluded with a word for himself, after the manner of his kind, and clearly demonstrated that no other lawyer was so capable as he to arrange the affairs of Mademoiselle Denise Lange.

"Jean Jacques Moreau," read Mademoiselle Brun, with some scorn, the signature of the Marseilles notary. "An imbecile, your Jean Jacques - an imbecile, like his great and mischievous namesake. He does not say of what malady your second cousin died, or what income the property will yield - if any."

"But we can ask him those particulars."

"And pay for each answer," retorted Mademoiselle Brun, folding the letter reflectively.

She was remembering that a few minutes earlier she had been thinking that their present existence was too narrow for Denise; and now, in the twinkling of an eye, life seemed to be opening out and spreading with a rapidity which only the thoughts of youth could follow and the energy of spring keep pace with.

"Then we will go to Marseilles and ask the questions ourselves, and then he cannot charge for each answer, for I know he could never keep count."

But Mademoiselle Brun only looked grave, and would not rise to Denise's lighter humour. It almost seemed, indeed, as if she were afraid - she who had never known fear through all the years of pinch and struggle, who had faced a world that had no use for her, that would not buy the poor services she had to sell. For to know the worst is always a relief, and to exchange it for something better is like exchanging an old coat for a new one.

"And in the mean time - " said Mademoiselle Brun, turning sharply upon her pupils, who had taken the opportunity of abandoning French literature.

"In the mean time," said Denise, turning reluctantly away - "in the mean time, I am filling a vat of so many cubic metres, from a well so many metres deep, with a pail containing four litres, and of course the pail has a leak in it, and the well becomes deeper as one draws from it, and the Casa Perucca is, I suppose, a dream."

She went back to her work, and in a few moments was quite absorbed in it. And it was Mademoiselle Brun who could not settle to her French literature, nor compose her thoughts at all. For change is the natural desire of youth, and the belief that it must be for the better, part and parcel of the astounding optimism of that state of life.

A few minutes later Denise remembered the enclosure - a letter in a thick white envelope, which was still lying on her desk. She opened it.

"MADEMOISELLE" (the letter ran),

"I think I have the pleasure of addressing the daughter of an old comrade-in-arms, and this must be my excuse for at once approaching my object. I hear by accident that you have inherited from the late Mattei Perucca his small property near Olmeta in Corsica. I knew Mattei Perucca, and the property you inherit is not unknown to one who has had official dealings with landowners in Corsica. I tell you frankly that it would be impossible, in the present disturbed state of the island, for you to live at Olmeta, and I ask you as frankly whether you are disposed to sell me your small estate. I have long cherished the scheme of buying a small parcel of land in Corsica for the purpose of showing the natives that agriculture may be made profitable in so fertile an island, by dint of industry and a firm and unswerving honesty. The Perucca property would suit my purpose. You may be doing a good action in handing over your tenants to one who understands the Corsican nature. I, in addition to relieving the monotony of my present exile at Bastia, may perhaps be inaugurating a happier state of affairs in this most unfortunate country.

"Awaiting your answer, I am, mademoiselle,

"Your obedient servant,

"LOUIS GILBERT (Colonel)."

The school bell rang as Denise finished reading the letter. The class was over.

"We shall descend into the well again to-morrow," she said, closing her books.

The girls trooped out into the forlorn courtyard, leaving Mademoiselle Brun and Denise alone in the schoolroom. Mademoiselle Brun read the second letter with a silent concentration. She glanced up when she had finished it.

"Of course you will sell," she said.

Denise was looking out of the tall closed windows at the few yards of sky that were visible above the roofs. Some fleecy clouds were speeding across the clear ether.

"No," she answered slowly; "I think I shall go to Corsica. Tell me," she added, after a pause - "I suppose I have Corsican blood in my veins?"

"I suppose so," admitted Mademoiselle Brun, reluctantly.

CHAPTER VI.

NEIGHBOURS.

"Chaque homme a trois caractères: celui qu'il a, celui qu'il montre, et celui qu'il croit avoir."

By one of the strokes of good fortune which come but once to the most ardent student of fashion, the Baroness de Mélide had taken up horsiness at the very beginning of that estimable craze. It was, therefore, in mere sequence to this pursuit that she fixed her abode on the south side of the Champs Elysées, and within a stone's throw of the Avenue du Bois de Boulogne, before the world found out that it was quite impossible to live elsewhere. It is so difficult, in truth, to foretell the course of fashion, that one cannot help wondering why the modern soothsayers, who eke out what appears to be a miserable existence in the smaller streets of the Faubourg St. Honoré and in the neighbourhood of Bond Street, do not turn their second-sight to the contemplation of the future of streets and districts, instead of telling the curious a number of vague facts respecting their past and vaguer prophecies as to the future.

If, for instance, Cagliostro had foretold that to-day the Chausée d'Antin would be deserted; that the faubourg would have completely ousted the Rue St. Honoré; that the Avenue de la Grande Armée should be, fashionably speaking, dead after a short and brilliant life; and that the little streets of the Faubourg St. Germain should be all that is most *chic* - what fortunes might have been made! Indeed, no one in a trance or in his right mind can tell to-day why it is right to walk on the right-hand side of the Boulevard des Italiens and the Boulevard des Capucines, and heinously wrong to walk on the left; while, on the contrary, no self-respecting Parisian would allow himself to be seen on the right-hand pavement of the Boulevard de la Madeleine. Indeed, these things are a mystery, and the wise seek only to obey, and not to ask the reason why.

It would be difficult to lay before the English reader the precise social position of the Baroness de Mélide. For there are wheels within wheels, or, more properly perhaps, shades within shades, in the social world of Paris, which are quite unsuspected on this side of the Channel. Indeed, our ignorance of social France is only surpassed by the French ignorance of social England. The Baroness de Mélide was rich, however, and the rich, as we all know, have nothing to fear in this world. As a matter of fact, Monsieur de Mélide dated his nobility from Napoleon's creation, and madame's grandfather was of the Emigration. By conviction, they belonged to the Anglophile school, and theirs was one of the prettiest little houses between the Avenue Victor Hugo and the Avenue du Bois de Boulogne, which is more important than ancestors.

It was to this miniature palace that Mademoiselle Brun and Denise were bidden, to the new function of afternoon tea, the day after the receipt of the lawyer's letter. Madame de Mélide would take no denial.

"I have already heard of Denise's good fortune; and from whom do you think?" she wrote. "From my dear good cousin, Lory de Vasselot, who is, if you will believe it, a Corsican neighbour - the Vasselot and Perucca estates actually adjoin. Both, I need hardly tell you, bristle with bandits, and are quite impossible. But I have quite decided that Lory shall marry Denise. Come, therefore, without fail. I need not tell you to see that Denise looks pretty. The good God has seen to that for you. And as for Lory, he is an angel. I cannot think why I did not marry him myself - except that he did not ask me. And then there is my stupid, whom nobody else would have, and who now sends his dear love to his oldest friend. - Your devoted JANE."

The Baroness de Mélide was called Jeanne, but she had enthusiastically changed that name for its English version at the period when England was, as it were, first discovered by social France.

When Mademoiselle Brun and Denise arrived, they found the baroness beautifully dressed as usual, and very French, for the empress was at this time the leader of the world's women, as the emperor - that clever *parvenu* - was undoubtedly the first monarch in Europe. It behoves not a masculine pen to attempt a description of Madame de Mélide's costume, which, moreover, was of a bygone mode, and nothing is so unsightly in death as a deceased fashion.

"How good of you to come!" she cried, embracing both ladies in turn, with a fervour which certainly seemed to imply that she had no other friends on earth.

In truth, she had, for the moment, none so dear; for there are certain warm hearts that are happy in always loving, not the highest, but the nearest.

"Let me see, now," she added, vigorously dragging forward chairs. "I asked some one to meet you - some one I particularly wanted you to become acquainted with, but I cannot remember who it is." As she spoke she consulted a little red morocco betting-book.

"Lory!" she cried, after a short search. "Yes, of course it was Lory de Vasselot - my cousin. And - will you believe it? - he saved my life the other day, all in a moment! Yes! I saw death, quite close, before my eyes. Ugh! And I, who am so wicked! You do not know what it is to be wicked and to know it, Denise - you who are so young. But that dear Mademoiselle Brun, she knows."

"Thank you," said mademoiselle.

"And Lory saved me, ah! so cleverly. There is no better horseman in the army, they say. Yes; he will certainly come this afternoon, unless there is a race at Longchamps. Now, is there a race, I wonder?"

"For the moment," said Mademoiselle Brun, very gravely, "I cannot tell you."

"She is laughing at me," cried the baroness, shaking a vivacious forefinger at Mademoiselle Brun. "But I do not mind; we cannot all be wise - eh?"

"And what a dull world for the rest of us if you were," said Mademoiselle Brun; and Lory de Vasselot, coming into the room at this moment, was met by her sour smile.

"Ah!" cried the baroness, "here he is. I present you, my dear Lory, to Mademoiselle Brun, a terrible friend of mine, and to Mademoiselle Lange, who, as you know, has just inherited the other half of Corsica."

"My congratulations," answered Lory, shaking hands with Denise in the English fashion. "An inheritance is so nice when it is quite new."

"And figure to yourself that this dear child has no notion how it has all come about! She only knows the bare fact that some one is dead, and she has gained - well, a white elephant, one may suppose."

De Vasselot's quick face suddenly turned grave.

"Ah," he said, "then I can tell you how it has all come about. Though I confess at once that I have never been to Corsica, and have never found myself a halfpenny the richer for owning land there."

He paused for a moment, and glanced at Mademoiselle Brun.

"Unless," he interpolated, "such personal matters will bore mademoiselle."

"But mademoiselle is the good angel of Mademoiselle Lange, my dear, dull Lory," explained the baroness; and the object of the elucidation looked at him more keenly than so trifling an incident would seem to warrant.

"You will not be betraying secrets to the first-comer," she said.

Still de Vasselot seemed to hesitate, as if choosing his words.

"And," he said at length, "they shot your cousin's agent in the back, almost in the streets of Olmeta, and Mattei Perucca himself died suddenly, presumably from apoplexy, brought on by a great anger at receiving a letter threatening his life - that is how it has come about, mademoiselle."

He broke off short, with a quick gesture and a flash of his eyes, usually so pleasant and smiling.

"I have that from a reliable source," he went on, after a pause, during which Mademoiselle Brun looked steadily at Denise and said nothing.

"Gracious heavens!" exclaimed the baroness, in a whisper; and for once was silenced.

"A faithful correspondent on the island," explained de Vasselot. "Though why he is faithful I cannot tell you. Some family legend, perhaps - I cannot tell. It is the Abbé Susini of Olmeta who has told me this. He it was who told me of your - well, I can only call it your misfortune, mademoiselle. For there is assuredly a curse upon Corsica as there is upon Ireland. It cannot govern itself, and no other can govern it. The Napoleons have been the only men to make anything of the island, but a man who is driving a pair of horses down the Champs Elysées cannot give much thought to his little dog that runs behind. And it is in the Bonaparte blood to drive, not only a pair, but a four-in-hand in the thickest traffic of the world. The Abbé Susini tells me that when the emperor's hand was firm, Corsica was almost orderly, justice was almost administered, banditism was for the moment made to feel the hand of the law, and the authorities could count the number of outlaws evading their grip in the mountains. But since the emperor's illness has taken a dangerous turn things have gone back again. Corsica is, it seems, a weather-glass by which one may tell the state of the political weather in France; and now it is disturbed, mademoiselle."

He had become graver as he spoke, and now found himself addressing Denise almost as if she were a man. There is as much difference in listeners as there is in talkers. And Lory de Vasselot, who belonged to the new school of Frenchmen - the open-air, the vigorous, the sportsmanlike - found his interlocutor listening with clear eyes fixed frankly on his face. Intelligence betrays itself in listening more than in talking, and de Vasselot, with characteristic and an eminently national intuition, perceived that this girl from a covent school in the Rue du Cherche-Midi was not a person to whom to address drawing-room generalities, and those insults to the feminine comprehension which a bygone generation called compliments.

"But a woman need surely have nothing to fear," said Denise, who had the habit of carrying her head rather high, and now spoke as if this implied more than a mere trick of deportment.

"A woman! You are not going to Corsica, mademoiselle?"

"But I am," she answered.

De Vasselot turned thoughtfully, and brought forward a chair. He sat down and gravely contemplated

Mademoiselle Brun, whose attitude - upright in a low chair, with crossed hands and a compressed mouth - betrayed nothing. A Frenchman is not nearly so artificial as the shallow British observer has been pleased to conclude. He is, in fact, much more a child of nature than either an Englishman or a German. Lory de Vasselot's expression said as plainly as words to Mademoiselle Brun -

"And what have *you* been about?"

It was so obvious that Mademoiselle Brun, almost imperceptibly, shrugged one shoulder. She was powerless, it appeared.

"But, if you will permit me to say so," said Lory, sitting down and drawing near to Denise in his earnestness, "that is impossible. I will not trouble you with details, but it is an impossibility. I understand that Mattei Perucca and his agent were the two strongest men in the northern district, and they only attempted to hold their own, nothing more. With the result that you know."

"But there are many ways of attempting to hold one's own," persisted Denise; and she shook her head with a wisdom which only belongs to youth.

De Vasselot spread out his hands in utter despair. The end of the world, it seemed, was at hand. And Denise only laughed.

"And when I have regulated my own affairs, I will undertake the management of your estate at a high salary," she said.

"There is only one thing to do," said Lory, gravely, "and I have done it myself. I have abandoned the idea of ever receiving a halfpenny of rent. I have allowed the land to go out of cultivation. The vine-terraces are falling, the olive trees are dying for want of cultivation. A few peasants graze their cattle in my garden, I understand. The house itself is only saved from falling down by the fact that it is strongly built of stone. I would sell for a mere song, if I could find a serious offer of that trifle; but nobody buys land in Corsica - for the peasants recognize no title deeds and respect no rights of ownership. I had indeed an offer the other day, but it was undoubtedly a joke, and I treated it as such."

"Denise also has had an offer to buy the Perucca property," said Mademoiselle Brun.

"Yes," said Denise, seeing his surprise. "And you would advise me to accept it?"

"If it is a serious one, most decidedly."

"It is serious enough," answered Denise. "It is from a Colonel Gilbert, an officer stationed at Bastia."

"Ah!" he exclaimed; and at that moment another caller entered the room, and he rose with eager politeness.

So it happened that Mademoiselle Brun could not see his face, and was left wondering what the exclamation meant.

Several other callers now appeared - persons of the Baroness de Mélide's own world, who had a hundred society tricks, and bowed or shook hands according to the latest mode. This was not Mademoiselle Brun's world, and she was not interested to hear the latest gossip from that hotbed of scandal, the Tuileries, nor did the ever-changing face of the political world command her attention. She therefore rose, and stiffly took her leave. De Vasselot accompanied them to the hall.

Denise paused in the entrance, and turned to him.

"Seriously," she said, "do you advise me to accept this offer to sell Perucca?"

"I scarcely feel authorized to give you any advice upon the subject," answered Lory, reluctantly. "Though, after all, we are neighbours."

"Then - "

"Then, I should say not, mademoiselle. At all events, do nothing in haste. And, if I may ask it, will you communicate with me before you finally decide?"

They had come in an open cab, which was waiting on the shady side of the street.

"A young man who changes his mind very quickly," commented Mademoiselle Brun, as they drove away.

CHAPTER VII.

JOURNEY'S END.

"The offender never pardons."

De Vasselot returned to the Baroness de Mélide's pretty drawing-room, and there, after the manner of his countrymen, made himself agreeable in that vivacious manner which earns the contempt of all honest and, if one may say so, thick-headed Englishmen. He laughed with one, and with another almost wept. Indeed, to see him sympathize with an elderly countess whose dog was grievously ill, one could only conclude that he too had placed all his affections upon a canine life.

He outstayed the others, and then, holding out his hand to the baroness, said curtly -

"Good-bye."

"Good-bye! What do you mean?"

"I am going to Corsica," he explained airily.

"But where did you get that idea, mon ami?"

"It came. A few moments ago, I made up my mind."

And, with a gesture, he described the arrival of the idea, apparently from heaven, upon his head, and then a sideward jerk of the arm seemed to indicate the sudden and irrevocable making up of his own mind.

"But what for?" cried the lady. "You were not even born there. Your father died thirty years ago - you will not even find his tomb. Your dear mother left the place in horror, just before you were born. Besides, you promised her that you would never return to Corsica - and she who has been dead only five years! Is it filial, I ask you, my cousin? Is it filial?"

"Such a promise, of course, only held good during her lifetime," answered Lory. "Since there is no one left behind to be anxious on my account, it is assuredly no one's affair whether I go or stay."

"And now you are asking me to say it will break my heart if you go," said the baroness, with a gay glance of her brown eyes; "and you may ask - and ask!"

She shook hands as she spoke.

"Go, ingratitude!" she said. "But tell me, what will bring you back?"

"War," he answered, with a laugh, pausing for a moment on the threshold.

And three days later Lory de Vasselot stood on the deck of a small trading steamer that rolled sideways into Calvi Bay, on the shoulder, as it were, of one of those March mistrals which serve as the last kick of the dying winter. De Vasselot had taken the first steamer he could find at Marseilles, with a fine disregard for personal comfort, which was part of his military training and parcel of his sporting instincts. He was, like many islanders, a good sailor, for, strange as it may seem, a man may inherit from his forefathers not only a taste for the sea, but a stout heart to face its grievous sickness.

There are few finer sights than Calvi Bay when the heavens are clear and the great mountains of the interior tower above the bare coast-hills. But now the clouds hung low over the island, and the shape of the heights was only suggested by a deeper shadow in the grey mist. The little town nestling on a promontory looked gloomy and deserted with its small square houses and medieval fortress - Calvi the faithful, that fought so bravely for the Genoese masters whose mark lies in every angle of its square stronghold; Calvi, where, if (as seems likely) the local historian is to be believed, the greatest of all sailors was born, within a day's ride of that other sordid little town where the greatest of all soldiers first saw the light. Assuredly Corsica has done its duty - has played its part in the world's history - with Christopher Columbus ´and Napoleon as leading actors.

De Vasselot landed in a small boat, carrying his own simple luggage. He had not been very sociable on the trading steamer; had dined with the captain, and now bade him farewell without an exchange of names. There is a small inn on the wharf facing the anchorage and the wave-washed steps where the fishing-boats lie. Here the traveller had a better lunch than the exterior of the house would appear to promise, and found it easy enough to keep his own counsel; for he was now in Corsica, where silence is not only golden, but speech is apt to be fatal.

"I am going to St. Florent," he said to the woman who had waited on him. "Can I have a carriage or a horse? I am indifferent which."

"You can have a horse," was the reply, "and leave it at Rutali's at St. Florent when you have done with it. The price is ten francs. There are parts of the road impassable for a carriage in this wind."

De Vasselot replied by handing her ten francs, and asked no further questions. If you wish to answer no questions, ask none.

The horse presently appeared, a little thin beast, all wires, carrying its head too high, boring impatiently - masterful, intractable.

"He wants riding," said the man who led him to the door, half sailor, half stableman, who made fast de Vasselot's portmanteau to the front of the high Spanish saddle with a piece of tarry rope and simple nautical knots.

He nodded curtly, with an upward jerk of the head, as Lory climbed into the saddle and rode away; for there is nothing so difficult to conceal as horsemanship.

"A soldier," muttered the stable-man. "A gendarme, as likely as not."

De Vasselot did not ask the way, but trusted to Fortune, who as usual favoured him who left her a free hand. There is but one street in Calvi, but one way out of the town, and a cross-road leading north and south. Lory turned to the north. He had a map in his pocket, which he knew almost by heart; for he was an officer of the finest cavalry in the world, and knew his business as well as any. And it is the business of the individual trooper to find his way in an unknown country. That a couple of hours' hard riding brought him to his own lands, de Vasselot knew not nor heeded, for he was aware that he could establish his rights only by force of martial law, and with a miniature army at his back; for civil law here is paralyzed by a cloud of false witnesses, while equity is administered by a jury which is under the influence of the two strongest of human motives, greed and fear.

At times the solitary rider mounted into the clouds that hung low upon the hills, shutting in the valleys beneath their grey canopy, and again descended to deep gorges; where brown water churned in narrow places. And at all times he was alone. For the Government has built roads through these rocky places, but it has not yet succeeded in making traffic upon them.

With the quickness of his race de Vasselot noted everything - the trend of the watersheds, the colour of the water, the prevailing wind as indicated by the growth of the trees - a hundred petty details of Nature which would escape any but a trained comprehension, or that wonderful eye with which some men are born, who cannot but be gipsies all their lives, whether fate has made them rich or poor; who cannot live in towns, but must breathe the air of open heaven, and deal by sea or land with the wondrous works of God.

It was growing dusk when de Vasselot crossed the bridge that spans the Aliso - his own river, that ran through and all around his own land - and urged his tired horse along the level causeway built across the old river-bed into the town of St. Florent. The field-workers were returning from vineyard and olive grove, but appeared to take little heed of him as he trotted past them on the dusty road. These were no heavy, agricultural boors, of the earth earthy, but lithe, dark-eyed men and women, who tilled the ground grud-gingly, because they had no choice between that and starvation. Their lack of curiosity arose, not from stupidity, but from a sort of pride which is only seen in Spain and certain South American States. The proudest man is he who is sufficient for himself.

A single inquiry enabled de Vasselot to find the house of Rutali; for St. Florent is a small place, with Ichabod written large on its crumbling houses. It was a house like another - that is to say, the ground floor was a stable, while the family lived above in an atmosphere of its own and the stable drainage.

The traveller gave Rutali a small coin, which was coldly accepted - for a Corsican never refuses money like a Spaniard, but accepts it grudgingly, mindful of the insult - and left St. Florent by the road that he had come, on foot, humbly carrying his own portmanteau. Thus Lory de Vasselot, went through his paternal acres with a map. His intention was to catch a glimpse of the Chateau de Vasselot, and walk on to the village of Olmeta, and there beg bed and board from his faithful correspondent, the Abbé Susini.

He followed the causeway across the marsh to the mouth of the river, and here turned to the left, leaving the *route nationale* to Calvi on the right. That which he now followed was the narrower *route departementale*, which borders the course of the stream Guadelle, a tributary to the Aliso. The valley is flat here - a mere level of river deposit, damp in winter, but dry and sandy in the autumn. Here are cornfields and vineyards all in one, with olives and almonds growing amid the wheat - a promised land of milk and honey. There are no walls, but great hedges of aloe and prickly pear serve as a sterner landmark. At the side of the road are here and there a few crosses - the silent witnesses that stand on either side of every Corsican road - marking the spot where such and such a one met his death, or was found dead by his friends.

Above, perched on the slope that rises abruptly on the left-hand side of the road, the village of Oletta looks out over the plain towards St. Florent and the sea - a few brown houses of dusky stone, with roofs of stone; a square-towered church, built just where the cultivation ceases and the rocks and the macquis begin.

De Vasselot quitted the road where it begins sharply to ascend, and took the narrow path that follows the course of the river, winding through the olive groves around the great rock that forms a shoulder of Monte Torre, and breaks off abruptly in a sheer cliff. He looked upward with a soldier's eye at this spot, designed by nature as the site of a fort which could command the whole valley and the roads to Corte and Calvi. Far above, amid chestnut trees and some giant pines, De Vasselot could see the roof and the chimneys of a house - it was the Casa Perucca. Presently he was so immediately below it that he could see it no longer as he followed the path, winding as the river wound through the narrow flat valley.

Suddenly he came out of the defile into a vast open country, spread out like a fan upon a gentle slope rising to the height of the Col St. Stefano, where the Bastia road comes through the Lancone defile - the road by which Colonel Gilbert had ridden to the Casa Perucca not so very long before. At the base of the fan runs the Aliso, without haste, bordered on either bank by oleanders growing like rushes. Halfway down the slope is a lump of land which looks like, and probably is, a piece of the mountain cast off by some subterranean disturbance, and gently rolled down into the valley. It stands alone, and on its summit, three hundred feet above the plain, are the square-built walls of what was once a castle.

Lory stood for a moment and looked at this prospect, now pink and hazy in the reflected light of the western sky. He knew that he was looking at the Chateau de Vasselot.

Within the crumbling walls, built on the sheer edge of the rock, stood, amid a disorderly thicket of bamboo and feathery pepper and deep copper beech, a square stone house with smokeless chimneys, and, so far as was visible, every shutter shut. The owner of it and all these lands, the bearer of the name that was written here upon the map, walked slowly out into the open country. He turned once and looked back at the towering cliff behind him, the rocky peninsula where the Casa Perucca stood amidst its great trees, and hid the village of Olmeta, perched on the mountain side behind it.

The short winter twilight was almost gone before de Vasselot reached the base of the mound of half-shattered rock upon which the chateau had been built. The wall that had once been the outer battlement of the old stronghold was so fallen into disrepair that he anticipated no difficulty in finding a gap through which to pass within the enclosure where the house

Henry Seton Merriman

was hidden; but he walked right round and found no such breach. Where the wall of rock proved vulnerable, the masonry, by some curious chance, was invariably sound.

It had not been de Vasselot's intention to disturb the old gardener, who, he understood, was left in charge of the crumbling house, but to return the next day with the Abbé Susini. But he was tired, and having failed to gain an entrance, was put out and angry, when at length he found himself near the great door built in the solid wall on the north-west side of the ruin. A rusty bell-chain was slowly swinging in the wind, which was freshening again at sunset, as the mistral nearly always does when it is dying. With some difficulty he succeeded in swinging the heavy bell suspended inside the door, so that it gave two curt clangs as of a rusty tongue against moss-grown metal.

After some time the door was opened by a grey-haired man in his shirt-sleeves. He wore a huge black felt hat, and the baggy corduroy trousers of a deep brown, which are almost universal in this country. He held the door half open and peered out. Then he slowly opened it and stood back.

"Good God!" he whispered. "Good God!"

De Vasselot stepped over the threshold with one quick glance at the single-barrelled gun in the man's hand.

"I am - " he began.

"Yes," interrupted the other, breathlessly. "Straight on; the door is open."

Half puzzled, Lory de Vasselot advanced towards the house alone; for the peasant was long in closing the door and readjusting chain and bolts. The shutters of the house were all closed, but the door, as he had said, was open. The place was neatly enough kept, and the house stood on a lawn of that brilliant green turf which is only seen in parts of England, in Ireland, and in Corsica.

De Vasselot went into the house, which was all dark by reason of the closed shutters. There was a large room, opposite to the front door, dimly indicated by the daylight behind him. He went into it, and was going straight to one of the windows to throw back the shutters, when a sharp click brought him round on his heels as if he had been shot. In a far corner of the room, in a dark doorway, stood a shadow. The click was that of a trigger.

Quick as thought de Vasselot ran to the window, snatched at the opening, opened it, threw back the shutter, and was round again with bright and flashing eyes facing the doorway. A man stood there watching him - a man of his own build, slight and quick, with close upright hair like his own, but it was white; with a neat upturned moustache like his own, but it was white; with a small quick face like his own, but it was bleached. The eyes that flashed back were dark like his own.

"You are a de Vasselot," said this man, quickly.

"Are you Lory de Vasselot?"

"Yes."

"Then I am your father."

"Yes," said Lory, slowly; "there is no mistaking it."

CHAPTER VIII.

AT VASSELOT.

"The life unlived, the deed undone, the tear unshed ... not judging those, who judges right?"

It was the father who spoke first.

"Shut that shutter, my friend," he said. "It has not been opened for thirty years."

He had an odd habit of jerking his head upwards and sideways with raised eyebrows. It would appear that a trick of thus deploring some unavoidable misfortune had crystallized itself, as it were, into a habit by long use. And the old man rarely spoke now without this upward jerk.

Lory closed the shutter and followed his father into an adjoining room - a small, round apartment lighted by a skylight and impregnated with tobacco-smoke. The carpet was worn into holes in several places, and the boards beneath were polished by the passage of smooth soles. Lory glanced at his father's feet, which were encased in carpet slippers several sizes too large for him, bought at a guess in the village shop.

Henry Seton Merriman

Here again the two men stood and looked at each other. And again it was the father who broke the silence.

"My son," he said, half to himself; "and a soldier. Your mother was a bad woman, mon ami. And I have lived thirty years in this room," he concluded simply.

"Name of God!" exclaimed Lory. "And what have you done all this time?"

"Carnations," replied the old man, gravely. "There is still daylight. Come; I will show you. Yes; carnations."

As he spoke he turned and opened the door behind him. It led out to a small terrace no larger than a verandah, and every inch of earth was occupied by the pale green of carnation-spikes. Some were budding, some in bloom. But there was not a flower among them at which a modern gardener would not have laughed aloud. And there were tears in Lory de Vasselot's eyes as he looked at them.

The father stood, jerking his head and looking at his son, waiting his verdict.

"Yes," was the son's reply at last; "yes - very pretty."

"But to-night you cannot see them," said the old man, earnestly. "To-morrow morning - we shall get up early, eh?"

"Yes," said Lory, slowly; and they went back into the little windowless room.

"We will get up early," said the count, "to see the

pinks. This cursed mistral beats them to pieces, but I
have no other place to grow them. It is the only spot
that is not overlooked by Perucca."

He spoke slowly and indifferently, as if his spirit had
been bleached, like his face, by long confinement. He
had lost his grip of the world and of human interests.
As he looked at his son, his black eyes had a sort of
irresponsible vagueness in their glance.

"Tell me," said Lory, gently, at length, as if he were
speaking to a child; "why have you done this?"

"Then you did not know that I was alive?" inquired his
father in return, with an uncanny, quiet laugh, as he sat
down.

"No."

"No; no one knows that - no one but the Abbé Susini
and Jean there. You saw Jean as you came in. He
recognized you or he would not have let you in; for he
is quick with his gun. He shot a man seven years ago -
one of Perucca's men, of course, who was creeping up
through the tamarisk trees. I do not know what he
came seeking, but he got more from Jean than he
looked for. Jean was a boy when your mother went to
France, and he was left in charge of the château. For
they all thought that I had gone to France with your
mother, and perhaps the police searched France for me;
I do not know. There is a warrant out against me still,
though the paper it is written on must be yellow
enough after thirty years."

As he spoke he carefully drew up his trousers, which
were of corduroy, like Jean's; indeed, the Count de

Vasselot was dressed like a peasant - but no rustic dress could conceal the tale told by the small energetic head, the clean-cut features. It was obvious that his thoughts were more concerned in his immediate environments - in the care, for instance, to preserve his trousers from bagging at the knee - than he was in the past. He had the curious, slow touch and contemplative manner of the prisoner.

"Yes; Jean was a boy when he first came here, and now he is a grey-haired man, as you see. He picks the olives and earns a little by selling them. Besides, I provided myself with money long ago, before - before I died. I thought I might live long, and I have, for thirty years, like a tree."

Which was nearly true, for his life must have been somewhere midway between the human and the vegetable.

"But why, my God!" cried Lory, impatiently, "why have you done it?"

"Why?" echoed the count, in his calm and suppressed way. "Why? Because I am a Corsican, and am not to be frightened into leaving the country by a parcel of Peruccas. They are no better than the Luccans you see working in the road, and the miserable Pisans who come in the winter to build the terraces. They are no Corsicans, but come from Pisa."

"But if they thought you were dead, what satisfaction could there be in living on here?"

But the count only looked at his son in silence. He did not seem to follow the hasty argument. He had the placid air of a child or a very old man, who will not argue.

"Besides, Mattei Perucca is dead."

"So they say. So Jean tells me. I have not seen the abbé lately. He does not dare to come more often than once in three months - four times a year. Mattei Perucca dead!" He shook his head with the odd, upward jerk and the weary smile. "I should like to see his carcass," he said.

Then, after a pause, he went back to his original train of thought.

"We are different," he said. "We are Corsicans. It was only when the Bonapartes changed their name to a French one that your great-grandfather Gallicized ours. We are not to be frightened away by the Peruccas."

"But since he is dead - " said Lory, with an effort to be patient.

He was beginning to realize now that it was all real and not a dream, that this was the Château de Vasselot, and this was his father - this little, vague, quiet man, who seemed to exist and speak as if he were only half alive.

"He may be," was the answer; "but that will make no difference, since for one adherent that we have the Peruccas have twenty. There are a thousand men between Cap Corse and Balagna who, if I went outside this door and was recognized, would shoot me like a rat."

"But why?"

"Because they are of Perucca's clan, my friend," replied the count, with a shrug of the shoulder.

"But still I ask why?" persisted Lory.

And the count spread out his thin white hands with a gesture of patient indifference.

"Well, of course I shot Andrei Perucca - the brother - thirty years ago. We all know that. That is ancient history."

Lory looked at the little white-haired, placid man, and said no word. It was perhaps the wisest thing to do. When you have nothing to say, say nothing.

"But he has had his revenge - that Mattel Perucca," said the count at length, in a tone of careless reminiscence - "by living in that house all these years, and, so they tell me, by making a small fortune out of the vines. The house is not his, the land is not his. They are mine. Only he and I knew it, and to prove it I should have to come to life. Besides, what is land in this country, unless you till it with a spade in one hand and a gun in the other?"

Lory de Vasselot leant forward in his chair.

"But now is the time to act," he said. "I can act if you will not. I can make use of the law." "The law," answered his father, calmly. "Do you think that you could get a jury in Bastia to give you a verdict? Do you think you could find a witness who would dare to appear in your favour? No, my friend. There is no law in this country, except that;" and he pointed to a gun in the corner of the room, an old-fashioned muzzle-loader, with which he had had the law of Andrei Perucca thirty years before.

"But now that there is no Perucca left the clan will cease to exist," said Lory.

"Not at all," replied the father. "The inheritor of the estate, whoever it is, will become the head of the clan, and things will be as they were before. They tell me it is a woman named Denise Lange."

Lory gave a start. He had forgotten Denise Lange, and all that world of Paris fad and fashion.

"And the women are always the worst," concluded his father.

They sat in silence for some moments. And then the count spoke again in his odd, detached way, as if he were contemplating his environments from afar.

"There was a man in Sartene who had an enemy. He was a shoemaker, and could therefore work at his trade indoors. He never crossed his threshold for sixteen years. One day they told him his enemy was dead, that the funeral was for the same afternoon. It passed his door, and when it had gone by, he stepped out, after sixteen, years, to watch it, and - Paff! He twisted himself round as he writhed on the ground, and there was his enemy, laughing, with the smoke still at the muzzle. The funeral was a trick. No; I shall not believe that Mattei Perucca is dead until the Abbé Susini tells me that he has seen the body. Not that it would make any difference. I should not go outside the door. I am accustomed to this life now."

He sat with his hands idly crossed on his knee, and looked at nothing in particular. Nothing could arouse him now from his apathy, except perhaps the culture of carnations - certainly not the arrival of the son whom he had never seen. He had that air of waiting without expectancy which is assuredly the dungeon mark, and a moral mourning worn for dead Hope.

Lory contemplated him as a strange old man who interested him despite himself. There was pity, but nothing filial in his feelings. For filial love only grows out of propinquity and a firm respect which must keep pace with the growing demands of a daily increasing comprehension.

"Why did you come?" asked the count, suddenly.

It seemed as if his mind lay hidden under the accumulated *débris* of the years, as the old château perhaps lay hidden beneath that smooth turf which only grows over ruins.

"I do not know," answered Lory, thoughtfully. Then he turned in his quick way, and looked at his father with a smile. "Perhaps it was the good God who put the idea into my head, for it came quite suddenly. We shall grow accustomed to each other, and then we may find perhaps that it was a good thing that I came."

The count looked at him with rather a puzzled air, as if he did not quite understand.

"Yes," he said at length - "yes; perhaps so. I thought it likely that you would come. Do you mean to stay?"

"I do not know. I have not thought yet. I have had no

time to think. I only know I am hungry. Perhaps Jean will get me something to eat."

"I have not dined yet," said the count, simply. "Yes; we will dine."

He rose, and, going to the door, called Jean, who came, and a whispered consultation ensued. From out of the *débris* of his mind the count seemed to have unearthed the fact that he was a gentleman, and as such was called upon to exercise an unsparing hospitality. He rather impeded than helped the taciturn man, who seemed to be gardener and servant all in one, and who now prepared the table, setting thereon linen and glass and silver of some value. There was excellent wine, and over the simple meal the father and son, in a jerky, explosive way, made merry. For Lory was at heart a Frenchman, and the French know, better than any, how near together tears and laughter must ever be, and have less difficulty in snatching a smile from sad environments than other men.

It was only as he finally cleared the table that Joan broke his habitual silence.

"The moon is up," he said to the count, and that was all.

The old man rose at once, and went to a window, which had hitherto been shuttered and barred.

"I sometimes look out," he said, "when there is a moon."

With odd, slow movements he opened the shutter and window, and, turning, invited Lory by a jerk of the head to come and look. The moon, which must have been at the full, was behind the château, and therefore invisible. Before them, in a framework of giant pines that have no match in Europe, lay a panorama of rolling plain and gleaming river. Far away towards Calvi and the south, range after range of rugged mountain melted into a distance, where the snow-clad summits of Cinto and Grosso stood majestically against the sky. The clouds had vanished. It was almost twilight under the southern moon. To the right the sea lay shimmering.

"I did not know that there was anything like it in Europe," said Lory, after a long pause.

"There is nothing like it," answered his father, gravely, "in the world."

Father and son were still standing at the open window, when Jean came hurriedly into the room.

"It is the abbé," he said, and went out again. The count stepped down from the raised window recess, and turned up the lamp, which he had lowered. Lory paused to close the shutter, and as he did so the Abbé Susini came into the room without looking towards the window, which was near the door by which he entered, without, therefore, seeing Lory. He hurried into the room, and stopped dead, facing the count. He threw out one finger, and pointed at his interlocutor as he spoke, in his quick dramatic way.

"I have just seen a man from Calvi. One landed there this morning whom he recognized. It could only have been your son. If one recognizes him, another may. Is the boy mad to return thus - "

He broke off, and made a step nearer, peering into the count's face.

"You know something. I see it in your face. You know where he is."

"He is there," said the count, pointing over the priest's shoulder.

"Then God bless him," said the Abbé Susini, turning on his heel.

Henry Seton Merriman

CHAPTER IX.

THE PROMISED LAND.

"I do not ask that flowers should always spring beneath my feet."

Colonel Gilbert was not one of those visionaries who think that the lot of the individual man is to be bettered by a change from, say, an empire to a republic. Indeed, the late transformation from a republic to an empire had made no difference to him, for he was neither a friend nor a foe of the emperor. He had nothing in common with those soldiers of the Second Empire who had won their spurs in the Tuileries, and owed promotion to a woman's favouritism. He was, in a word, too good a soldier to be a good courtier; and politics represented for him, as they do for most wise men, an after-breakfast interest, and an edifying study of the careers of a certain number of persons who mean to make themselves a name in the easiest arena that is open to ambition.

The colonel read the newspapers because there was little else to do in Bastia, and the local gossip "on tap," as it were, at the cafés and the "Réunion des Officiers," had but a limited interest for him. He was, however, at heart a gossip, and rode or walked through the streets of Bastia with that leisurely air which seems to invite the passer-by to stop and exchange something more than a formal salutation.

The days, indeed, were long enough; for his service often got the colonel out of bed at dawn, and his work was frequently done before civilians were awake. It thus happened that Colonel Gilbert was riding along the coast-road from Brando to Bastia one morning before the sun had risen very high above the heights of Elba. The day was so clear that not only were the rocky islands of Gorgona and Capraja and Monte Cristo visible, but also the mysterious flat Pianosa, so rarely seen, so capricious and singular in its comings and goings that it fades from sight before the very eyes, and in clear weather seems to lie like a raft on the still water.

The colonel was contemplating the scene with a leisurely, artistic eye, when some instinct made him turn his head and look over his shoulder towards the north.

"Ah!" he muttered, with a nod of satisfaction.

A steamer was slowly pounding down towards Bastia. It was the Marseilles boat - the old *Persévérance*. And for Colonel Gilbert she was sure to bring news from France, possibly some one with whom to while away an hour or so in talk. He rode more leisurely now, and the steamer passed him. By the time he reached the dried-fruit factory on the northern outskirt of the town, the *Persévérance* had rounded the pier-head, and was gently edging alongside the quay. By the time he reached the harbour she was moored, and her captain enjoying a morning cigar on the wharf.

Henry Seton Merriman

Of course Colonel Gilbert knew the captain of the *Persévérance*. Was he not friendly with the driver of the St. Florent diligence? All who brought news from the outside world were the friends of this idle soldier.

"Good morning, captain," he cried. "What news of France?"

The captain was a jovial man, with unkempt hair and a smoke-grimed face.

"News, colonel," he answered. "It is not quite ready yet. The emperor is always brewing it in the Tuileries, but it is not ripe for the public palate yet."

"Ah!"

"And in the mean time," said the captain, testing with his foot the tautness of the hawser that moored the *Persévérance* to the quay - "in the mean time they are busy at Cherbourg and Toulon. As to the army, you probably know that better than I, mon colonel."

And he finished with his jovial laugh. Then he jerked his thumb in the direction of the steamer.

"Your newspapers are, no doubt, in the mail-bags," he said. "We had a good passage, and are a full ship. Of passengers I have two - and ladies. One, by the way, is the heiress of Mattei Perucca over at Olmeta, whom you doubtless knew."

The colonel turned, and looked towards the steamer with some interest.

"Is that so?" he said reflectively.

"Yes; a pinched old maid in a black dress. None will marry her for her acres. It will be a *pré salé* with a vengeance. I caught a glimpse of her as we came out of harbour. I did not see the other, who is young - her niece, I understand. There she is, coming on deck now - the heiress, I mean. She will not look her best after a night at sea."

And, with a jerk of the head, he indicated a black-clad form on the deck of the *Persévérance*. It happened to be Mademoiselle Brun, who, as a matter of fact, looked no different after a night at sea to what she had looked in the drawing-room of the Baroness de Mélide. She was too old or too tough to take her colour from her environments. She was standing with her back towards the quay, talking to the steward, and did not, therefore, see the colonel until the clank of his spurred heel on the deck made her turn sharply.

"You, mademoiselle!" exclaimed the colonel, on seeing her face as he stood, *képi* in hand, staring at her in astonishment.

"Yes; I am the ogre chosen by Fate to watch over Denise Lange," she answered, holding out her withered hand.

"But this is indeed a pleasure," said the colonel, with his ready smile. "I came by a mere accident to offer my services, as any Frenchman would, to ladies arriving at such a place as Bastia, as a friend, moreover, of Mattel Perucca, and never expected to see a face I knew. It is years, mademoiselle, since we met - since before the war - before Solferino."

"Yes," said Mademoiselle Brun; "since before Solferino."

And she glanced suspiciously at him, as if she had something to hide. A chance word often is the "open sesame" to that cupboard where we keep our cherished skeleton. Colonel Gilbert saw the quick glance, and misconstrued it.

"I wrote a letter some time ago," he said, "to Mademoiselle Lange, making her an offer for her property, little dreaming that I had so old a friend as yourself at hand, as one may say, to introduce us to each other."

"No," said Mademoiselle Brun.

"And I was surprised to receive a refusal."

"Yes," said Mademoiselle Brun, looking across the harbour towards the old town.

"There are not many buyers of land in Corsica," he explained, half indifferently, "and there are plenty of other plots which would serve my purpose. However, I will not buy elsewhere until you and Mademoiselle Lange have had an opportunity of seeing Perucca - that is certain. No; it is only friendly to keep my offer open."

He was standing with his face turned towards the deck-house and the saloon stairway, and tapped his boot idly with his whip. There was something expectant and almost anxious in his demeanour. Mademoiselle Brun was looking at his face, and he was perhaps not aware that it changed at this moment.

"Yes," she said, without looking round; "that is my niece. You find her pretty?"

"Present me," answered the colonel, turning to hook his sword to his belt.

Denise came hurriedly across the deck, her eyes bright with anticipation and happiness. This was a better life than that of the Rue du Cherche-Midi, and the stir and bustle of the sailors, already at work on the cargo, were contagious. She noticed that Mademoiselle Brun was speaking to an officer, but was more interested in the carriage, which, in accordance with an order sent by the captain, was at this moment rattling across the stones towards the steamer.

"This," said Mademoiselle Brun, "is Colonel Gilbert, whose letter you answered a few weeks ago."

"Ah, yes," said Denise, returning his bow, and looking at him with frank eyes. "Thank you very much, monsieur, but we are going to live at Perucca ourselves."

"By all means," laughed the colonel, "try it, mademoiselle; try it. It is an impossibility, I tell you frankly. And Corsica is not a country in which to attempt impossibilities. See here! I perceive you have your carriage ready, and the sailors are now carrying your baggage ashore. You are going to drive to Perucca. Good! Now, as you pass along the road, you will perceive on either side quite a number of small crosses, simply planted at the roadside - some of iron, some of wood, some with a name, some with initials. They are to be found all over Corsica, at the side of every road. Those are people, mademoiselle, who have attempted impossibilities in this country and have failed - at the very spot where the cross is planted. You understand? I speak as a soldier to a soldier's daughter."

He looked at her, and nodded slowly and gravely with compressed lips.

"Rest assured that we shall not attempt impossibilities," replied Denise, gaily. "We only ask to be left alone to feed our poultry and attend to our garden. I am told that the house and servants are as my father's cousin left them, and we are expected to-day."

"And you, colonel, shall be our protector," added Mademoiselle Brun, with one of her straight looks.

The colonel laughed, shrugged his shoulders, and accompanied them to the carriage which awaited them.

"If one only knew whether you approve or disapprove of these hair-brained proceedings," he took an opportunity of saying to Mademoiselle Brun, when Denise was out of earshot.

"If I only knew myself," she replied coldly.

They climbed into the high, old-fashioned carriage, and drove through the new Boulevard du Palais, upward to the hills above the town. And if they observed the small crosses on either side of the road, marking the spot where some poor wight had come to what is here called an accidental death, they took care to make no mention of it. For Denise persisted in seeing everything in that rose light which illumines the world when we are young. She had even a good word to say for the *Persévérance*, which vessel had assuredly need of such, and said that the captain was a good French sailor, despite his grimy face.

"This," she cried, "is better than your stuffy schoolroom!"

And she stood up in the carriage to inhale the breeze that hummed through the macquis from the cool mountain-tops. There is no air like that which comes as through a filter made of a hundred scented trees - a subtle mingling of their clean woody odours.

"Look!" she added, pointing down to the sea, which looked calm from this great height. "Look at that queer flat island there. That is Pianosa. And there is Elba. Elba! Cannot the magic of that word rouse you? But no, you have no Corsican blood in you; and you sit there with your uncompromising old face and your black bonnet a little bit on one side, if I may mention it" - and she proceeded to put Mademoiselle Brun's bonnet straight - "you, who are always in mourning for something - I don't know what," she added half reflectively, as she sat down again.

The road to St. Florent mounts in a semi-circle behind Bastia through orange-groves and vineyards, and the tiny private burial-grounds so dear to Corsican families of position. These, indeed, are a proud people, for they are too good to await the last day in the company of their humbler brethren, but must needs have a small garden and a hideous little mausoleum of their own, with a fine view and easy access to the highroad.

With many turns the great road climbs round the face of the mountain, and soon leaving Bastia behind, takes a southern trend, and suddenly commands from a height a matchless view of the Lake of Biguglia and the little hillside village where a Corsican parliament once sat, which was once, indeed, the capital of this war-torn island. For every village can boast of a battle, and the rocky earth has run with the blood of almost every European nation, as well as that of Turk and Moor. Beyond the lake, and stretching away into a blue haze where sea and land melt into one, lies the great salt marsh where the first Greek colony was located, where the ruins of Mariana remain to this day.

Soon the road mounts above the level of the semi-tropical vegetation, and passes along the face of bare and stony heights, where the pines are small and the macquis no higher than a man's head.

Denise, tired with so long a drive at a snail's pace, jumped from the carriage.

"I will walk up this hill," she cried to the driver, who had never turned in his seat or spoken a word to them.

"Then keep close to the carriage," he answered.

"Why?"

But he only indicated the macquis with his whip, and made no further answer. Mademoiselle Brun said nothing, but presently, when the driver paused to rest the horses, she descended from the carriage and walked with Denise.

It was nearly midday when they at last reached the summit of the pass. The heavy clouds, which had been long hanging over the mountains that border the great plain of Biguglia, had rolled northward before a hot and oppressive breeze, and the sun was now hidden. The carriage descended at a rapid trot, and once the man got down and silently examined his brakes. The road was a sort of cornice cut on the bare mountain side, and a stumble or the slipping of a brake-block would inevitably send the carriage rolling into the valley below.

Denise sat upright, and looked quickly, with eager movements of the head, from side to side. Soon they reached the region of the upper pines, which are small, and presently passed a piece of virgin forest - of those great pines which have no like in Europe.

"Look!" said Denise, gazing up at the great trees with a sort of gasp of excitement.

But mademoiselle had only eyes for the road in front. Before long they passed into the region of chestnuts, and soon saw the first habitation they had seen for two hours. For this is one of the most thinly peopled lands of Europe, and four great nations of the Continent have at one time or other done their best to exterminate this untameable race. Then a few more houses and a smaller road branching off to the left from the highway. The carriage swung round into this, which led straight to a wall built right across it. The driver pulled up, and, turning, brought the horses to a standstill at a door built in the solid wall. With his whip he indicated a bell-chain, rusty and worn, that swung in the breeze.

There was nobody to be seen. The clouds had closed down over the mountains. Even the tops of the great pines were hidden in a thin mist.

Denise got down and rang the bell. After a long pause the door was opened by a woman in black, with a black silk handkerchief over her head, who looked gravely at them.

"I am Denise Lange," said the girl.

"And I," said the woman, stepping back to admit them, "am the widow of Pietro Andrei, who was shot at Olmeta."

And Denise Lange entered her own door followed by Mademoiselle Brun.

CHAPTER X.

THUS FAR.

"There are some occasions on which a man must sell half his secret in order to conceal the rest."

"There is some one moving among the oleanders down by the river," said the count, coming quickly into the room where Lory de Vasselot was sitting, one morning some days after his unexpected arrival at the château.

The old man was cool enough, but he closed the window that led to the small terrace where he cultivated his carnations, with that haste which indicates a recognition of undeniable danger, coupled with no feeling of fear.

"I know every branch in the valley," he said, "every twig, every leaf, every shadow. There is some one there."

Lory rose, and laid aside the pen with which he was writing for an extended leave of absence. In four days these two had, as one of them had predicted, grown accustomed to each other. And the line between custom and necessity is a fine drawn one.

"Show me," he said, going towards the window.

"Ah!" murmured the count, jerking his head. "You will hardly perceive it unless you are a hunter - or the hunted."

Lory glanced at his father. Assuredly the sleeping mind was beginning to rouse itself.

"It is nothing but the stirring of a leaf here, the movement of a branch there, which are unusual and unnatural."

As he spoke, he opened the window with that slow caution which had become habitual to his every thought and action.

"There," he said, pointing with a steady hand; "to the left of that almond tree which is still in bloom. Watch those willows which have come there since the wall fell away, and the terrace slipped into the flooded river twenty-one years this spring. You will see the branches move. There - there! You see. It is a man, and he comes too slowly to have an honest purpose."

"I see," said Lory. "Is that land ours?"

The count gave an odd little laugh.

"You can see nothing from this window that is not ours," he answered. "As much as any other man's," he added, after a pause. For the conviction still holds good in some Corsican minds that the mountains are common property.

"He is coming slowly, but not very cautiously," said

Lory. "Not like a man who thinks that he may be watched from here. He probably is taking no heed of these windows, for he thinks the place is deserted."

"It is more probable," replied the count, "that he is coming here to ascertain that fact. What the abbé has heard, another may hear, though he would not learn it from the abbé. If you want a secret kept, tell it to a priest, and of all priests, the Abbé Susini. Some one has heard that you are here in Corsica, and is creeping up to the castle to find out."

"And I will go and find him out. Two can play at that game in the bushes," said Lory, with a laugh.

"If you go, take a gun; one can never tell how a game may turn."

"Yes; I will take a gun if you wish it." And Lory went towards the door. "No," he said, pausing in answer to a gesture made by his father, "not that one. It is of too old a make."

And he went out of the room, leaving his father holding in his hand the gun with which he had shot Andrei Perucca thirty years before. He stood looking at the closed door with dim, reflective eyes. Then he looked at the gun, which he set slowly back in its corner.

"It seems," he said to himself, "that I am of too old a make also."

He went to the window, and, opening it cautiously, stood looking down into the valley. There he perceived that, though two may play at the same game, it is usually given to one to play it better than the other. For he who was climbing up the hill might be followed by a careful eye, by the chance displacement of a twig, the bending of a bough; while Lory, creeping down into the valley, remained quite invisible, even to his father, upon whose memory every shadow was imprinted.

"Aha!" laughed the old man, under his breath. "One sees that the boy is a Corsican. And," he added, after a pause, "one would almost say that the other is not."

In which the count's trained eye - trained as only is the vision of the hunted - was by no means deceived. For Lory, who was far down in the valley, had already caught sight of a braided sleeve, and, a moment later, recognized Colonel Gilbert. The colonel not only failed to perceive him, but was in nowise looking for him. He appeared to be entirely absorbed, first in the examination of the ground beneath his feet, and then in the contemplation of the rising land. In his hand he seemed to be carrying a note-book, and, so far as the watcher could see, consulted from time to time a compass.

"He is only engaged in his trade," said Lory to himself, with a laugh; and, going out into the open, he sat down on a rock with the gun across his knee and waited.

Thus it happened that Colonel Gilbert, working his way up through the bushes, note-book in hand, looked up and saw, within a few yards of him, the owner of the land upon which they stood, whom he had every reason to believe to be in Paris.

His ruddy face was of a deeper red as he slipped his note-book within his tunic and came forward, holding out his hand. But his smile was as ready and good-natured as ever.

"Well met!" he said. "You find me, count, taking a professional and business-like survey of the laud that you promised to sell me."

"You are welcome to take the survey," answered Lory, taking the outstretched, cordial hand, "but I must ask you to let me keep the land. I did not take your offer seriously."

"It was intended seriously, I assure you."

"Then it was my mistake," answered Lory, quite pleasantly.

He tapped himself vigorously on the chest, and made a gesture indicating that at a word from the colonel he was ready to lay violent hands upon himself for having been so foolish. The colonel laughed, and shrugged his shoulders as if the matter were but a small one. The pitiless Mediterranean, almost African, sun poured down on them, and one of those short spells of absolute calm, which are characteristic of these latitudes, made it unbearably hot. The colonel took off his cap, and, sitting down in quite a friendly way near de Vasselot on a rock, proceeded to mop his high forehead, pressing back the thin smooth hair which was touched here and there with grey.

"You have come here at the wrong time," he said. "The heats have begun. One longs for the cool breezes of Paris or of Normandy."

And he paused, giving Lory an opportunity of

explaining why he had come at this time, which opportunity was promptly neglected.

"At all events, count," said the colonel, replacing his cap and lighting a cigarette, "I did not deceive you as to the nature of the land which I wished to buy. It is a desert, as you see. And yet I cannot help thinking that something might be made of this land."

He sat and gazed lazily in front of him. Presently, leaving his cigarette to smoulder, he began to buzz through his teeth, in the bucolic manner, an air of Offenbach. He was, in a word, entirely agricultural, and consequently slow of speech.

"Yes, count," he said, with conviction, after a long pause; "there is only one drawback to Corsica."

"Ah?"

"The Corsicans," said the colonel, gravely. "You do not know them as I do; for I suppose you have only been here a few days?"

De Vasselot's quick eyes glanced for a moment at the colonel's face, but no reply was made to the supposition. Then the colonel fell to his guileless Offenbach again. There is nothing so innocent as the meditative rendering of a well-known tune. A popular air is that which echoes in empty heads.

Colonel Gilbert glanced sideways at his companion. He had not thought that this was a silent man. Nature was singularly at fault in her mouldings if this slightly made, dark-eyed Frenchman was habitually taciturn. And the colonel was vaguely uneasy.

"My horse," he said, "is up at Olmeta. I took a walk round by the river. It is my business to answer innumerable questions from the Ministry of the Interior. Railway projects are still in the air, you understand. I must know my Corsica. Besides, as I tell you, I thought I was on my own land."

"I am sorry that I cannot hold to my joke, for it was nothing else, as you know."

"Yes, yes, of course," acquiesced the colonel. "And in the mean time, it is a great pleasure to see you here, as well as a surprise. I need hardly tell you that your presence here is quite unknown to your neighbours. We have little to talk about at this end of the island now that the Administration is centred more than ever at Ajaccio; and were it known in the district that you are at Vasselot, you may be sure I should have heard of it at the café or at the hotel where I dine."

"Yes. I came without drum or trumpet."

"You are wise."

The remark was made so significantly that Lory could not ignore it even if such a course had recommended itself to one of his quick and impulsive nature.

"What do you mean, colonel?"

Gilbert made a little gesture of the hand that held the half-burnt cigarette. He deprecated, it would appear, having been drawn to talk on so serious a topic.

"Well, I speak as one Frenchman to another, as one soldier to another. If the emperor does not die, he will declare war against Germany. There is the situation in a nutshell, is it not? And do you think the army can afford to lose one man at the present time, especially a man who has made good use of such small opportunities of distinction as the fates have offered him? And, so far as I have been able to follow the intricacies of the parochial politics, your life is not worth two sous in this country, my dear count. There, I have spoken. A word to the wise, is it not?"

He rose, and threw away his cigarette with a nod and a smile.

"And now I must be returning. You will allow me to pass up that small pathway that leads past the chateau. Some day I should, above all things, like to see the chateau. I am interested in old houses, I tell you frankly."

"I will walk part of the way with you," answered Lory, with a stiffness which was entirely due to a sense of self-reproach. For it was his instinct to be hospitable and open-handed and friendly. And Lory would have liked to ask the colonel then and there to come to the chateau.

"By the way," said the colonel, as they climbed the hill together, "I did not, of course, mean to suggest that you should sell me the old house which bears your name - only a piece of land, a few hectares on this south-west slope, that I may amuse myself with agriculture, as I told you. Perhaps some day you may reconsider your decision?"

He waited for a reply to this suggestion, or an invitation in response to the hint that he was interested in the old house. But neither came.

"I am much obliged to you for your warning as to the unpopularity of my name in this district," said Lory, rather laboriously changing the subject. "I had, of course, heard something of the same sort before; but I do not attach much importance to local tradition, do you?"

The colonel paused for a few minutes. He had the leisurely conversational manner of an old man.

"These people have undergone a change," he said at length, "since their final subjugation by ourselves - exactly a hundred years ago, by the way. They were a turbulent, fighting, obstinate people. Those qualities - good enough in times of war - go bad in times of peace. They are a lawless, idle, dishonest people now. Their grand fighting qualities have run to seed in municipal disagreements and electioneering squabbles. And, worst of all, we have grafted on them our French thrift, which has run to greed. There is not a man in the district who would shoot you, count, from any idea of the vendetta, but there are a hundred who would do it for a thousand-franc note, or in order to prevent you taking back the property which he has stolen from you. That is how it stands. And that is why Pietro Andrei came to grief at Olmeta."

"And Mattei Perucca?" asked Lory, thereby causing the colonel to trip suddenly over a stone.

"Oh, Perucca," he answered, "that was different. He died a more or less natural death. He was a very stout man, and on receiving a letter, gave way to such ungovernable rage that he fell in a fit. True, it was a threatening letter; but such are common enough in this country. It may have been a joke or may have had some comparatively harmless object. None could have foreseen such a result."

They were now near the chateau, and the colonel rather suddenly shook hands and went away.

"I am always to be found at Bastia, and am always at your service," he said, waving a farewell with his whip.

Lory found the door of the chateau ajar, and Jean watching behind it. His father, however, seemed to have forgotten upon what mission he had gone forth, and was sitting placidly in the little room, lighted by a skylight, where they always lived. The sight of Lory reminded him, however.

"Who was it?" he asked, without showing a very keen interest.

"It was a man called Gilbert," answered Lory, "whom I have met in Paris. An engineer. He is stationed at Bastia, and is connected with the railway scheme. A man I should like to like, and yet - He ought to be a good fellow. He has every qualification, and yet - "

Lory did not finish the sentence, but stood reflectively looking at his father.

"He has more than once offered to buy Vasselot," he said, watching for the effect.

"You must never sell Vasselot," replied the old man. He did not seem to conceive it possible that there should be any temptation to do so.

"I do not quite understand Colonel Gilbert," continued Lory. "He has also offered to buy Perucca; but there I think he has to deal with a clever woman."

Henry Seton Merriman

CHAPTER XI.

BY SURPRISE.

"C'est ce qu'on ne dit pas qui explique ce qu'on dit."

From the Rue du Cherche-Midi in Paris to the Casa Perucca in Corsica is as complete a change as even the heart of woman may desire. For the Rue du Cherche-Midi is probably the noisiest corner of that noisy Paris that lies south of the Seine; and the Casa Perucca is one of the few quiet corners of Europe where the madding crowd is non-existent, and that crowning effort of philanthropic folly, the statute holiday, has yet to penetrate.

"Yes," said Mademoiselle Brun, one morning, after she and Denise had passed two months in what she was pleased to term exile - "yes; it is peaceful. Give me war," she added grimly, after a pause.

They were standing on the terrace that looked down over the great valley of Vásselot. There was not a house in sight except the crumbling chateau. The month was June, and the river, which could be heard in winter, was now little more than a trickling stream. A faint breeze stirred the young leaves of the copper-beech, which is a silent tree by nature, and did not so much as whisper now. There are few birds in Corsica, for the natives are great sportsmen, and will shoot, sitting, anything from a man to a sparrow in season and out.

"Listen," said Mademoiselle Brun, holding up one steady, yellow finger; but the silence was such as will make itself felt. "And the neighbours do not call much," added mademoiselle, in completion of her own thoughts.

Denise laughed. She had been up early, for they were almost alone in the Casa Perucca now. The servants who had obeyed Mattei Perucca in fear and trembling, had refused to obey Denise, who, with much spirit, had dismissed them one and all. An old man remained, who was generally considered to be half-witted; and Maria Andrei, the widow of Pietro, who was shot at Olmeta. Denise superintended the small farm.

"That cheery Maria," said Mademoiselle Brun, "she is our only resource, and reminds me of a cheap funeral."

"There is the colonel," said Denise. "You forget him."

"Yes; there is the colonel, who is so kind to us."

And Mademoiselle Brun slowly contemplated the whole landscape, taking in Denise, as it were, in passing.

"And there is our little friend," she added, "down in the valley there who does not call."

"Why do you call him little?" asked Denise, looking down at the Chateau de Vasselot. "He is not little."

"He is not so large as the colonel," explained mademoiselle.

"I wonder why he does not call?" said Denise, presently, looking down into the valley, as if she could perhaps see the explanation there.

"It has something to do with the social geography of the district," said mademoiselle, "which we do not understand. The Cheap Funeral alone knows it. Half of the country she colours red, the other half black. Theoretically, we hate a number of persons who reciprocate the feeling heartily. Practically, we do not know of their existence. I imagine the Count de Vasselot hates us on the same principle."

"But we are not going to be dictated to by a number of ignorant peasants," cried Denise, angrily.

"I rather fancy we are."

Denise was standing by the low wall, with her head thrown back. She was naturally energetic, and had the carriage that usually goes with that quality.

"Are you sure he is there?" she asked, still looking down at the château.

"No, I am not. I have only Maria's word for it."

"Then I am going to the village of Olmeta to find out," said Denise.

And mademoiselle followed her to the house without comment. Indeed, she seemed willing enough to do that which they had been warned not to do.

On the road that skirts the hill and turns amid groves of chestnut trees, they met two men, loitering along with no business in hand, who scowled at them and made no salutation.

"They may scowl beneath their great hats," said Denise; "I am not afraid of them." And she walked on with her chin well up.

Below them, on the left, the terraces of vine and olive were weed-grown and neglected; for Denise had found no one to work on her land, and the soil here is damp and warm, favouring a rapid growth.

Colonel Gilbert had been unable to help them in this matter. His official position necessarily prevented his taking an active part in any local differences. There were Luccans, he said, to be hired at Bastia, hard-working men and skilled vine-dressers, but they would not come to a commune where such active hostility existed, and to induce them to do so would inevitably lead to bloodshed.

The Abbé Susini had called, and told a similar tale in more guarded language. Finding the ladies good Catholics, he pleaded for and abused his poor in one breath, and then returned half the money that Denise gave him.

"As likely as not you will be given credit for the whole in heaven, mademoiselle, but I will only take part of it," he said.

"A masterful man," commented Mademoiselle Brun, when he was gone.

But the abbé had suggested no solution to Denise's difficulties. The estate seemed to be drifting naturally into the hands of the only man who wanted it, and, after all, had offered a good price for it.

"I will find out from the Abbé Susini or the mayor whether the Count de Vasselot is really here," Denise said, as they approached the village. "And if he is, we will go and see him. We cannot go on like this. He says do not sell, and then he does not come near us. He must give his reasons. Why should I take his advice?"

"Why, indeed?" said Mademoiselle Brun, to whom the question was not quite a new one.

She knew that though Denise would rebel against de Vasselot's advice, she would continue to follow it.

"It seems to be luncheon-time," said Denise, when they reached the village. "The place is deserted. It must be their *déjeuner*."

"It may be," responded mademoiselle, with her manlike curtness of speech.

They went into the church, which was empty, and stayed but a few minutes there, for Mademoiselle Brun was as short in her speech with God as with men. When they came out to the market-place, that also was deserted, which was singular, because the villagers in Corsica spend nearly the whole day on the market-place, talking politics and whispering a hundred intrigues of parochial policy; for here a municipal councillor is a great man, and usually a great scoundrel, selling his favour and his vote, trafficking for power, and misappropriating the public funds. Not only was the market-place empty, but some of the house-doors were closed. The door of a small shop was even shut from within as they approached, and surreptitiously barred. Mademoiselle Brun noticed it, and Denise did not pretend to ignore it.

"One would say that we had an infectious complaint," she said, with a short laugh.

They went to the house of the Abbé Susini. Even this door was shut.

"The abbé is out," said the old woman, who came in answer to their summons, and she closed the door again with more speed than politeness.

Denise did not need to ask which was the mayor's house, for a board, with the word "Mairie" painted upon it (appropriately enough a movable board), was affixed to a house nearly opposite to the church. As they walked towards it, a stone, thrown from the far corner of the Place, under the trees, narrowly missed Denise, and rolled at her feet. Mademoiselle Brun walked on, but Denise swung round on her heel. There was no one to be seen, so she had to follow Mademoiselle Brun, after all, in silence. She was rather pale, but it was anger that lighted her eyes, and not fear.

Almost immediately a volley of stones followed, and a laugh rang out from beneath the trees. And, strange to say, it was the laugh that at last frightened Denise, and not the stones; for it was a cruel laugh - the laugh of a brutal fool, such as one may still hear in a few European countries when boys are torturing dumb animals.

"Let us hurry," said Denise, hastily. "Let us get to the Mairie."

"Where we shall find the biggest scoundrel of them all, no doubt," added mademoiselle, who was alert and cool.

But before they reached the Mairie the stones had ceased, and they both turned at the sound of a horse's feet. It was Colonel Gilbert riding hastily into the Place. He saw the stones lying there and the two women standing alone in the sunlight. He looked towards the trees, and then round at the closed houses. With a shrug of the shoulders, he rode towards Denise and dismounted.

"Mademoiselle", he said, "they have been frightening you."

"Yes", she answered. "They are not men, but brutes."

The colonel, who was always gentle in manner, made a deprecatory gesture with the great riding-whip that he invariably carried.

"You must remember", he said, "that they are but half civilized. You know their history - they have been conquered by all the greedy nations in succession, and they have never known peace from the time that history began until a hundred years ago. They are barbarians, mademoiselle, and barbarians always distrust a new-comer."

"But why do they hate me?"

"Because they do not know you, mademoiselle,"

replied the colonel, with perhaps a second meaning in his blue eyes.

And, after a pause, he explained further.

"Because they do not understand you. They belong to one of the strongest clans in Corsica, and it is the ambition of every one to belong to a strong clan. But the Peruccas are in danger of falling into dissension and disorder, for they have no head. You are the head, mademoiselle. And the work they expect of you is not work for such hands as yours."

And again Colonel Gilbert looked at Denise slowly and thoughtfully. She did not perceive the glance, for she was standing with her head half turned towards the trees.

"Ah!" he said, noting the direction of her glance, "they will throw no more stones, mademoiselle. You need have no anxiety. They fear a uniform as much as they hate it."

"And if you had not come at that moment?"

"Ah!" said the colonel, gravely; and that was all. "At any rate, I am glad I came," he added, in a lighter tone, after a pause. "You were going to the Mairie, mesdemoiselles, when I arrived. Take my advice, and do not go there. Go to the abbé if you like - as a man, not as a priest - and come to me whenever you desire a service, but to no one else in Corsica."

Denise turned as if she were going to make an exception to this sweeping restriction, but she checked herself and said nothing. And all the while

Mademoiselle Brun stood by in silence, a little, patient, bent woman, with compressed lips, and those steady hazel eyes that see so much and betray so little.

"The abbé is not at home," continued the colonel. "I saw him many miles from here not long ago; and although he is quick on his legs - none quicker - He cannot be here yet. If you are going towards the Casa Perucca, you will perhaps allow me to accompany you".

He led the way as he spoke, leading loosely by the bridle the horse which followed him, and nuzzled thoughtfully at his shoulder. The colonel was, it appeared, one whose gentle ways endeared him to animals.

It was glaringly hot, and when they reached the Casa Perucca, Denise asked the colonel to come in and rest. It was, moreover, luncheon-time, and in a thinly populated country the great distances between neighbours are conducive to an easier hospitality than that which exists in closer quarters. The colonel naturally stayed to luncheon.

He was kind and affable, and had a hundred little scraps of gossip such as exiles love. He made no mention of his offer to buy Perucca, remembered only the fact that he was a gentleman accepting frankly a lady's frank hospitality, and if the conversation turned to local matters, he gracefully guided it elsewhere.

Immediately after luncheon he rose from the table, refusing even to wait for coffee.

"I have my duties," he explained. "The War Office is,

for reasons known to itself, moving troops, and I have gradually crept up the ladder at Bastia, till I am nearly at the top there."

Denise went with him to the stable to see that his horse had been cared for.

"They have only left me the decrepit and the half-witted," she said, "but I am not beaten yet."

Colonel Gilbert fetched the horse himself and tightened the girths. They walked together towards the great gate of solid wood which fitted into the high wall so closely that none could peep through so much as a crack. At the door the colonel lingered, leaning against his great horse and stroking its shoulder thoughtfully with a gloved finger.

"Mademoiselle," he said at length.

"Yes," answered Denise, looking at him so honestly in the face that he had to turn away.

"I want to ask you," he said slowly, "to marry me."

Denise looked at him in utter astonishment, her face suddenly red, her eyes half afraid.

"I do not understand you," she said.

"And yet it is simple enough," answered the colonel, who himself was embarrassed and ill at ease. "I ask you to marry me. You think I am too old - " He paused, seeking his words. "I am not forty yet, and, at all events, I am not making the mistake usually made by very young men. I do not imagine that I love you - I know it."

They stood for a minute in silence; then the colonel spoke again.

"Of what are you thinking, mademoiselle?"

"That it is hard to lose the only friend we have in Corsica."

"You need not do that," replied the colonel. "I do not even ask you to answer now."

"Oh, I can answer at once."

Colonel Gilbert bit his lip, and looked at the ground in silence.

"Then I am too old?" he said at length.

"I do not know whether it is that or not," answered Denise; and neither spoke while the colonel mounted and rode slowly away. Denise closed the door quite softly behind him.

CHAPTER XII.

A SUMMONS.

"One stern tyrannic thought that made
All other thoughts its slave."

All round the Mediterranean Sea there dwell people
who understand the art of doing nothing. They do it
unblushingly, peaceably, and of a set purpose.
Moreover, their forefathers must have been addicted to
a similar philosophy; for there is no Mediterranean
town or village without its promenade or lounging-
place, where the trees have grown quite large, and the
shade is quite deep, and the wooden or stone seats are
shiny with use. Here those whom the French call
"worth-nothings" congregate peacefully and happily, to
look at the sea and contemplate life from that reflective
and calm standpoint which is only to be enjoyed by the
man who has nothing to lose. To begin at Valentia, one
will find these human weeds almost Oriental in their
apathy. Farther north, at Barcelona, they are given to
fitful lapses into activity before the heat of the day. At
Marseilles they are almost energetic, and are even
known to take the trouble of asking the passer for alms.
But eastward, beyond Toulon, they understand their
business better, and do not even trouble to talk among
themselves. The French worth-nothing is, in a word,

Henry Seton Merriman

worth less than any of his brothers - much less than the Italian, who is quite easily roused to a display of temper and a rusty knife - and more nearly approaches the supreme calm of the Moor, who, across the Mediterranean, will sit all day and stare at nothing with any man in the world. And between these dreamy coasts there lie half a dozen islands which, strange to say, are islands of unrest. In Majorca every man works from morn till eve. In Minorca they do the same, and quarrel after nightfall. In Iviza they quarrel all day. In Corsica they do nothing, restlessly; while Sardinia, as all the world knows, is a hotbed of active discontent.

At Ajaccio there are half a dozen idlers on the Place Bonaparte, who sit under the trees against the wall; but they never sit there long, and do not know their business. At St. Florent, in the north of the island, which has a western aspect - the best for idling - there are but two real, unadulterated knights of industry, who sit on the low wall of that which is called the New Quay, and conscientiously do nothing from morning till night.

"Of course I know him," one was saying to the other. "Do I not remember his father, and are not all the de Vasselots cut with the same knife? I tell you there was a moon, and I saw him get off his horse, just here at the very door of Rutali's stable, and unstrap his sack, which he carried himself, and set off towards Olmeta."

The speaker lapsed into silence, and Colonel Gilbert, who had lunched, and was now sitting at the open window of the little inn, which has neither sign nor license, leant farther forward. For the word "Olmeta" never failed to bring a light of energy and enterprise into his quiet eyes.

The inn has its entrance in the main street of St. Florent, and only the back windows look out upon the quay and across the bay. It was at one of these windows that Colonel Gilbert was enjoying a cigarette and a cup of coffee, and the loafers on the quay were unaware of his presence there. And for the sixth time at least, the story of Lory de Vasselot's arrival at St. Florent and departure for Olmeta was told and patiently heard. Has not one of the great students of human nature said that the *canaille* of all nations are much alike? And the dull or idle of intellect assuredly resemble each other in the patience with which they will listen to or tell the same story over and over again.

The colonel heard the tale, listlessly gazing across the bay with dreamy eyes, and only gave the talker his full attention when more ancient history was touched upon.

"Yes," said the idler; "and I remember his father when he was just at that age - as like this one as one sheep is like another. Nor have I forgotten the story which few remember now."

He pressed down the tobacco into his wooden pipe - for they are pipe-smokers in a cigarette latitude - and waited cunningly for curiosity to grow. His companion showed no sign, though the colonel set his empty coffee-cup noiselessly aside and leant his elbow on the window-sill.

The speaker jerked his thumb in the direction of Olmeta over his left shoulder far up on the mountainside.

"That story was buried with Perucca," he said, after a long pause. "Perhaps the Abbé Susini knows it. Who can tell what a priest knows? There were two Peruccas once - fine, big men - and neither married. The other - Andrei Perucca - who has been in hell these thirty years, made sheep's eyes, they told me, at de Vasselot's young wife. She was French, and willing enough, no doubt. She was dull, down there in that great chateau; and when a woman is dull she must either go to church or to the devil. She cannot content herself with tobacco or the drink, like a man. De Vasselot heard of it. He was a quiet man, and he waited. One day he began to carry a gun, like you and me - a bad example, eh? Then Andrei Perucca was seen to carry a gun also. And, of course, in time they met - up there on the road from Pruneta to Murato. The clouds were down, and the gregale was blowing cold and showery. It is when the gregale blows that the clouds seem to whisper as they crowd through the narrow places up among the peaks, and there was no other sound while these two men crept round each other among the rocks, like two cats upon a roof. De Vasselot was quicker and smaller, and as agile as a goat, and Andrei Perucca lost him altogether. He was a fool. He went to look for him. As if any one in his senses would go to look for a Corsican in the rocks! That is how the gendarmes get killed. At length Andrei Perucca raised his head over a big stone, and looked right into the muzzle of de Vasselot's gun. The next minute there was no head upon Perucca's shoulders."

The narrator paused, and relighted his pipe with a foul-smelling sulphur match.

"Yes," he said reflectively; "they are fine men, the de Vasselots."

He tapped himself on the chest with the stem of his

pipe, and made a gesture towards the mountains and the sky, as if calling upon the gods to hear him.

"I am all for the de Vasselots - I," he said.

Colonel Gilbert leant out of the window, and quietly took stock of this valuable adherent.

"At that time," continued the speaker, "we had at Bastia a young prefect who took himself seriously. He was going to reform the world. They decided to arrest the Count de Vasselot, though they had not a scrap of evidence, and the clan was strong in those days, stronger than the Peruccas are to-day. But they never caught him. They disappeared bag and baggage - went to Paris, I understand; and they say the count died there, or was perhaps killed by the Peruccas, who grew strong under Mattei, so that in a few years it would have been impossible for a de Vasselot to show his face in this country. Then Mattei Perucca died, and was hardly in his grave before this man came. I tell you, I saw him myself, a de Vasselot, with his father's quick way of turning his head, of sitting in the saddle lightly like a Spaniard or a Corsican. That was in the spring, and it is now July - three months ago. And he has never been seen or heard of since. But he is here, I tell you; he is here in the island. As likely as not he is in the old chateau down there in the valley. No honest man has set his foot across the threshold since the de Vasselots left it thirty years ago - only Jean is there, who has the evil eye. But there are plenty of Perucca's people up at Olmeta who would risk Jean's eye, and break down the doors of the chateau at a word from the Casa Perucca. But the girl there who is the head of the clan will not say the word. She does not understand that she is powerful if she would only go to work in the right way, and help her people. Instead of that, she quarrels with them over such small matters as the right of grazing or of cutting wood. She will make the place too hot for her - " He broke off suddenly. "What is that?" he said, turning on the wall, which was polished smooth by constant friction.

He turned to the north and listened, looking in the direction of Cap Corse, from whence the Bastia road comes winding down the mountain slopes.

"I hear nothing," said his companion.

"Then you are deaf. It is the diligence half an hour before its time, and the driver of it is shouting as he comes - shouting to the people on the road. It seems that there is news - "

But Colonel Gilbert heard no more, for he had seized his sword, and was already halfway down the stone stairs. It appeared that he expected news, and when the diligence drew up in the narrow street, he was there awaiting it, amid a buzzing crowd, which had inexplicably assembled in the twinkling of an eye. Yes; there was assuredly news, for the diligence came in at a gallop though there was no one on it but the driver. He shouted incoherently, and waved his whip above his head. Then, quite suddenly, perceiving Colonel Gilbert, he snapped his lips together, threw aside the reins, and leapt to the ground.

"Mon colonel," he said, "a word with you."

And they went apart into a doorway. Three words sufficed to tell all that the diligence driver knew, and a minute later the colonel hurried towards the stable of the inn, where his horse stood ready. He rode away at a sharp trot, not towards Bastia, but down the valley of Vasselot. Although it was evident that he was pressed for time, the colonel did not hurry his horse, but rather relieved it when he could by dismounting, at every sharp ascent, and riding where possible in the deep shade of the chestnut trees. He turned aside from the main road that climbs laboriously to Oletta and Olmeta, and followed the river-path. In order to gain time he presently left the path, and made a short cut across the open land, glancing up at the Casa Perucca as he did so. For he was trespassing.

He was riding leisurely enough when his horse stumbled, and, in recovering itself, clumsily kicked a great stone with such force that he shattered it to a hundred pieces, and then stood on three legs, awkwardly swinging his hoof in a way that horses have when the bone has been jarred. In a moment the colonel dismounted, and felt the injured leg carefully.

"My friend," he said kindly, "you are a fool. What are you doing? Name of a dog" - he paused, and collecting the pieces of broken quartz, threw them away into the brush - "name of a dog, what are you doing?"

With an odd laugh Colonel Gilbert climbed into the saddle again, and although he looked carefully up at the Casa Perucca, he failed to see Mademoiselle Brun's grey face amid the grey shadows of an olive tree. The horse limped at first, but presently forgot his grievance against the big stone that had lain in his path. The colonel laughed to himself in a singular way more than once at the seemingly trivial accident, and on regaining the path, turned in his saddle to look again at the spot where it had occurred.

On nearing the chateau he urged his horse to a better pace, and reached the great door at a sharp trot. He rang the bell without dismounting, and leisurely quitted the saddle. But the summons was not immediately answered. He jerked at the chain again, and rattled on the door with the handle of his riding whip. At length the bolts were withdrawn, and the heavy door opened sufficiently to admit a glance of that evil eye which the peasants did not care to face.

Before speaking the colonel made a step forward, so that his foot must necessarily prevent the closing of the door.

"The Count de Vasselot," said he.

"Take away your foot," replied Jean.

The colonel noted with a good-natured surprise the position of his stout riding-boot, and withdrew it.

"The Count de Vasselot," he repeated. "You need not trouble, my friend, to tell any lies or to look at me with your evil eye. I know the count is here, for I saw him in Paris just before he came, and I spoke to him at this very door a few weeks ago. He knows me, and I think you know me too, my friend. Tell your master I have news from France. He will see me."

Jean unceremoniously closed the door, and the colonel, who was moving away towards his horse, turned sharply on his heel when he heard the bolts being surreptitiously pushed back again.

"Ah!" he said, and he stood outside the door with his hand at his moustache, reflectively following Jean's movements, "they are singularly careful to keep me out, these people."

He had not long to wait, however, for presently Lory came, stepping quickly over the high threshold and closing the door behind him. But Gilbert was taller than de Vasselot, and could see over his head. He looked right through the house into the little garden on the terrace, and saw someone there who was not Jean. And the light of surprise was still in his eyes as he shook hands with Lory de Vasselot.

"You have news for me?" inquired de Vasselot.

"News for every Frenchman."

"Ah!"

"Yes. The emperor has declared war against Germany."

"War!" echoed Lory, with a sudden laugh.

"Yes; and your regiment is the first on the list."

"I know, I know!" cried de Vasselot, his eyes alight with excitement. "But this is good news that you tell me. How can I thank you for coming? I must get home - I mean to France - at once. But this is great news!" He seized the colonel's hand and shook it. "Great news, mon colonel - great news!"

"Good news for you, for you are going. But I shall be left behind as usual. Yes; it is good news for you."

"And for France," cried Lory, with both hands

outspread, as if to indicate the glory that was awaiting them.

"For France," said the colonel, gravely, "it cannot fail to be bad. But we must not think of that now."

"We shall never think of it," answered Lory. "This is Monday; there is a boat for Marseilles to-night. I leave Bastia to-night, colonel."

"And I must get back there," said the colonel, holding out his hand.

He rode thoughtfully back by the shortest route through the Lancone Defile, and, as he approached Bastia, from the heights behind the town he saw the steamer that would convey Lory to France coming northward from Bonifacio.

"Yes," he said; "he will leave Bastia to-night; and assuredly the good God, or the devil, helps me at every turn of this affair."

CHAPTER XIII.

WAR.

"Since all that I can ever do for thee
Is to do nothing, may'st thou never see,
Never divine, the all that nothing costeth me!"

It is for kings to declare war, for nations to fight and pay. Napoleon III declared war against Russia, and France fought side by side with England in the Crimea, not because the gayest and most tragic of nations had aught to gain, but to ensure an upstart emperor a place among the monarchs of Europe. And that strange alliance was merely one move in a long game played by a consummate intriguer - a game which began disastrously at Boulogne and ended disastrously at Sedan, and yet was the most daring and brilliant feat of European statesmanship that has been carried out since the adventurer's great uncle went to St. Helena.

But no one knows why in July, 1870, Napoleon III declared war against Germany. The secret of the greatest war of modern times lies buried in the Imperial mausoleum at Frognal.

There is a sort of surprise which is caused by the sudden arrival of the long expected, and Germany experienced it in that hot midsummer, for there seemed to be no reason why war should break out at the moment. Shortly before, the Spanish Government had offered the crown to the hereditary Prince Leopold of Hohenzollern, and France, ever ready to see a grievance, found herself suited. But the hereditary prince declined that throne, and the incident seemed about to close. Then quite suddenly France made a demand, with reference to any possible recurrence of the same question, which Germany could not be expected to grant. It was an odd demand to make, and in a flash of thought the great German chancellor saw that this meant war. Perhaps he had been waiting for it. At all events, he was prepared for it, as were the silent soldier, von Roon, and the gentle tactician, von Moltke. These gentlemen were away for a holiday, but they returned, and, as history tells, had merely to fill in a few dates on already prepared documents.

If France was not ready she thought herself so, and was at all events willing. Nay, she was so eager that she shouted when she should have held her tongue. And who shall say what the schemer of the Tuileries thought of it all behind that pleasant smile, those dull and sphinx-like eyes? He had always believed in his star, had always known that he was destined to be great; and now perhaps he knew that his star was waning - that the greatness was past. He made his preparations quietly. He was never a flustered man, this nephew of the greatest genius the world has seen. Did he not sit three months later in front of a cottage at Donchery and impassively smoke cigarette after cigarette while waiting for Otto von Bismarck? He was a fatalist.

"The Moving Finger writes; and, having writ,

Moves on."

And it must be remembered to his credit that he asked no man's pity - a request as foolish to make for a fallen emperor as for the ordinary man who has, for instance, married in haste, and is given the leisure of a whole lifetime in which to repent. For the human heart is incapable of bestowing unadulterated pity: there must be some contempt in it. If the fall of Napoleon III was great, let it be remembered that few place themselves by their own exertions in a position to fall at all.

The declaration of war was, on the whole, acclaimed in France; for Frenchmen are, above all men, soldiers. Does not the whole world use French terms in the technicalities of warfare? The majority received the news as Lory de Vasselot received it. For a time he could only think that this was a great and glorious moment in his life. He hurried in to tell his father, but the count failed to rise to the occasion.

"War!" he said. "Yes; there have been many in my time. They have not affected me - or my carnations."

"And I go to it to-night," announced Lory, watching his father with eyes suddenly grave and anxious.

"Ah!" said the count, and made no farther comment.

Then, without pausing to consider his own motives, Lory hurried up to the Casa Perucca to tell the ladies there his great news. He must, it seemed, tell somebody, and he knew no one else within reach, except perhaps the Abbé Susini, who did not pretend to be a Frenchman.

"Is it peace?" asked Mademoiselle Brun, who, having seen him climbing the steep slope in the glaring sunshine, was waiting for him by the open side-door when he arrived there.

He took her withered hand, and bowed over it as gallantly as if it had been soft and young.

"What do you mean?" he asked, looking at her curiously.

"Well, it seems that the Casa Perucca and the Château de Vasselot are not on visiting terms. We only call on each other with a gun."

"It is odd that you should have asked me that," said Lory, "for it is not peace, but war."

And as he looked at her, her face hardened, her steady eyes wavered for once.

"Ah!" she said, her hands dropping sharply against her dingy black dress in a gesture of despair. "Again!"

"Yes, mademoiselle," answered Lory, gently; for he had a quick intuition, and knew at a glance that war must have hurt this woman at one time of her life.

She stood for a moment tapping the ground with her foot, looking reflectively across the valley.

"Assuredly," she said, "Frenchwomen must be the bravest women in the world, or else there would never be a light heart in the whole country. Come, let us go in and tell Denise. It is Germany, I suppose?"

"Yes, mademoiselle. They have long wanted it, and we are obliging them at last. You look grave. It is not bad news I bring you, but good."

"Women like soldiers, but they hate war," said mademoiselle, and walked on slowly in silence.

After a pause, she turned and looked at him as if she were going to ask him a question, but checked herself.

"I almost did a foolish thing," she explained, seeing his glance of surprise. "I was going to ask you if you were going?"

"Ah, yes, I am going," he answered, with a laugh and a keen glance of excitement. "War is a necessary evil, mademoiselle, and assists promotion. Why should you hate it?"

"Because we cannot interfere in it," replied Mademoiselle Brun, with a snap of the lips. "We shall find Denise in the garden to the north of the house, picking green beans, Monsieur le Comte," continued Mademoiselle Brun, with a glance in his direction.

"Then I shall have time to help with the beans before I go to the war," answered Lory; and they walked on in silence.

The garden was but half cultivated - a luxuriant thicket of fruit and weed, of trailing vine and wild clematis. The air of it was heavy with a hundred scents, and, in the shade, was cool, and of a mossy odour rarely found in Southern seas.

They did not see Denise at first, and then suddenly she

emerged at the other end of the weed-grown path where they stood. Lory hurried forward, hat in hand, and perceived that Denise made a movement, as if to go back into the shadow, which was immediately restrained.

Mademoiselle Brun did not follow Lory, but turned back towards the house.

"If they must quarrel," she said to herself, "they may do it without my assistance."

And Denise seemed, indeed, ready to fall out with her neighbour, for she came towards him with heightened colour and a flash of annoyance in her eyes.

"I am sorry they put you to the trouble of coming out here," she said.

"Why, mademoiselle? Because I find you picking green beans?"

"No; not that. But one has one's pride. This is my garden. I keep it! Look at it!" And she waved her hand with a gesture of contempt.

De Vasselot looked gravely round him. Then, after a pause, he made a movement of the deepest despair.

"Yes, mademoiselle," he said, with a great sigh, "it is a wilderness."

"And now you are laughing at me."

"I, mademoiselle?" And he faced her tragic eyes.

"You think I am a woman."

De Vasselot spread out his hands in deprecation, as if, this time, she had hit the mark.

"Yes," he said slowly.

"I mean you think we are only capable of wearing pretty clothes and listening to pretty speeches, and that anything else is beyond our grasp altogether."

"Nothing in the world, mademoiselle, is beyond your grasp, except" - he paused, and looked round him - "except a spade, perhaps, and that is what this garden wants."

They were very grave about it, and sat down on a rough seat built by Mattei Perucca, who had come there in the hot weather.

"Then what is to be done?" said Denise, simply.

For the French - the most intellectually subtle people of the world - have a certain odd simplicity which seems to have survived all the changes and chances of monarchy, republic, and empire.

"I do not quite know. Have you not a man?"

"I have nobody, except a decrepit old man, who is half an imbecile," said Denise, with a short laugh. "I get my provisions surreptitiously by the hand of Madame Andrei. No one else comes near the Casa. We are in a state of siege. I dare not go into Olmeta; but I am holding on because you advised me not to sell."

"I, mademoiselle?"

"Yes; in Paris. Have you forgotten?"

"No," answered Lory, slowly - "no; I have not forgotten. But no one takes my advice - indeed, no one asks it - except about a horse. They think I know about a horse." And Lory smiled to himself at the thought of his proud position.

"But you surely meant what you said?" asked Denise.

"Oh yes. But you honour me too much by taking my opinion thus seriously without question, mademoiselle."

Denise was looking at him with her clear, searching eyes, rather veiled by a suggestion of disappointment.

"I thought - I thought you seemed so decided, so sure of your own opinion," she said doubtfully.

De Vasselot was silent for a moment, then he turned to her quickly, impulsively, confidentially.

"Listen," he said. "I will tell you the truth. I said 'Don't sell.' I say 'Don't sell' still. And I have not a shred of reason for doing so. There!"

Denise was not a person who was easily led. She laughed at the stern, strong Mademoiselle Brun to her face, and treated her opinion with a gay contempt. She had never yet been led.

"No," she said, and seemed ready to dispense with reasons. "You will not sell, yourself?" she said, after a pause.

"No; I cannot sell," he said quickly; and she remembered his answer long afterwards.

After a pause he explained farther.

"I tell you frankly," he said earnestly, for he was always either very earnest or very gay - "I tell you frankly, when we both received an offer to buy, I thought there must be some reason why the places are worth buying, but I have found none."

He paused, and, looking round, remembered that this also was his, and did not belong to Denise at all, who claimed it, and held it with such a high hand.

"As Corsica at present stands, Perucca and Vasselot are valueless, mademoiselle, I claim the honour of being in the same boat with you. And if the empire falls - *bonjour la paix!*"

And he sketched a grand upheaval with a wave of his two hands in the air.

"But why should the empire fall?" asked Denise, sharply.

"Ah, but I have the head of a sparrow!" cried Lory, and he smote himself grievously on the forehead. "I forgot to tell you the very thing that I came to tell you. Which is odd, for until I came into this garden I could think of nothing else. I was ready to shout it to the trees. War has been declared, mademoiselle."

"War!" said Denise; and she drew in one whistling

Henry Seton Merriman

breath through her teeth, as one may who has been burnt by contact with heated metal, and sat looking straight in front of her. "When do you go, Monsieur le Comte?" she asked, in a steady voice, after a moment.

"To-night."

He rose, and stood before her, looking at the tangled garden with a frown.

"Ah!" he said, with a sudden laugh, "if the emperor had only consulted me, he would not have done it just yet. I want to go, of course, for I am a soldier. But I do not want to go now. I should have liked to see things more settled, here in Olmeta. If the empire falls, mademoiselle, you must return to France; remember that. I should have liked to have offered you my poor assistance; but I cannot - I must go. There are others, however. There is Mademoiselle Brun, with a man's heart in that little body. And there is the Abbé Susini. Yes; you can trust him as you can trust a little English fighting terrier. Tell him - - No; I will tell him. He is a Vasselot, mademoiselle, but I shall make him a Perucca."

He held out his hand gaily to say good-bye.

"And - stay! Will you write to me if you want me, mademoiselle? I may be able to get to you."

Denise did not answer for a moment. Then she looked him straight in the eyes, as was her wont with men and women alike.

"Yes," she said.

A few minutes later, Mademoiselle Brun came into the garden. She looked round but saw no one. Approaching the spot where she had left Denise, she found the basket with a few beans in it, and Denise's gloves lying there. She knew that Lory had gone, but still she could see Denise nowhere. There were a hundred places in the garden where any who did not wish to be discovered could find concealment.

Mademoiselle Brun took up the basket and continued to pick the French beans.

"My poor child! my poor child!" she muttered twice, with a hard face.

CHAPTER XIV.

GOSSIP.

"Cupid is a casuist,
A mystic, and a cabalist.
Can your lurking thought surprise,
And interpret your device?"

That which has been taken by the sword must be held by the sword. In Corsica the blade is sheathed, but it has never yet been laid aside. The quick events of July thrust this sheathed weapon into the hand of Colonel Gilbert, who, as he himself had predicted, was left behind in the general exodus.

"If you are placed in command at Bastia, how many, or how few men will suffice?" asked the civil authority, who was laid on the shelf by the outbreak of war.

And Colonel Gilbert named what appeared to be an absurd minimum.

"We must think of every event; things may go badly, the fortune of war may turn against us."

"Still I can do it," answered the colonel.

"The empire may fall, and then Corsica will blaze up like tow."

"Still I can do it," repeated the colonel.

It is the natural instinct of man to strike while his blood is up, and the national spirit on either side of the Rhine was all for immediate action. The leaders themselves were anxious to begin, so that they might finish before the winter. So the preparations were pushed forward in Germany with a methodical haste, a sane and deliberate foresight. In France it was more a question of sentiment - the invincibility of French arms, the heroism of French soldiers, the Napoleonic legend. But while these abstract aids to warfare may make a good individual soldier of that untidy little man in the red trousers, who has, in his time, overrun all Europe, it will not move great armies or organize a successful campaign. For the French soldier must have some one to fight for - some one towering man in whom he trusts, who can turn to good account some of the best fighting material the human race has yet produced. And Napoleon III was not such a man.

It is almost certain that he counted on receiving assistance from Austria or Italy, and when this was withheld, the disease-stricken, suffering man must assuredly have realized that his star was sinking. He had made the mistake of putting off this great war too long. He should have fought it years earlier, before the Prussians had made sure of those steady, grumbling Bavarians, who bore the brunt of all the fighting, before his own hand was faltering at the helm, and the face of God was turned away from the Napoleonic dynasty.

The emperor was no tactician, but he knew the human heart. He knew that at any cost France must lead off with a victory, not only for the sake of the little man in the red trousers, but to impress watching Europe, and perhaps snatch an ally from among the hesitating powers. And the result was Saarbrück. The news of it filtered through to Colonel Gilbert, who was now quartered in the grey, picturesque Watrin barracks at Bastia, which jut out between the old harbour and the plain of Biguglia. The colonel did not believe half of it. It is always safe to subtract from good news. But he sat down at once and wrote to Denise Lange. He had not seen her, had not communicated with her, since he had asked her to marry him, and she had refused. He was old enough to be her father. He had asked her to marry him because she would not sell Perucca, and he wanted that estate; which was not the right motive, but it is the usual one with men who are past the foolishness of youth - that foolishness which is better than all the wisdom of the ages.

From having had nothing to do, Colonel Gilbert found himself thrown into a whirl of work, or what would have been a whirl with a man less calm and placid. Very much at ease, in white linen clothes, he sat in his room in the bastion, and transacted the affairs of his command with a leisurely good nature which showed his complete grasp of the situation.

With regard to Denise, this middle-aged, cynical Frenchman grasped the situation also. He was slowly and surely falling in love with her. And she herself had given him the first push down that facile descent when she had refused to be his wife.

"Mademoiselle," he wrote, "to quarrel is, I suppose, in

the air of Corsica, and when we parted at your gate some time ago, I am afraid I left you harbouring a feeling of resentment against me. At this time, and in the adverse days that I foresee must inevitably be in store for France, none can afford to part with friends who by any means can preserve them. In our respective positions, you and I must rise above small differences of opinion; and I place myself unreservedly at your service. I write to tell you that I have this morning good news from France. We have won a small victory at Saarbrück. So far, so good. But, in case of a reverse, there is only too much reason to fear that internal disturbances will arise in France, and consequently in this unfortunate island. It is, therefore, my duty to urge upon you the necessity of quitting Perucca without delay. If you will not consent to leave the island, come at all events into Bastia, where, at a few minutes' notice, I shall be able to place you in a position of safety. I trust I am not one who is given to exaggerating danger. Ask Mademoiselle Brun, who has known me since, as a young man, I had the privilege of serving under your father, a general who had the gift of drawing out from those about him such few soldierly qualities as they might possess."

Denise received this letter by post the next morning, and, after reading it twice, handed it to Mademoiselle Brun, who was much too wise a woman to ask for an explanation of those parts of it which she did not comprehend. Indeed, she was manlike enough to pass on with an unimpaired understanding to the second part of the letter, whereas most women would have been so consumed by curiosity as to be unable to give more than half their mind to the colonel's further news.

"And - ?" inquired mademoiselle - a Frenchwoman's

way of asking a thousand questions in one. Mademoiselle Brun knew all the conversational tricks that serve to economize words.

"It is all based upon supposition," said the erstwhile mathematical instructress of the school in the Rue du Cherche-Midi. "It will be time enough to arrive at a decision when the reverse comes. The Count de Vasselot or the Abbé Susini will, no doubt, warn us in time."

"Ah!" said Mademoiselle Brun.

"But, if you like, I will write to the Count de Vasselot," said Denise, in the voice of one making a concession.

Mademoiselle Brun thought deeply before replying. It is so easy to take a wrong turning at the cross-roads of life, and assuredly Denise stood at a *carrefour* now.

"Yes," said mademoiselle at length; "it would be well to do that."

And Denise went away to write the letter that Lory had asked for in case she wanted him. She did not show it to Mademoiselle Brun, but went out and posted it herself in the little square box, painted white, affixed to the white wall on the high-road, and just within sight of Olmeta. When she returned she went into the garden again, where she spent so great a part of these hot days that her face was burnt to a healthy brown, which was in keeping with her fearless eyes and carriage. Mademoiselle Brun, on the other hand, spent most of her days indoors, divining perhaps that Denise had of late fallen into an unconscious love of solitude.

Denise returned to the house at luncheon-time, entered by the window, and caught Mademoiselle Brun hastily shutting an atlas.

"I was wondering," she said, "where Saarbrück might be, and whether any one we know had time to get there before the battle."

"Yes."

"But Colonel Gilbert will tell us."

"Colonel Gilbert?" inquired Denise, turning rather sharply.

"Yes. I think he will come to-day or to-morrow."

And Mademoiselle Brun was right. In the full heat of the afternoon the great bell at the gate gave forth a single summons; for the colonel was always gentle in his ways.

"I made an opportunity," he said, "to escape from the barracks this hot day."

But he looked cool enough, and greeted Denise with his usual leisurely, friendly bow. His manner conveyed, better than any words, that she need feel no uneasiness on his account, and could treat him literally at his word, as a friend.

"In order to tell you, with all reserve, the good news," he continued.

"With all reserve!" echoed Mademoiselle Brun.

"Good news in a French newspaper, Mademoiselle - " And he finished with a gesture eloquent of the deepest distrust.

"I was wondering," said Mademoiselle Brun, speaking slowly, and in a manner that demanded for the time the colonel's undivided attention, "whether our friend the Count de Vasselot could have been at Saarbrück."

"The Count de Vasselot," said Colonel Gilbert, with an air of friendly surprise. "Has he quitted his beloved château? He is so attached to that old house, you know."

"He has joined his regiment," replied Mademoiselle Brun, upon whom the burden of the conversation fell; for Denise had gone to the open window, and was closing the shutters against the sun.

"Ah! Then I can tell you that he was not at Saarbrück. The count's regiment is not in that part of the country. I was forgetting that he was a soldier. He is, by the way, your nearest neighbour."

The colonel rose as he spoke, and went to the window - not to that where Denise was standing, but to the other, of which the sun-blinds were only half closed.

"You can, of course, see the château from here?" he said musingly.

"Yes," answered Mademoiselle Brun, with an uneasy glance.

What was Colonel Gilbert going to say?

He stood for a moment looking down into the valley, while Denise and Mademoiselle Brun waited.

"And you have perceived nothing that would seem to confirm the gossip current regarding your - enemy?" he asked, with a good-natured, deprecatory laugh.

"What gossip?" asked mademoiselle, bluntly.

The colonel shrugged his shoulders without looking round.

"Oh," he answered, "one does not believe all one hears. Besides, there are many who think that in such a remote spot as Corsica, it is not necessary to observe the ordinary - what shall I say? - etiquette of society."

He laughed uneasily, and spread out his hands as if, for his part, he would rather dismiss the subject. But Mademoiselle Brun could be frankly feminine at times.

"What is the gossip to which you refer?" she asked again.

"Oh, I do not believe a word of it - though I, myself, have seen. Well, mademoiselle - you will excuse my frankness? - they say there is some one in the château - some one whom the count wishes to conceal, you understand."

"Ah!" said mademoiselle, indifferently.

Denise said nothing. She was looking out of the window with a face as hard as the face of Mademoiselle Brun. She looked at her watch, seemed to make a quick mental calculation, and then turned and spoke to Colonel Gilbert with steady, smiling eyes.

"You have not told us your war news yet," she said.

So he told them what he knew, which, as a matter of fact, did not amount to much. Then he took his leave, and rode home in the cool of the evening - a solitary, brooding man, who had missed his way somehow early on the road of life, and lacked perhaps the strength of mind to go back and try again.

Denise said good-bye to him in the same friendly spirit which he had inaugurated. She was standing with her back to the window from which she had looked down on to the château of Vasselot while Colonel Gilbert related his idle gossip respecting that house. And Mademoiselle Brun, who remembered such trifles, noted that she never looked out of that window again, but avoided it as one would avoid a cupboard where there is a skeleton.

Denise, who consulted her watch again so soon as the colonel had left, wrote another letter, which she addressed in an open envelope to the postmaster at Marseilles, and enclosed a number of stamps. She went out on to the high-road, and waited there in the shade of the trees for the diligence, which would pass at four o'clock on its way to Bastia.

The driver of the diligence, like many who are on the road and have but a passing glimpse of many men and many things, was a good-natured man, and willingly charged himself with Denise's commission. For that which she had enclosed was not a letter, but a telegram to be despatched from Marseilles on the arrival of the mail steamer there. It was addressed to Lory de Vasselot at the Cercle Militaire in Paris, and contained the words -

"Please return unopened the letter posted to-day."

CHAPTER XV.

WAR.

"When half-gods go,
The gods arrive."

"Then," said the Baroness de Mélide, "I shall go down to St. Germain en Pré, and say my prayers." And she rang the bell for her carriage.

On all great occasions in life, the Baroness de Mélide had taken her overburdened heart in a carriage and pair to St. Germain en Pré. For she had always had a carriage and pair for the mere ringing of a bell ever since her girlhood, when the Baron de Mélide had, with much assistance from her, laid his name and fortune at her feet. When she had helped him to ask her to be his wife, she had ordered the carriage thus, as she was ordering it now in the month of August, 1870, on being told by her husband that the battle of Wörth had been fought and lost, and that Lory de Vasselot was safe.

"The Madeleine is nearer," suggested the baron, a large man, with a vacant face which concealed a very mine of common sense, "and you could give me a lift as far as the club."

"The Madeleine is all very well for a wedding or a funeral or a great public festivity of any sort," said the baroness, with a harmless, light manner of talking of grave subjects which is a closed book to the ordinary stolid British mind; "but when one has a prayer, there is nowhere like St. Germain en Pré, which is old and simple and dirty, so that one feels like a poor woman. I shall put on an old dress."

She looked at her husband with a capable nod, as if to convey the comforting assurance that he could leave this matter entirely to her.

"Yes," said the baron; "do as you will."

Which permission the world was pleased to consider superfluous in the present marital case.

"It is," he said, "the occasion for a prayer; and say a word for France. And Lory is safe - one of very, very few survivors. Remember that in your prayers, ma mie, and remember me."

"I will see about it," answered the baroness. "If I have time, I will perhaps put in a word for one who is assuredly a great stupid - no name mentioned, you understand."

So the Baroness de Mélide went to the gloomy old church of her choice, and sent up an incoherent prayer, such as were arising from all over France at this time. On returning by the Boulevard St. Germain, she met a friend, a woman whose husband had fallen at Weissembourg, who gave her more news from the front. The streets were crowded and yet idle. The men stood apart in groups, talking in a low voice: the women stood apart and watched them - for it is only in times of peace that the women manage France.

The baroness went home, nervous, ill at ease. She hardly noticed that the door was held open by a maid-servant. The men had all gone out for news - some to enroll themselves in the National Guard. She went up to the drawing-room, and there, seated at her writing-table with his back turned towards her, was Lory de Vasselot. All the brightness had gone from his uniform. He turned as she entered the room.

"Mon Dieu!" she said, "what is it?"

"What is what?" he answered gravely.

"Why, your face," said the baroness. "Look - look at it!" She took him by the arm, and turned him towards a mirror, half hidden in hot-house flowers. "Look!" she cried again. "Mon Dieu! it is a tragedy, your face. What is it?"

Lory shrugged his shoulders.

"I was at Wörth," he explained, "two days ago. I suppose Wörth will be written for life in the face of every Frenchman who was there. They were three to one. They are three to one wherever we turn."

He sat down again at the writing-table, and the baroness stood behind him.

"And this is war," she said, tapping slowly on the carpet with her foot.

She laid her hand on his shoulder, and, noting a quick

movement of withdrawal, glanced down.

"Ach!" she exclaimed, in a whisper, as she drew back.

The shoulder and sleeve of his tunic were stained a deep brown. The gold lace was green in places and sticky. In an odd silence she unbuttoned her glove, and laid it quietly aside.

"It seems, mon ami, that we have only been playing at life up to now," she said, after a pause.

And Lory did not answer her. He had several letters lying before him, and had taken up his pen again.

"What brings you to Paris?" asked the baroness, suddenly.

"The emperor," he answered. "It is a queer story, and I can tell you part of it. After Wörth, I was given a staff appointment - and why? Because my occupation was gone; I had no men left." With a quick gesture he described the utter annihilation of his troop. "And I was sent into Metz with despatches. While I was still there - judge of my surprise! - the emperor sent for me. You know him. He was sitting at a table, and looked a big man. Afterwards, when he stood up, I saw he was small. He bowed as I entered the room - for he is polite even to the meanest private of a line regiment - and as he bowed he winced. Even that movement gave him pain. And then he smiled, with an effort. 'Monsieur de Vasselot,' he said; and I bowed. 'A Corsican,' he went on. 'Yes, sire.' Then he took up a pen, and examined it. He wanted something to look at, though he might safely have looked at me. He could look any man in the face at any time, for his eyes tell no tales. They are dull and veiled; you know them, for you have spoken to him often."

"Yes; and I have seen the great snake at the Jardin d'Acclimatation," answered the Baroness de Mélide, quietly.

"Then," continued Lory, "still looking at the pen, he spoke slowly as if he had thought it all out before I entered the room. 'When my uncle fell upon evil times he naturally turned to his fellow-countrymen.' 'Yes, sire.' 'I do not know you, Monsieur de Vasselot, but I know your name. I am going to trust you entirely. I want you to go to Paris for me.'"

"And that is all you are going to tell me?" said the baroness.

"That is all I can tell you. Whatever he may be, he is more than a brave man - he is a stoic. I arrived an hour ago, and went to the club for my letters, but I did not dare to go in, because it is evident that I am from the front. Look at my clothes. That is why I come here and present myself before you as I am. I must beg your hospitality for a few hours and the run of your writing-table."

The baroness nodded her head repeatedly as she looked at him. It was not only from his gold-laced uniform that the brightness had gone, but from himself. His manner was abrupt. He was almost stern. This, again, was war.

"You know that now, as always, our house is yours," she said quietly; for it is not all light hearts that have nothing in them.

Then, being a practical Frenchwoman - and there is no more practical being in the world - she rang for luncheon.

"One sees," she said, "that you are hungry. One must eat though empires fall."

"Ah!" said Lory, turning sharply to look at her. "You talk like that in Paris, do you?"

"In the streets, my cousin, they speak plainer language than that. But Henri will tell you what they are saying on the pavement. I have sent for him to the club to come home to luncheon. He forgives me much, that poor man, but he would never forgive me if I did not tell him that you were in Paris."

"Thank you," answered Lory. "I shall be glad to see him. There are things which he ought to know, which I cannot tell you."

"You think I am not discreet," said the baroness, slowly drawing the pins from her smart hat.

Lory looked up at her with a laugh, which was perhaps what she wanted, for there is no cunning like the cunning of a woman who seeks to charm a man from one humour to another. And when the baroness had first seen Lory, she thought that his heart was broken - by Wörth.

"You are beautiful, but not discreet," he answered.

"That is the worst of men," she said reflectively, as she laid her hat aside - "they always want an impossible combination."

She looked back at him over her shoulder and laughed, for she saw that she was gaining her point. The quiet of this luxurious house, her own personality, the subtle domesticity of her action in taking off her hat in his presence - all these were soothing a mind rasped and torn by battle and defeat. But there was something yet which she had not grasped, and she knew it. She glanced at the letters on the table before him. As if the thought were transmitted across the room to him, Lory took up an open telegram, and read it with a puzzled face. He half turned towards her as if about to speak, but closed his lips again.

"Yes," said the baroness, lightly. "What is it?"

"It is," he explained, after a pause, "that I have had so little to do with women."

"Except me, mon cousin," said the baroness, coming nearer to the writing-table.

"Except you, ma cousine," he answered, turning in his chair and taking her hand.

He glanced up at her with eyes that would appear to the ordinary British mind to express a passionate devotion, eminently French and thrilling and terrible, but which really reflected only a very honest and brotherly affection. For a Frenchman never hates or loves as much as he thinks he does.

"Well," said the baroness, practically, "what is it?"

"At the club," explained Lory, "I found a letter and a telegram from Corsica."

"Both from Denise?" asked the baroness, rather bluntly.

"Both from Mademoiselle Lange. See how things hinge upon a trifling chance - how much, we cannot tell! I happened to open the telegram first, and it told me to return the letter unopened."

As he spoke he handed her the grey sheet upon which were pasted the narrow blue paper ribbons bearing the text. The baroness read the message slowly and carefully. She glanced over the paper, down at his head, with a little wise smile full of contempt for his limited male understanding.

"And the letter?" she inquired.

He showed her a sealed envelope addressed by himself to Denise at Perucca. She took it up and turned it over slowly. It was stamped and ready for the post. She then threw it down with a short laugh.

"I was thinking," she explained, "of the difference between men and women. A woman would have filled a cup with boiling water and laid that letter upon it. It is quite easy. Why, we were taught it at the convent school! You could have opened the letter and read it, and then closed it again and returned it. By that simple subterfuge you would have known the contents, and would still have had the credit for doing as you were told. And I think three women out of five would have done it, and the whole five would have wanted to do it. Ah! you may laugh. You do not know what wretches we are compared to men - compared especially to some few of them; to a Baron Henri de Melide or a Count de Vasselot - who are honourable men, my cousin."

She touched him lightly on the shoulder with one finger, and then turned away to look with thoughtful eyes out of the window.

"I wonder what is in that letter," said Lory, returning to his pen.

The baroness turned on her heel and looked at him with her contemptuous smile again.

"Oh," she said carelessly, "she was probably in a difficulty, which solved itself after the letter was posted. Or she was afraid of something, and found that her fears were unnecessary. That is all, no doubt."

There is, it appears, an *esprit de sexe* which prevents women from giving each other away.

"So you merely placed the letter in an envelope and are returning it, thus, without comment?" inquired the baroness.

"Yes," answered Lory, who was writing a letter now.

And his cousin stood looking at him with an amused and yet tender smile in her gay eyes. She remained silent until he had finished.

"There," he said, taking an envelope and addressing it hurriedly, "that is done. It is to the Abbé Susini at Olmeta; and it contains some of those things, my cousin, that I cannot tell you."

"Do you think I care," said the baroness, "for your

stupid politics? Do you think any woman cares for politics who has found some stupid man to care for her? There is *my* stupid in the street - on his new horse."

In a moment Lory was at the window.

"A new horse," he said earnestly. "I did not know that. Why did you not tell me?"

"We were talking of empires," replied the baroness. "By the way," she added, in after-thought, "is our good friend Colonel Gilbert in Corsica?"

"Yes - he is at Bastia."

"Ah," said the baroness, looking reflectively at Denise's telegram, which she still held in her hand, "I thought he was."

Then that placid man, the Baron Henri de Mélide, came into the room, and shook hands in the then novel English fashion, looking at his lifelong friend with a dull and apathetic eye.

"From the frontier?" he inquired.

Lory laughed curtly. He had returned from that Last Frontier, where each one of us shall inevitably be asked "Si monsieur a quelque chose à déclarer?"

"I shall give you ten minutes for your secrets, and then luncheon will be ready," said the baroness, quitting the room.

And Lory told his friend those things which were not

for a woman's hearing.

At luncheon both men were suspiciously cheerful; and, doubtless, their companion read them like open books. Immediately after coffee Lory took his leave.

"I leave Paris to-night," he said, with his old cheerfulness. "This war is not over yet. We have not the shadow of a chance of winning, but we shall perhaps be able to show the world that France can still fight."

Which prophecy assuredly came true.

CHAPTER XVI.

A MASTERFUL MAN.

"Tous les raisonnements des hommes ne valent pas un sentiment d'une femme."

It would seem that Lory de Vasselot had played the part of a stormy petrel when he visited Paris, for that calm Frenchman, the Baron de Mélide, packed his wife off to Provence the same night, and the letter that Lory wrote to the Abbé Susini, reaching Olmeta three days later, aroused its recipient from a contemplative perusal of the *Petit Bastiais* as if it had been a bomb-shell.

The abbé threw aside his newspaper and cigarette. He was essentially a man of action. He had been on his feet all day, hurrying hither and thither over his widespread parish, interfering in this man's business and that woman's quarrels with that hastiness which usually characterizes the doings of such as pride themselves upon their capability for action and contempt for mere passive thought. It was now evening, and a blessed cool air was stealing down from the mountains. Successive days of unbroken sunshine had burnt all the western side of the island, had almost dried up the Aliso, which crept, a mere rivulet in its stormy bed, towards St. Florent and the sea.

Susini went to-the window of his little room and opened the wooden shutters. His house is next to the church at Olmeta and faces north-west; so that in the summer the evening sun glares across the valley into its windows. He was no great scholar, and had but a poor record in the archives of the college at Corte. Lory de Vasselot had written in a hurry, and the letter was a long one. Susini read it once, and was turning it to read again, when, glancing out of the window, he saw Denise cross the Place, and go into the church.

"Ah!" he said aloud, "that will save me a long walk."

Then he read the letter again, with curt nods of the head from time to time, as if Lory were making points or giving minute instructions. He folded the letter, placed it in the pocket of his cassock, and gave himself a smart tap on the chest, as if to indicate that this was the moment and himself the man. He was brisk and full of self-confidence, managing, interfering, comman-ding, as all true Corsicans are. He took his hat, hardly paused to blow the dust off it, and hurried out into the sunlit Place. He went rather slowly up the church steps, however, for he was afraid of Denise. Her youth, and something spring-like and mystic in her being, disturbed him, made him uneasy and shy; which was perhaps his reason for drawing aside the heavy leather curtain and going into the church, instead of waiting for her outside. He preferred to meet her on his own ground - in the chill air, heavy with the odour of stale incense, and in the dim light of that place where he laid down, in blunt language, his own dim reading of God's law.

He stood just within the curtain, looking at Denise, who was praying on one of the low chairs a few yards away from him; and he was betrayed into a characteristic impatience when she remained longer on her knees than he (as a man) deemed necessary at that moment. He showed his impatience by shuffling with his feet, and still Denise took no notice.

The abbé, by chance or instinct, slipped his hand within his cassock, and drew out the letter which he had just received. The rustle of the thin paper brought Denise to her feet in a moment, facing him.

"The French mail has arrived," said the priest.

"Yes," replied Denise, quickly, looking down at his hands.

They were alone in the church which, as a matter of fact, was never very well attended; and the abbé, who had not that respect for God or man which finds expression in a lowered voice, spoke in his natural tones.

"And I have news which affects you, mademoiselle."

"I suppose that any news of France must do that," replied Denise, with some spirit.

"Of course - of course," said the abbé, rubbing his chin with his forefinger, and making a rasping sound on that shaven surface.

He reflected in silence for a moment, and Denise made, in her turn, a hasty movement of impatience. She had only met the abbé once or twice; and all that she knew of him was the fact that he had an imperious way with him which aroused a spirit of opposition in herself.

"Well, Monsieur l'Abbé," she said, "what is it?"

"It is that Mademoiselle Brun and yourself will have but two hours to prepare for your departure from the Casa Perucca," he answered. And he drew out a large silver watch, which he consulted with the quiet air of a commander.

Denise glanced at him with some surprise, and then smiled.

"By whose orders, Monsieur l'Abbe?" she inquired with a dangerous gentleness.

Then the priest realized that she meant fight, and all his combativeness leapt, as it were, to meet hers. His eyes flashed in the gloom of the twilit church.

"I, mademoiselle," he said, with that humility which is nought but an aggravated form of pride. He tapped himself on the chest with such emphasis that a cloud of dust flew out of his cassock, and he blew defiance at her through it. "I - who speak, take the liberty of making this suggestion. I, the Abbé Susini - and your humble servant."

Which was not true: for he was no man's servant, and only offered to heaven a half-defiant allegiance. Denise wanted to know the contents of the letter he held crushed within his fingers; so she restrained an impulse to answer him hastily, and merely laughed. The priest thought that he had gained his point.

"I can give you two hours," he said, "in which to make your preparations. At seven o'clock I shall arrive at the Casa Perucca with a carriage, in which to conduct Mademoiselle Brun and yourself to St. Florent, where a yacht is awaiting you."

Denise bit her lip impatiently, and watched the thin brown fingers that were clenched round the letter.

"Then what is your news from France?" she asked. "From whence is your letter - from the front?"

"It is from Paris," answered the abbé, unfolding the paper carelessly; and Denise would not have been human had she resisted the temptation to try and decipher it.

"And - ?"

"And," continued the abbé, shrugging his shoulders, "I have nothing to add, mademoiselle. You must quit Perucca before the morning. The news is bad, I tell you frankly. The empire is tottering to its fall, and the news that I have in secret will be known all over Corsica to-morrow. Who knows? the island may flare up like a heap of bracken, and no one bearing a French name, or known to have French sympathies, will be safe. You know how you yourself are regarded in Olmeta. It is foolhardy to venture here this evening."

Denise shrugged her shoulders. She had plenty of spirit, and, at all events, that courage which refuses to admit the existence of danger. Perhaps she was not thinking of danger, or of herself, at all.

"Then the Count Lory de Vasselot has ordered us out

of Corsica?" she asked.

"Mademoiselle, we are wasting time," answered the priest, folding the letter and replacing it in his pocket. "A yacht is awaiting you off St. Florent. All is organized - "

"By the Count Lory de Vasselot?"

The abbé stamped his foot impatiently.

"Bon Dieu, mademoiselle!" he cried, "you will make me lose my temper. The yacht, I tell you, is at the entrance of the bay, and by to-morrow morning it will be halfway to France. You cannot stay here. You must make your choice between returning to France and going into the Watrin barracks at Bastia. Colonel Gilbert will, I fancy, know how to make you obey him. And all Corsica is in the hands of Colonel Gilbert - though no one but Colonel Gilbert knows that."

He spoke rapidly, thrusting forward his dark, eager face, forgetting all his shyness, glaring defiance into her quiet eyes.

"There, mademoiselle - and now your answer?"

"Would it not be well if the Count Lory de Vasselot attended to his own affairs at the Château de Vasselot, and the interests he has there?" replied Denise, turning away from his persistent eyes.

And the abbé's face dropped as if she had shot him.

"Good!" he said, after a moment's hesitation. "I wash my hands of you. You refuse to go?"

"Yes," answered Denise, going towards the door with a high head, and, it is possible, an aching heart. For the two often go together.

And the abbé, a man little given to the concealment of his feelings, shook his fist at the leather curtain as it fell into place behind her.

"Ah - these women!" he said aloud. "A secret that is thirty years old!"

Denise hurried down the steps and away from the village. She knew that the postman, having passed through Olmeta, must now be on the high-road on his way to Perucca, and she felt sure that he must have in his bag the letter of which she had followed, in imagination, the progress during the last three days.

"Now it is in the train from Paris to Marseilles; now it is on board the Persévérance, steaming across the Gulf of Lyons," had been her thought night and morning. "Now it is at Bastia," she had imagined on waking at dawn that day. And at length she had it now, in thought, close to her on the Olmeta road in front of her.

At a turn of the road she caught sight of the postman, trudging along beneath the heavy chestnut trees. Then at length she overtook him, and he stopped to open the bag slung across his shoulder. He was a silent man, who saluted her awkwardly, and handed her several letters and a newspaper. With another salutation he walked on, leaving Denise standing by the low wall of the road alone. There was only one letter for her. She turned it over and examined the seal: a bare sword with a gay French motto beneath it - the device of the Vasselots.

She opened the envelope after a long pause. It contained nothing but her own travel-stained letter, of which the seal had not been broken. And, as she thoughtfully examined both envelopes, there glistened in her eyes that light which it is vouchsafed to a few men to see, and which is the nearest approach to the light of heaven that ever illumines this poor earth. For love has, among others, this peculiarity: that it may live in the same heart with a great anger, and seems to gain only strength from the proximity.

Denise replaced the two letters in her pocket and walked on. A carriage passed her, and she received a curt bow and salutation from the Abbé Susini who was in it. The carriage turned to the right at the crossroads, and rattled down the hill in the direction of Vasselot. Denise's head went an inch higher at the sight of it.

"I met the Abbé Susini at Olmeta," she said to Mademoiselle Brun, a few minutes later in the great bare drawing-room of the Casa Perucca. "And he transmitted the Count de Vasselot's command that we should leave the Casa Perucca to-night for France. I suggested that the order should be given to the Château de Vasselot instead of the Casa Perucca, and the abbé took me at my word. He has gone to the Château de Vasselot now in a carriage."

Mademoiselle Brun, who was busy with her work near the window, laid aside her needle and looked at Denise. She had a faculty of instantly going, as it were, to the essential part of a question and tearing the heart out of it: which faculty is, with all respect, more a masculine than a feminine quality. She ignored the side-issues and pounced, as it were, upon the central thread - the reason that Lory de Vasselot had had for sending such an order. She rose and tore open the newspaper, glanced at the war-news, and laid it aside. Then she opened a letter addressed to herself. It was on superlatively thick paper and bore a coronet in one corner.

"My Dear" (it ran),

"This much I have learnt from two men who will tell me nothing - France is lost. The Holy Virgin help us!

"Your devoted

"Jane De Mélide."

Mademoiselle Brun turned away to the window, and stood there with her back to Denise for some moments. At length she came back, and the girl saw something in the grey and wizened face which stirred her heart, she knew not why; for all great thoughts and high qualities have power to illumine the humblest countenance.

"You may stay here if you like," said Mademoiselle Brun, "but I am going back to France to-night."

"What do you mean?"

For reply Mademoiselle Brun handed her the Baroness do Mélide's letter.

"Yes," said Denise, when she had read the note. "But I do not understand."

"No. Because you never knew your father - the bravest man God ever created. But some other man will teach you some day."

"Teach me what?" asked Denise, looking with wonder at the little woman. "Of what are you thinking?"

"Of that of which Lory de Vasselot, and Henri de Mélide, and Jane, and all good Frenchmen and Frenchwomen are thinking at this moment - of France, and only France," said Mademoiselle Brun; and out of her mouse-like eyes there shone, at that moment, the soul of a man - and of a brave man.

Her lips quivered for a moment, before she shut them with a snap. Perhaps Denise wanted to be persuaded to return to France. Perhaps the blood that ran in her veins was stirred by the spirit of Mademoiselle Brun, whose arguments were short and sharp, as became a woman much given to economy in words. At all events, the girl listened in silence while mademoiselle explained that even two women might, in some minute degree, help France at this moment. For patriotism, like courage, is infectious; and it is a poor heart that hurries to abandon a sinking ship.

It thus came about that, soon after sunset, Mademoiselle Brun and Denise hurried down to the cross-roads to intercept the carriage, of which they could perceive the lights slowly approaching across the dark valley of Vasselot.

CHAPTER XVII.

WITHOUT DRUM OR TRUMPET.

"We do squint each through his loophole,
And then dream broad heaven
Is but the patch we see."

It was almost dark when the abbé's carriage reached
the valley, and the driver paused to light the two
stable-lanterns tied with string to the dilapidated lamp-
brackets. The abbé was impatient, and fidgeted in his
seat. He was at heart an autocrat, and hated to be
defied even by one over whom he could not pretend to
have control. He snapped his finger and thumb as he
thought of Denise.

"She puzzles me," he muttered. "What does she want?
Bon Dieu, what does she want?"

Then he spoke angrily to the driver, whose movements
were slow and clumsy.

"At all events my task is easier here," he consoled
himself by saying as the carriage approached the
château, "now that I am rid of these women."

At last they reached the foot of the slope leading up to

Henry Seton Merriman

the half-ruined house, which loomed against the evening sky immediately above them; and the driver pulled up his restive horses with an air significant of arrival.

"Right up to the château," cried the Abbé from beneath the hood.

But the man made no movement, and sat on the box muttering to himself.

"What!" cried the abbé, who had caught some words. "Jean has the evil eye! What of Jean's evil eye? Here, I will give you my rosary to put round your coward's neck. No! Then down you get, my friend. You can wait here till we come back."

As he spoke he leapt out, and, climbing into the box, pushed the driver unceremoniously from his seat, snatching the reins and whip from his hands.

"He!" he cried. "Allons, my little ones!"

And with whip and voice he urged the horses up the slope at a canter, while the carriage swayed across from one great tree to another. They reached the summit in safety, and the priest pulled the horses up at the great door - the first carriage to disturb the quiet of that spot for nearly a generation. He twisted the reins round the whip-socket, and clambering down rang the great bell. It answered to his imperious summons by the hollow clang that betrays an empty house. No one came. He stood without, drumming with his fist on the doorpost. Then he turned to listen. Some one was approaching from the darkness of the trees. But it was only the driver following sullenly on foot.

"Here!" said the priest, recognizing him. "Go to your horses!"

As he spoke he was already untying one of the stable-lanterns that swung at the lamp-bracket. His eyes gleamed beneath the brim of his broad hat. He was quick and anxious.

"Wait here till I come back," he said; and, keeping close to the wall, he disappeared among the low bushes.

There was another way in by a door half hidden among the ivy, which Jean used for his mysterious comings and goings, and of which the abbé had a key. He had brought it with him to-night by a lucky chance. He had to push aside the ivy which hung from the walls in great ropes, and only found the keyhole after a hurried search. But the lock was in good order. Jean, it appeared, was a careful man.

Susini hurried through a long passage to the little round room where the Count de Vasselot had lived so long. He stopped with his nose in the air, and sniffed aloud. The atmosphere was heavy with the smell of stale tobacco, and yet there could be detected the sweeter odour of smoke scarcely cold. The room must have been inhabited only a few hours ago. The abbé opened the window, and the smell of carnations swept in like the breath of another world. He returned to the room, and, opening his lantern, lighted a candle that stood on the mantelpiece. He looked round. Sundry small articles in daily use - the count's pipe, his old brass tobacco-box: a few such things that a man lives with, and puts in his pocket when he goes away - were missing.

"Buon Diou! Buon Diou! Buon Diou - gone!" muttered the priest, lapsing into his native dialect. He looked around him with keen eyes - at the blackened walls, at the carpet worn into holes. "That Jean must have known something that I do not know. All the same, I shall look through the house."

He blew out the candle, and taking the lantern quitted the room. He searched the whole house - passing from empty room to empty room. The reception-rooms were huge and sparingly furnished with those thin-legged chairs and ancient card-tables which recall the days of Letitia Ramolino and that easy-going Charles Buonaparte, who brought into the world the greatest captain that armies have ever seen. The bedrooms were small: all alike smelt of mouldering age. In one room the abbé stopped and raised his inquiring nose; the room had been inhabited by a woman - years and years ago.

He searched the house from top to bottom, and there was no one in it. The abbé had failed in the two missions confided to him by Lory, and he was one to whom failure was peculiarly bitter. With respect to the two women, he had perhaps scarcely expected to succeed, for he had lived fifty years in the world, and his calling had brought him into daily contact with that salutary chastening of the spirit which must assuredly be the lot of a man who seeks to enforce his will upon women. But his failure to find the old Count de Vasselot was a more serious matter.

He returned slowly to the carriage, and told the driver to return to Olmeta.

"I have changed my plans," he said, still mindful of the secret he had received with other pastoral charges from his predecessor. "Jean is not in the château, so I shall not go to St. Florent to-night."

He leant forward, and looked up at the old castle outlined against the sky. A breeze was springing up with the suddenness of all atmospheric changes in these latitudes, and the old trees creaked and groaned, while the leaves had already that rustling brittleness of sound that betokens the approach of autumn.

As they crossed the broad valley the wind increased, sweeping up the course of the Aliso in wild gusts. It was blowing a gale before the horses fell to a quick walk up the hill; and Mademoiselle Brun's small figure, planted in the middle of the road, was the first indication that the driver had of the presence of the two women, though the widow Andrei, who accompanied them and carried their travelling-bags, had already called out more than once.

"The Abbé Susini?" cried Mademoiselle Brun, in curt interrogation.

In reply, the driver pointed to the inside of the carriage with the handle of his whip.

"You are alone?" said mademoiselle, in surprise.

The light of the lantern shone brightly on her, and on the dimmer form of Denise, silent and angry in the background; for Denise had allowed her inclination to triumph over her pride, which conquest usually leaves a sore heart behind it.

"But, yes!" answered the abbé; alighting quickly enough.

He guessed instantly that Denise had changed her mind, and was indiscreet enough to put his thoughts into words.

"So mademoiselle has thought better of it?" he said; and got no answer for his pains.

Both Mademoiselle Brun and Denise were looking curiously at the interior of the carriage from which the priest emerged, leaving it, as they noted, empty.

"There is yet time to go to St. Florent?" inquired the elder woman.

The priest grabbed at his hat as a squall swept up the road, whirling the dust high above their heads.

"Whether we shall get on board is another matter," he muttered by way of answer. "Come, get into the carriage; we have no time to lose. It will be a bad night at sea."

"Then, for my sins I shall be sea-sick," said Mademoiselle Brun, imperturbably.

She took her bag from the hand of the widow Andrei, and would have it nowhere but on her lap, where she held it during the rapid drive, sitting bolt upright, staring straight in front of her into the face of the abbé.

No one spoke, for each had thoughts sufficient to occupy the moment. Susini perhaps had the narrowest vein of reflection upon which to draw, and therefore fidgeted in his seat and muttered to himself, for his mental range was limited to Olmeta and the Château de Vasselot. Mademoiselle Brun was thinking of France -

of her great past and her dim, uncertain future. While Denise sat stiller and more silent than either, for her thoughts were at once as wide as the whole world, and as narrow as the human heart.

At a turn in the road she looked up, and saw the sharp outline of the Casa Perucca, black and sombre against a sky now lighted by a rising moon, necked and broken by heavy clouds, with deep lurking shadows and mountains of snowy whiteness. In the Casa Perucca she had learnt what life means, and no man or woman ever forgets the place where that lesson has been acquired.

"I shall come back," she whispered, looking up at the great rock with its giant pines and the two square chimneys half hidden in the foliage.

And the Abbé Susini, seeing a movement of her lips, glanced curiously at her. He was still wondering what she wanted. "Mon Dieu," he was reflecting a second time, "what *does* she want?"

He stopped the carriage outside the town of St. Florent at the end of the long causeway built across the marsh, where the wind swept now from the open bay with a salt flavour to it. He alighted, and took Denise's bag, rightly concluding that Mademoiselle Brun would prefer to carry her own.

"Follow me," he said, taking a delight in being as curt as Mademoiselle Brun herself, and in denying them the explanations they were too proud to demand.

They walked abreast through the narrow street dimly lighted by a single lamp swinging on a gibbet at the corner, turned sharp to the left, and found themselves suddenly at the water's edge. A few boats bumped lazily at some steps where the water lapped. It was blowing hard out in the bay, but this corner was protected by a half-ruined house built on a projecting rock.

The priest looked round.

"Hé! là-bas!" he called out, in a guarded voice. But he received no answer.

"Wait here," he said to the two women. "I will fetch him from the café." And he disappeared.

Denise and mademoiselle stood in silence listening to the lapping of the water and the slow, muffled bumping of the boats until the abbé returned, followed by a man who slouched along on bare feet.

"Yes," he was saying, "the yacht was there at sunset. I saw her myself lying just outside the point. But it is folly to try and reach her to-night; wait till the morning, Monsieur l'Abbé."

"And find her gone," answered the priest. "No, no; we embark to-night, my friend. If these ladies are willing, surely a St. Florent man will not hold back?"

"But you have not told these ladies of the danger. The wind is blowing right into the bay; we cannot tack out against it. It will take me two hours to row out single-handed with some one baling out the whole time."

"But I will pull an oar with you," answered Susini. "Come, show us which is your boat. Mademoiselle

Brun will bale out, and the young lady will steer. We shall be quite a family party."

There was no denying a man who took matters into his own hands so energetically.

"You can pull an oar?" inquired the boatman, doubtfully.

"I was born at Bonifacio, my friend. Come, I will take the bow oar if you will find me an oilskin coat. It will not be too dry up in the bows to-night."

And, like most masterful people - right or wrong - the abbé had his way, even to the humble office assigned to Mademoiselle Brun.

"You will need to remove your glove and bare your arm," explained the boatman, handing her an old tin mug. "But you will not find the water cold. It is always warmer at night. Thus the good God remembers poor fishermen. The seas will come over the bows when we round this corner; they will rise up and hit the abbé in the back, which is his affair; then they will wash aft into this well, and from that you must bale it out all the time. When the seas come in, you need not be alarmed, nor will it be necessary to cry out."

"Such instructions, my friend," said the priest, scrambling into his oilskin coat, "are unnecessary to mademoiselle, who is a woman of discernment."

"But I try not to be," snapped Mademoiselle Brun. She knew which women are most popular with men.

"As for you, mademoiselle," said the boatman to

Henry Seton Merriman

Denise, "keep the boat pointed at the waves, and as each one comes to you, cut it as you would cut a cream cheese. She will jerk and pull at you, but you must not be afraid of her; and remember that the highest wave may be cut."

"That young lady is not afraid of much," muttered the abbé, settling to his oar.

They pulled slowly out to the end of the rocky promontory, upon which a ruined house still stands, and shot suddenly out into a howling wind. The first wave climbed leisurely over the weather-bow, and slopped aft to the ladies' feet; the second rose up, and smote the abbé in the back.

"Cut them, mademoiselle; cut them!" shouted the boatman.

And at intervals during that wild journey he repeated the words, unceremoniously spitting the salt water from his lips. The abbé, bending his back to the work and the waves, gave a short laugh from time to time, that had a ring in it to make Mademoiselle Brun suddenly like the man - the fighting ring of exaltation which adapts itself to any voice and any tongue. For nearly an hour they rowed in silence, while mademoiselle baled the water out, and Denise steered with steady eyes piercing the darkness.

"We are quite close to it," she said at length; for she had long been steering towards a light that flickered feebly across the broken water.

In a few moments they were alongside, and, amidst confused shouting of orders, the two ladies were half lifted, half dragged on board. The abbé followed them,

"A word with you," he said, taking Mademoiselle Brun unceremoniously by the arm, and leading her apart. "You will be met by friends on your arrival at St. Raphael to-morrow. And when you are free to do so, will you do me a favour?"

"Yes."

"Find Lory de Vasselot, wherever he may be."

"Yes," answered Mademoiselle Brun.

"And tell him that I went to the Chateau de Vasselot and found it empty."

Mademoiselle reflected for some moments.

"Yes; I will do that," she said at length.

"Thank you."

The abbé stared hard at her beneath his dripping hat for a moment, and then, turning abruptly, moved towards the gangway, where his boat lay in comparatively smooth water at the lee-side of the yacht. Denise was speaking to a man who seemed to be the captain.

Mademoiselle Brun followed the abbé.

"By the way - " she said.

Susini stopped, and looked into her face, dimly lighted by the moon, which peeped at times through riven clouds.

"Whom should you have found in the château?" she asked.

"Ah! that I will not tell you."

Mademoiselle Brun gave a short laugh.

"Then I shall find out. Trust a woman to find out a secret."

The abbé was already over the bulwark, so that only his dark face appeared above, with the water running off it. His eyes gleamed in the moonlight.

"And a priest to keep one," he answered. And he leapt down into the boat.

CHAPTER XVIII.

A WOMAN OF ACTION.

"Love ... gives to every power a double power
Above their functions and their offices."

"Ah!" said Mademoiselle Brun, as she stepped on deck the next morning. And the contrast between the gloomy departure from Corsica and the sunny return to France was strong enough, without further comment from this woman of few words.

The yacht was approaching the little harbour of St. Raphael at half speed on a sea as blue and still as the Mediterranean of any poet's dream. The freshness of morning was in the air - the freshness of Provence, where the days are hot and the nights cool, and there are no mists between the one and the other. Almost straight ahead, the little town of Fréjus (where another Corsican landed to set men by the ears) stood up in sharp outline against the dark pinewoods of Valescure, with the thin wood-smoke curling up from a hundred chimneys. To the left, the flat lands of Les Arcs half hid the distant heights of Toulon; and, to the right, headland after headland led the eye almost to the frontier of Italy along the finest coast-line in the world. Every shade of blue was on sky or sea or mountain, while the deep morning shadows were transparent and almost luminous. From the pinewoods a scent of resin swept seaward, mingled with the subtle odour of the tropic foliage near the shore. The sky was cloudless. This was indeed the smiling land of France.

Denise, who had followed mademoiselle on deck, stood still and drank it all in; for such sights and scents have a deep eloquence for the young, which older hearts can only touch from the outside, vaguely and intangibly, like the memory of a perfume.

Denise had slept well, and Mademoiselle Brun said she had slept enough for an old woman. A cheery little stewardess had brought them coffee soon after daylight, and had answered a few curt questions put to her by Mademoiselle Brun.

"Yes; the yacht was the yacht of the Baron de Mélide, and the *bête-noire*, by the same token, of madame, who hated the sea."

And madame was at the château near Fréjus, where Monsieur le Baron had installed her on the outbreak of the war, and would assuredly be on the pier at St. Raphael to meet them. And God only knew where Monsieur le Baron was. He had gone, it was said, to the war in some civil capacity.

As they stood on deck, Denise soon perceived the little pier where there were, even at this early hour, a few of those indefatigable Mediterranean Waltons who fish and fish and catch nothing, all through the sunny day. Presently Mademoiselle Brun caught sight of a small dot of colour which seemed to move spasmodically up and down.

"I see the parasol," she said, "of Jane de Mélide. What good friends we have!"

And presently they were near enough to wave a handkerchief in answer to the Baroness de Mélide's vigorous salutations. The yacht crept round the pier-head, and was soon made fast to a small white buoy. While a boat was being lowered, the baroness, in a gay Parisian dress, walked impatiently backwards and forwards, waved her parasol, and called out incoherent remarks, which Mademoiselle Brun answered by a curt gesture of the hand.

"My poor friend!" exclaimed the baroness, as she embraced Mademoiselle Brun. "My dear Denise, you are a brave woman. I have heard all about you."

And her quick, dancing eyes took in at a glance that Denise had come against her will, and Mademoiselle Brun had brought her. Of which Denise was ignorant, for the sunshine and brightness of the scene affected her and made her happy.

"Surely," she said, as they walked the length of the pier together, "the bad news has been exaggerated. The war will soon be over and we shall be happy again."

"Do not talk of it," cried the baroness. "It is a horror. I saw Lory, after Wörth, and that was enough war for me. And, figure to yourself! - I am all alone in this great house. It is a charity to come and stay with me. Lory has gone to the front. My husband, who said he loved me - where is he? Bonjour, and he is gone. He leaves me without a regret. And I, who cry my eyes out; or would cry them out if I were a fool - such as mademoiselle thinks me. Ah! I do not know what has come to all the men."

"But I do," said mademoiselle, who had seen war before.

And the baroness, looking at that still face, laughed her gay little inconsequent laugh.

A carriage was waiting for them in the shade of the trees on the market-place, its smart horses and men forming a strong contrast to the untidy town and slip-shod idlers. As usual, a game of bowls was in progress, and absorbed all the attention of the local intelligence.

"We have half an hour through the pine trees," said the baroness, settling herself energetically on the cushions. "And, do you know, I am thankful to see you. I thought you would be prevented coming."

She glanced at Denise as she spoke, and with a suddenly grave face, leant forward, and whispered -

"The news is bad - the news is bad. All this has been organized by Lory and my husband, who told me, in so many words, that they must have us where they can find us at a moment's notice. In case - ah, mon Dieu! I do not know what is going to happen to us all."

"Then are we to be moved about, like ornaments, from one safe place to another?" asked Denise, with a laugh which was not wholly spontaneous.

"I have never been treated as an ornament yet," put in Mademoiselle Brun, "and it is perhaps rather late to begin now."

Denise looked at her inquiringly.

"Yes," said the little woman, quietly. "I am going to the war - if Jane will take care of you while I am away."

"And why should not I go too?" asked Denise.

"Because you are too young and too pretty, my dear - since you ask a plain question," replied the baroness, impulsively. Then she turned towards mademoiselle. "You know," she said, "that my precious stupid is organizing a field hospital."

"I thought he would find something to do," answered mademoiselle, curtly.

"Yes," said the baroness, slowly, "yes - because when he was a boy he had for governess a certain little woman whose teaching was deeds, not words. And he is paying for it himself. And we shall all be ruined."

She spread out her rich dress, lay back in her luxurious carriage, and smiled on Mademoiselle Brun with something that was not mirth at the back of her brown eyes.

"I shall go to him," said mademoiselle. And the baroness made no reply for some moments.

"Do you know what he said?" she asked. "He said we shall want women - old ones. I know one old woman who will come!"

Mademoiselle was buttoning her cotton gloves and did not seem to hear.

"It was, of course, Lory," went on the baroness, "who encouraged him and told him how to go about it. And then he went back to the front to fight. Mon Dieu! he can fight - that Lory!"

"Where is he?" asked mademoiselle. And the baroness spread out her gloved hands.

"At the front - I cannot tell you more."

And mademoiselle did not speak again. She was essentially a woman of her word. She had undertaken to find Lory and give him that odd, inexplicable message from the abbé. She had not undertaken much in her narrow life; but she had usually accomplished, in a quiet, mouse-like way, that to which she set her hand. And now, as she drove through the smiling country, with which it was almost impossible to associate the idea of war, she was planning how she could get to the front and work there under the Baron de Mélide, and find Lory de Vasselot.

"They are somewhere near a little place called Sedan," said the baroness.

And Mademoiselle Brun set out that same day for the little place called Sedan; then known vaguely as a fortress on the Belgian frontier, and now for ever written in every Frenchman's heart as the scene of one of those stupendous catastrophes to which France seems liable, and from which she alone has the power of recovery. For, whatever the history of the French may be, it has never been dull reading, and she has shown the whole world that one may carry a brave and a light heart out of the deepest tragedy.

By day and night Mademoiselle Brun, sitting upright in a dark corner of a second-class carriage, made her way northward across France. No one questioned her, and she asked no one's help. A silent little old woman assuredly attracts less attention to her comings and goings than any other human being. And on the third day mademoiselle actually reached Chalons, which many a more important traveller might at this time have failed to do. She found the town in confusion, the civilians bewildered, the soldiers sullen. No one knew what an hour might bring forth. It was not even known who was in command. The emperor was somewhere near, but no one knew where. General officers were seeking their army-corps. Private soldiers were wandering in the streets seeking food and quarters. The railway station was blocked with stores which had been hastily discharged from trucks wanted elsewhere. And it was no one's business to distribute the stores.

Mademoiselle Brun wandered from shop to shop, gathering a hundred rumours but no information. "The emperor is dying - Macmahon is wounded," a butcher told her, as he mechanically sharpened his knife at her approach, though he had not as much as a bone in his shop to sell her.

She stopped a cuirassier riding a lame horse, his own leg hastily bandaged with a piece of coloured calico.

"What regiment?" she asked.

"I have no regiment. There is nothing left. You see in me the colonel, and the majors, and the captains. I am the regiment," he answered with a laugh that made mademoiselle bite her steady lip.

"Where are you going?"

"I don't know. Can you give me a little money?"

"I can give you a franc. I have not too much myself. Where have you come from?"

"I don't know. None of us knew where we were."

He thanked her, observed that he was very hungry, and rode on. She found a night's lodging at a seed-chandler's who had no seeds to sell.

"They will not need them this year," he said. "The Prussians are riding over the corn."

The next morning the indomitable little woman went on her way towards Sedan in a forage-cart which was going to the front. She told the corporal in charge that she was attached to the Baron de Mélide's field hospital and must get to her work.

"You will not like it when you get there, my brave lady," said the man, good-humouredly, making room for her.

"I shall like it better than doing nothing here," she replied.

And so they set forth through the country heavy with harvest. It was the second of September. The corn was ripe, the leaves were already turning; for it had been a dry summer, and since April hardly any rain had fallen.

It was getting late in the afternoon when they met a

man in a dog-cart driving at a great pace. He pulled up when he saw them. His face was the colour of lead, his eyes were startlingly bloodshot.

"This parishioner has been badly scared," muttered the soldier who was driving Mademoiselle Brun.

"Where are you going?" asked the stranger in a high, thin voice.

"To Sedan."

"Then turn back," he cried; "Sedan is no place for a woman. It is a hell on earth. I saw it all, mon Dieu. I saw it all. I was at Bazeilles. I saw the children thrown into the windows of the burning houses. I saw the Bavarians shoot our women in the streets. I saw the troops rush into Sedan like rabbits into their holes, and then the Prussians bombarded the town. They had six hundred guns all round the town, and they fired upon that little place which was packed full like a sheep-pen. It is not war - it is butchery. What is the good God doing? What is He thinking of?"

And the man, who had the pasty face of a clerk or a commercial traveller, raised his whip to heaven in a gesture of fierce anger. Mademoiselle Brun looked at him with measuring eyes. He was almost a man at that moment. But perhaps her standard of manhood was too high.

"And is Sedan taken?" she asked quietly.

"Sedan is taken. Macmahon is wounded. The emperor is prisoner, and the whole French army has surrendered. Ninety thousand men. The Prussians had two

hundred and forty thousand men. Ah! That emperor -
that scoundrel!"

Mademoiselle Brun looked at him coldly, but without
surprise. She had dealt with Frenchmen all her life, and
probably expected that the fallen should be reviled - an
unfortunate characteristic in an otherwise great
national spirit.

"And the cavalry?" she asked.

"Ah!" cried the man, and again his dull eye flashed.
"The cavalry were splendid. They tried to cut their way
out. They passed through the Prussian cavalry and
actually faced the infantry, but the fire was terrible. No
man ever saw or heard anything like it. The cuirassiers
were mown down like corn. The cavalry exists no
longer, madame, but its name is immortal."

There was nothing poetic about Mademoiselle Brun,
who listened rather coldly.

"And you," she asked, "what are you? you are
assuredly a Frenchman?"

"Yes - I am a Frenchman."

"And yet your back is turned," said Mademoiselle
Brun, "towards the Prussians."

"I am a writer," explained the man - "a journalist. It is
my duty to go to some safe place and write of all that I
have seen."

"Ah!" said Mademoiselle Brun. "Let us, my friend,"
she said, turning to her companion on the forage-cart,

"proceed towards Sedan. We are fortunately not in the position of monsieur."

Henry Seton Merriman

CHAPTER XIX.

THE SEARCH.

"Wisdom is ofttimes nearer when we stoop
Than when we soar."

There were many who thought the war was over that rainy morning after the fall of Sedan. For events were made to follow each other quickly by those three sleepless men who moved kings and emperors and armies at their will. Bismarck, Moltke, and Roon must have slept but little - if they closed their eyes at all - between the evening of the first and the morning of the third day of September. For human foresight must have its limits, and the German leaders could hardly have dreamt, in their most optimistic moments, of the triumph that awaited them. Bismarck could hardly have foreseen that he should have to provide for an imperial prisoner. Moltke's marvellous plans of campaign could scarcely have embraced the details necessary to the immediate disposal of ninety thousand prisoners of war, with many guns and horses and much ammunition.

It was but twenty-four hours after he had left Sedan to seek, and seek in vain, the King of Prussia, that the third Napoleon - the modern man of destiny who had climbed so high and fallen so very low - set out on his journey to the Palace of Wilhelmshöhe, never to set foot on French soil again. For he was to seek a home, and finally a grave, in England, where his bones will lie till that day when France shall think fit to deposit them by those of the founder of the adventurous dynasty.

Among those who stood in the muddy street of Donchéry that morning, and watched in silence the departure of the simple carriage, was Mademoiselle Brun, whose stern eyes rested for a moment on the sphinx-like face, met for an instant the dull and extinct gaze of the man who had twisted all France round his little finger.

When the cavalcade had passed by, she turned away and walked towards Sedan. The road was crowded with troops, coming and going almost in silence. Long strings of baggage-carts splashed past. Here and there an ambulance waggon of lighter build was allowed a quicker passage. Messengers rode, or hurried on foot, one way and the other; but few spoke, and a hush seemed to hang over all. There was no cheering this morning - even that was done. The rain splashed pitilessly down on these men who had won a great victory, who now hurried hither and thither, afraid of they knew not what, cowering beneath the silence of Heaven.

Mademoiselle was stopped outside the gates of Sedan.

"You can go no further!" said an under-officer of a Bavarian regiment in passable French, the first to question the coming or going of this insignificant and self-possessed woman.

"But I can stay here?" returned mademoiselle in German. In teaching, she had learnt - which is more than many teachers do.

"Yes, you can stay here," laughed the German.

And she stayed there patiently for hours in the rain and mud. It was afternoon before her reward came. No one heeded her, as, standing on an overturned gun-carriage, beneath her shabby umbrella, she watched the first detachment of nearly ten thousand Frenchmen march out of the fortress to their captivity in Germany.

"No cavalry?" she said to a bystander when the last detachment had gone.

"There is no cavalry left, ma bonne dame," replied the old man to whom she had spoken.

"No cavalry left! And Lory de Vasselot was a cuirassier. And Denise loved Lory." Mademoiselle Brun knew that, though perhaps Denise herself was scarcely aware of it. In these three thoughts mademoiselle told the whole history of Sedan as it affected her. Solferino had, for her, narrowed down to one man, fat and old at that, riding at the head of his troops on a great horse specially chosen to carry bulk. The victory that was to mar one empire and make another, years after Solferino, was summed up in three thoughts by the woman who had the courage to live frankly in her own small woman's world, who was ready to fight - as resolutely as any fought at Sedan - for Denise. She turned and went down that historic road, showing now, as ever, a steady and courageous face to the world, though all who spoke to her stabbed her with the words, "There is no cavalry left - no cavalry left, ma bonne dame."

She hovered about Donchéry and Sedan, and the ruins
of Bazeilles, for some days, and made sure that Lory
de Vasselot had not gone, a prisoner, to Germany. The
confusion in the French camp was greater than any had
anticipated, and no reliable records of any sort were
obtainable. Mademoiselle could not even ascertain
whether Lory had fought at Sedan; but she shrewdly
guessed that the mad attempt to cut a way through the
German lines was such as would recommend itself to
his heart. She haunted, therefore, the heights of
Bazeilles, seeking among the dead one who wore the
cuirassier uniform. She found, God knows, enough, but
not Lory de Vasselot.

All this while she never wrote to Fréjus, judging, with
a deadly common sense, that no news is better than bad
news. Day by day she continued her self-imposed task,
on the slippery hill-sides and in the muddy valleys,
until at last she passed for a peasant-woman, so
bedraggled was her dress, so lined and weather-beaten
her face. Her hair grew white in those days, her face
greyer. She had not even enough to eat. She lay down
and slept whenever she could find a roof to cover her.
And always, night and day, she carried with her the
burthen of that bad news of which she would not seek
to relieve herself by the usual human method of telling
it to another.

And one day she wandered into a church ten miles on
the French side of Sedan, intending perhaps to tell her
bad news to One who will always listen. But she found
that this was no longer a house of prayer, for the dead
and dying were lying in rows on the floor. As she
entered, a tall man, coming quickly out, almost

knocked her down. His arms were full of cooking utensils. He was in his shirt-sleeves: blood-stained, smoke-grimed, unshaven and unwashed. He turned to apologize, and began explaining that this was no place for a woman; but he stopped short. It was the millionaire Baron de Melide.

Mademoiselle Brun sat suddenly down on a bench near the door. She did not look at him. Indeed, she purposely looked away and bit her lip with her little fierce teeth because it would quiver. In a moment she had recovered herself.

"I have come to help you," she said.

"God knows, we want you," replied the baron - a phlegmatic man, who, nevertheless, saw the quivering lip, and turned away hastily. For he knew that mademoiselle would never forgive herself, or him, if she broke down now.

"Here," he said, with a clumsy gaiety, "will you wash these plates and dishes? You will find the pump in the cure's garden. We have nurses and doctors, but we have no one to wash up. And it is I who do it. This is my hospital. I have borrowed the building from the good God."

Mademoiselle was naturally a secretive woman. She could even be silent about her neighbours' affairs. Susini had been guided by a quick intuition, characteristic of his race, when he had confided in this Frenchwoman. She had been some hours in the baron's hospital before she even mentioned Lory's name.

"And the Count de Vasselot?" she inquired, in her

usual curt form of interrogation, as they were taking a hurried and unceremonious meal in the vestry by the light of an altar candle.

The baron shook his head and gulped down his food.

"No news?" inquired Mademoiselle Brun.

"None."

They continued to eat for some minutes in silence.

"Was he at Sedan?" asked mademoiselle, at length.

"Yes," replied the baron, gravely. And then they continued their meal in silence by the light of the flickering candle.

"Have you any one looking for him?" asked mademoiselle, as she rose from the table and began to clear it.

"I have sent two of my men to do so," replied the baron, who was by nature no more expansive than his old governess. And for some days there was no mention of de Vasselot between them.

Mademoiselle found plenty of work to do besides the menial labours of which she had relieved the man who deemed himself fit for nothing more complicated than washing dishes and providing funds. She wrote letters for the wounded, and also for the dead. She had a way of looking at those who groaned unnecessarily and out of idle self-pity, which was conducive to silence, and therefore to the comfort of others. She smoothed no pillows and proffered no soft words of sympathy. But it was she who found out that the cure had a piano. She it was who took two hospital attendants to the priest's humble house and brought the instrument away. She had it placed inside the altar rails, and fought the cure afterwards in the vestry as to the heinousness of the proceeding.

"You will not play secular airs?" pleaded the old man.

"All that there is of the most secular," replied she, inexorably. "And the recording angels will, no doubt, enter it to my account - and not yours, monsieur le curé".

So Mademoiselle Brun played to the wounded all through the long afternoons until her fingers grew stiff. And the doctors said that she saved more than one fretting life. She was not a great musician, but she had a soothing, old-fashioned touch. She only played such ancient airs as she could remember. And the more she played the more she remembered. It seemed to come back to her - each day a little more. Which was odd, for the music was, as she had promised the curé, secular enough, and could not, therefore, have been inspired by her sacred surroundings within the altar rails. Though, after all, it may have been that those who recorded this sacrilege against Mademoiselle Brun, not only made a cross-entry on the credit side, but helped her memory to recall that forgotten music.

Thus the days slipped by, and little news filtered through to the quiet Ardennes village. The tide of war had rolled on. The Germans, it was said, were already halfway to Paris. And from Paris itself the tidings were well-nigh incredible. One thing alone was certain; the Bonaparte dynasty was at an end and the mighty schemes of an ambitious woman had crumbled like ashes within her hands. All the plotting of the Regency had fallen to pieces with the fall of the greatest schemer of them all, whom the Paris government fatuously attempted to hookwink. Napoleon the Third was indeed a clever man, since his own wife never knew how clever he was. So France was now a howling Republic - a Republic being a community wherein every man is not only equal to, but better than his neighbour, and may therefore shout his loudest.

No great battles followed Sedan. France had but one army left, and that was shut up in Metz, under the command of another of the Paris plotters who was a bad general and not even a good conspirator.

Poor France had again fallen into bad hands. It seemed the end of all things. And yet for Mademoiselle Brun, who loved France as well as any, all these troubles were one day dispersed by a single note of a man's voice. She was at the piano, it being afternoon, and was so used to the shuffling of the bearer's feet that she no longer turned to look when one was carried in and another, a dead one perhaps, was carried out.

She heard a laugh, however, that made her music suddenly mute. It was Lory de Vasselot who was laughing, as they carried him into the little church. He was explaining to the baron that he had heard of his hospital, and had caused himself to be carried thither as soon as he could be moved from the cottage, where he had been cared for by some peasants.

The laugh was silenced, however, at the sight of Mademoiselle Brun.

"You here, mademoiselle?" he said. "Alone, I hope," he added, wincing as the bearers set him down.

"Yes, I am alone. Denise is safe at Fréjus with Jane de Mélide."

"Ah!"

"And your wounds?" said Mademoiselle Brun.

"A sabre-cut on the right shoulder, a bullet through the left leg - voila tout. I was in Sedan, and we tried to get out. That is all I know, mademoiselle."

Mademoiselle stood over him with her hands crossed at her waist, looking down at him with compressed lips.

"Not dangerous?" she inquired, glancing at his bandages, which indeed were numerous enough.

"I shall be in the saddle again in three weeks, they tell me. If the war only lasts - " He gave an odd, eager laugh. "If the war only lasts - "

Then he suddenly turned white and lost consciousness.

CHAPTER XX.

WOUNDED.

"Le temps fortifle ce qu'il n'ébranle pas."

That night mademoiselle wrote to Denise at Fréjus, breaking at last her long silence. That she gave the barest facts, may be safely concluded. Neither did she volunteer a thought or a conclusion. She was as discreet as she was secretive. There are some secrets which are infinitely safer in a woman's custody than in a man's. You may tell a man in confidence the amount of your income, and it will go no further; but in affairs of the heart, and not of the pocket, a woman is safer. Indeed, you may tell a woman your heart's secret, provided she keeps it where she keeps her own. And Mademoiselle Brun had only one thought night and day: the happiness of Denise. That, and a single memory - the secret, perhaps, which was such a standing joke at the school in the Rue du Cherche-Midi - made up the whole life of this obscure woman.

Two days later she gave Lory Susini's message; and de Vasselot sent for the surgeon.

"I am going," he said. "Patch me up for a journey."

The surgeon had dealt so freely with life and death that he only shrugged his shoulders.

"You cannot go alone," he said - "a man with one arm and one leg."

Mademoiselle looked from one to the other. She was willing enough that Lory should undertake this journey, for he must needs pass through Provence to get to Corsica. She did not attempt to lead events, but was content to follow and steer them from time to time.

"I am going to the south of France," she said. "The baron needs me no longer since the hospital is to be moved to Paris. I can conduct Monsieur de Vasselot - a part of the way, at all events."

And the rest arranged itself. Five days later Lory de Vasselot was lifted from the railway carriage to the Baroness de Melide's victoria at Frejus station.

"Madame's son is, no doubt, from Sedan?" said the courteous station-master, who personally attended to the wounded man.

"He is from Sedan - but he is not my son. I never had one," replied mademoiselle with composure.

She was tired, for she had hardly slept since Lory came under her care. She sat open-eyed, with that knowledge which is given to so few - the knowledge of the gradual completion of a set purpose.

They had travelled all night, and it was not yet midday when mademoiselle first saw, and pointed out to Lory, the white turret of the chateau among the pines.

The baroness was on the steps to greet them. Like many persons of a gay exterior, she had a kind heart and a quick sympathy. She often did, and said, the right thing, when cleverer people found themselves at fault. She laughed when she saw Lory lying full length across her smart carriage - laughed, despite his white cheeks and the grey weariness of mademoiselle's face. She seemed part of the sunshine and the brisk resinous air.

"Ah, my cousin," she cried, "it does the eyes good to see you! I should like to carry you up these steps."

"In three weeks," answered de Vasselot, "I will carry you down."

"His room is on the ground floor," said the baroness to mademoiselle, in an aside. "You are tired, my dear - I see it. Your room is the same as before; you must lie down this afternoon. I will take care of Lory, and Denise will - but, where is Denise? I thought she was behind me."

She paused to guide the men who were carrying de Vasselot through the broad doorway.

"Denise!" she cried without looking round, "Denise! where are you?"

Then turning, she saw Denise coming slowly down the stairs. Her face was whiter than Mademoiselle Brun's. Her eyes, clear and clever, were fixed on Lory's face as if seeking something there. There was an odd silence for a moment - such as the superstitious say, is caused by the passage of an angel among human beings - even the men carrying Lory seemed to tread softly. It was he who broke the spell.

"Ah, mademoiselle!" he said gaily, "the fortune of war, you see!"

"But it might have been so much worse," said the baroness in a whisper to Mademoiselle Brun. "Bon Dieu, it might have been so much worse!"

And at luncheon they were gay enough. For a national calamity is, after all, secondary to a family calamity. Only de Vasselot and Mademoiselle Brun had been close to war, and it was no new thing to them. Theirs was, moreover, that sudden gaiety which comes from re-action. The contrast of their present surroundings to that little hospital in a church within cannon-sound of Sedan - the quiet of this country house, the baroness, Denise herself young and grave - were sufficient to chase away the horror of the past weeks.

It was the baroness who kept the conversation alert, asking a hundred questions, and, as often as not, disbelieving the answers.

"And you assure me," she said for the hundredth time, "that my poor husband is well. That he does not miss me, I cannot of course believe with the best will in the world, though Mademoiselle Brun assert it with her gravest air. Now, tell me, how does he spend his day?"

"Mostly in washing up dishes," replied mademoiselle, looking severely at the baron's butler, whose hand happened to shake at that moment as he offered a plate. "But he is not good at it. He was ignorant of the properties of soda until I informed him."

"But there is no glory in that," protested the baroness. "It was only because he assured me that he would not run into danger, and would inevitably be made a grand commander of the Legion of Honour, that he was allowed to go. I do not see the glory in washing up dishes, my friends, I tell you frankly."

"No; but it is there," said mademoiselle.

After luncheon Lory, using his crutches, made his way laboriously to the verandah that ran the length of the southern face of the house. It was all hung with creepers, and shaded from the sun by a dense curtain of foliage. Here heliotrope grew like a vine on a trellis against the wall, and semi-tropical flowers bloomed in a bewildering confusion. A little fountain trickled sleepily near at hand, in the mossy basin of which a talkative family of frogs had their habitation.

Half asleep in a long chair, de Vasselot was already coming under the influence of this most healing air in the world, when the rustle of a skirt made him turn.

"It is only I, my poor Lory," said the baroness, looking down at him with an odd smile. "You turned so quickly. Is there anything you want - anything in my power to give you, I mean?"

"I am afraid you have parted with that already."

"To that - scullery-man, you mean. Yes, perhaps you are too late. It is so wise to ask too late, mon cousin."

She laughed gaily, and turned away towards the house.

Then she stopped suddenly and came back to him.

"Seriously," she said, looking down at him with a grave face - "seriously. My prayers should always be for any woman who became your wife - you, and your soldiering. Ciel! it would kill any woman who really cared - "

She broke off and contemplated him as he lay at full length.

"And she might care - a little - that poor woman."

"She would have to care for France as well," said de Vasselot, momentarily grave at the thought of his country.

"I know," said the baroness, with a wise shake of the head. "Mon ami, I know all about that."

"I have some new newspapers from Paris," she added, going towards the house. "I will send them to you."

And it was Denise who brought the newspapers. She handed them to him in silence. Their eyes met for an instant, and both alike had that questioning look which had shone in Denise's eyes as she came downstairs. They seemed to know each other now better than they had done when they last parted at the Casa Perucca.

There was a chair near to his, and Denise sat down there as if it had been placed on purpose - as perhaps it had - by Fate. They were silent for a few moments, gathering perhaps the threads that connected one with the other. For absence does not always break such threads, and sometimes strengthens them. Then Lory spoke without looking at her.

"You received the letter?" he said.

"Which letter?" she asked hurriedly; and then closed her lips and slowly changed colour.

There was only one letter, of course. There could be no other. For it had never been suggested that Lory should write to her.

"Yes; I received it," she answered. "Thank you."

"Will you answer one question?" asked Lory.

"If it is a fair one," she answered with a laugh.

"And who is to decide whether it is a fair one or not?"

"Oh! I will do that," replied Denise with decision.

She knew the weakness of her position, and was prepared to defend it. Her eyes were shining, and the colour had not faded from her cheeks yet. Lory held his lip between his teeth as he looked at her. She waited for the question, without meeting his eyes, with a baffling little smile tilting the corners of her lips.

"Well," she said, after a pause, "I suppose you have decided not to ask it?"

"I have decided to draw conclusions instead, mademoiselle."

"Ah!"

"What does 'Ah!' mean?"

"It means that you will draw them wrong," she answered; and yet the tone of her voice seemed to suggest that she would rather like to hear the conclusions.

"One may conclude then, simply, that you changed your mind after you wrote, and claimed a woman's privilege."

"Yes - "

"That you were good enough to trust me to send the letter back unopened; and yet you would not trust me with the contents. One may conclude that it is, therefore, also a woman's privilege to be of two minds at the same time."

"If she likes," answered Denise. To which wise men know that there is no answer.

De Vasselot made a tragic gesture with his one available hand, and cast his eyes upwards in a mute appeal to the gods. He sighed heavily, and the expression of his face seemed to indicate a hopeless despair.

"What is the matter?" she asked, with a solicitude which was perhaps slightly exaggerated.

"What is one to understand? I ask you that?" said Lory, turning towards her almost fiercely.

"What do you want to understand, monsieur?" asked Denise, quietly.

"Mon Dieu - you!"

"Me!"

"Yes. I cannot understand you at all. You ask my advice, and then you act contrary to it. You write me a letter, and you forbid me to open it. Ah! I was a fool to send that letter back. I have often thought so since - "

Denise was looking gravely at him with an expression in her eyes which made him stop, and laugh, and contradict himself suddenly.

"You are quite right, mademoiselle, I was not a fool to send it back. It was the only thing I could do; and yet I almost thought, just now, that you were not glad that I had done so."

"Then you thought quite wrong," said Denise, sharply, with a gleam of anger in her eyes. "You think that it is only I who am difficult to understand. You are no easier. They say in Balagna that, if you liked, you could be a sort of king in Northern Corsica, and I am quite sure you have the manners of one."

"Thank you, mademoiselle," he said with a laugh.

"Oh - I do not mean the agreeable side of the character. I meant that you are rather given to ordering people about. You send an incompetent and stupid little priest to take us by the hand, and lead us out of the Casa Perucca like two school-children, without so much as a word of explanation."

"But I had not your permission to write to you."

Denise laughed gaily.

"So far as that goes you had not my permission to order me out of my own house; to send a steamer to St. Florent to fetch me; to treat me as if I were a regiment, in a word - and yet you did it, monsieur."

Lory sat up in his desire to defend himself, winced and lay down again.

"I fancy it is your Corsican blood," said Denise, reflectively. She rose and re-arranged a very sporting dustcloth which the baroness had laid across the wounded man's legs, and which his movement had cast to one side. "However, it remains for me to thank you," she said, and did not sit down again.

"It may have been badly done, mademoiselle," he said earnestly, "but I still think that it was the wisest thing to do."

"And still you give me no reasons," she said without turning to look at him. She was standing at the edge of the verandah, looking thoughtfully out at the matchless view. For the house stood above the pines which lay like a dusky green carpet between it and the Mediterranean. "And I am not going to ask you for them," she added with an odd little smile, not devoid of that deep wisdom with which it is to be presumed women are born; for they have it when it is most useful to them, and at an age when their masculine contemporaries are singularly ignorant of human nature.

"I am going," she said after a pause. "Jane told me that I must not tire you."

"Then stay," he said. "It is only when you are not there that I find it tiring."

She did not answer, and did not move until a servant came noiselessly from the house and approached Lory.

"It is a man," he said, "who will not be denied, and says he must speak to Monsieur le Comte. He is from Corsica."

Denise turned, and her face was quite changed. She had until that moment forgotten Corsica.

CHAPTER XXI.

FOR FRANCE.

"Lov'd I not honour more."

The servant retired to bring the new arrival to the verandah. Denise followed him, and, after a few paces, returned to Lory.

"If it is one of my people," she said, "I should like to see him before he goes."

The man who followed the servant to the verandah a minute later had a dark, clean-shaven face, all drawn into fine lines and innumerable minute wrinkles. Such lines mean starvation; but in this case they told a tale of the past, for the dark eyes had no hungry look. They looked hunted - that was all. The glitter of starvation had left them. He glanced uneasily around, took off his hat and bowed curtly to Lory. The hat and the clothes were new. Then he turned and looked at the servant, who lingered, with a haughty stare which must have been particularly offensive to that respectable Parisian menial. For the Corsicans are bad servants, and despise good servitude in others. When the footman had gone, the new-comer turned to Lory, and said, in a low voice -

I saw you at Toulon. I have not seen many faces in my life - for I have spent most of it in the macquis - so I remember those I have once met. I knew the Count de Vasselot when he was a young man, and he was what you are now. You are a de Vasselot."

"Yes," answered Lory.

"I thought so. That is why I followed you from Toulon - spending my last sou to do so."

He stopped. His two hands were in the pockets of his dark corduroy trousers, and he jerked them out with a sudden movement, bringing the empty pockets to view.

"Voilà!" he said, "and I want to go to the war. So I came to you."

"Good," said Lory, looking him up and down. "You look tough, mon ami."

"I am," answered the Corsican. "Ten years of macquis, winter and summer - for one thing or another - do not make a man soft. I was told - the Abbé Susini told me - that France wants every man she can get, so I thought I would try a little fighting."

"Good," said Lory again. "You will find it very good fun."

The man gave a twisted grin. He had forgotten how to laugh. He drew forward the chair that Denise had just quitted, and sat down close to Lory in quite a friendly way, for there is a bond that draws fighting men and roaming men together despite accidental differences of station.

"One sees," he said, "that you are a de Vasselot. And I belong to the de Vasselots - ! Whenever I have got into trouble it has been on that side."

He looked round to make sure that none could overhear.

"It was I who shot that Italian dog, Pietro Andrei," he mentioned in confidence, "on the road below Olmeta - but that was a personal matter."

"Ah!" said Lory, who had heard the story of Andrei's death on the market-place at Olmeta, and the stern determination of his widow to avenge it.

"Yes - I was starving, and Andrei had money on him. In the old days it was easy enough to get food in the macquis. One could come down into the villages at night. But now it is different. It is a hard life there now, and one may easily die of starvation. There are many who, like Pietro Andrei, are friendly with the gendarmes."

He finished with a gesture of supreme disgust, as if friendship with a gendarme were the basest of crimes.

"When did you see the Abbé Susini?" asked Lory. "and where - if you can tell me that?"

"I saw him in the macquis. He often goes up into the mountains alone, dressed like one of us. He is a queer man, that abbé. He says that he sometimes thinks it well to care for the wanderers from his flock - a jest, you see."

And the man gave his crooked grin again.

"It was above Asco, in the high mountains near Cinto," he continued, "and about a week ago. It was he who gave me money, and told me to come and fight for France. He was arranging for others to do the same."

"The abbé is a practical man," said Lory.

"Yes - and he told me news of Olmeta," said the man, glancing sideways at his companion.

"What news?"

"You have no doubt heard it - of Vasselot."

"I have heard nothing, my friend, but cannon. I am from Sedan to-day."

The man seemed to hesitate. He turned uneasily in his chair, glanced this way and that among the trees - a habit acquired in the macquis, no doubt. He took off his hat and passed his hand pensively over his hair. Then he turned to Lory.

"There is no longer a Château de Vasselot - it is gone - burnt to the ground, mon brave monsieur."

"Who burnt it?" asked de Vasselot.

"Who knows?" replied the man. "The Peruccas, no doubt. They have a woman to lead them now!"

The man finished with a short laugh, which was unpleasant to the ear.

Lory thought of the woman who was leading the Peruccas now, who had quitted the chair in which her accuser now sat, a few minutes earlier, and smiled.

"Have you a cigarette?" asked the Corsican, bluntly.

"Yes - but I cannot offer it to you. It is in my right-hand pocket, and my right arm is disabled."

"An arm and a leg, eh?" said the man, seeking in the pocket indicated by Lory, for the neat silver cigarette-case, which he handled with a sort of grand air - this gentleman of the mountain side. "You will smoke also?"

And with his own brown fingers he was kind enough to place a cigarette between de Vasselot's lips. The tobacco-smoke seemed to make him feel still more at home with the head of his clan. For he sat down again and began the conversation in quite a familiar way.

"Who is this Colonel Gilbert of Bastia, who mixes himself up in affairs?" he inquired.

"What affairs, my friend?"

"Well, the affairs of others, it would appear. We hear strange stories in the macquis - and things that one would never expect to reach the mountains. They say that Colonel Gilbert busies himself in stirring up the Peruccas and the de Vasselots against each other - an affair that has slept these thirty years."

"Ah!"

"Yes, and you should know it, you who are the chief of the de Vasselots, and have this woman to deal with; the women are always the worst. The château, they say, was burnt down, and the women disappeared from the Casa Perucca in the same week. The Casa Perucca is empty now, and the Château de Vasselot is gone - at Olmeta they are bored enough, I can tell you."

"They have nothing to quarrel about," suggested Lory.

"Nothing," replied the Corsican, quite gravely.

"And the château was empty when they burnt it?" inquired Lory.

"Yes; it has been empty since I was a boy. I remember it when I went to St. Florent to school, and it was then that I used to see your father, the count. He was powerful in those days - before the Peruccas began to get strong. But they overrun that country now, which is no doubt the reason why you have never been there."

"Pardon me - I was there when the war broke out two months ago."

"Ah! We never heard that in the macquis, though the Abbé Susini must have known it. He knows so much that he does not tell - that abbé."

"Which makes him the strong man he is, mon ami."

"You are right - you are right," said the Corsican, rising energetically. "But I am wasting your time with my talk, and tiring you as well, no doubt."

"Wait a minute," replied Lory, touching the bell that stood on a table by his side. "I will give you a letter to a friend of mine, commanding a regiment in Paris."

The servant brought the necessary materials, and Lory prepared awkwardly to write. His arm was still weak, but he could use his hand without pain. While he was writing, the man sat watching him, and at last muttered an exclamation of wonderment.

"It is a marvel how you resemble the count," he said, "as I remember him thirty years ago, when I was a boy. And do you know, monsieur, I saw an old man the other day for a moment, in passing on the road, above Asco, who brought my heart into my throat. If he had not been dead this score of years it might have been your father - not as I remember him, but as the years would have made him. I was hidden in the trees at the side of the road, and he passed by on foot. He had the air of going into the macquis. But I do not know who he was."

"When was that?" asked de Vasselot, pausing with his pen on the paper.

"That must have been a month ago."

"And you never saw or heard of him again?"

"No," answered the man.

Lory continued to write, his arm moving laboriously on the paper.

"I must have a name - of some sort," he said, "to give my friend, the commandant."

"Ah! I cannot give you my own. Jean Florent - since I came from St. Florent - that will do."

De Vasselot wrote the name, folded and addressed the letter.

"There", he said, "and I wish you good luck. Good luck in war-time may mean gold lace on your sleeve in a few months. I shall join you as soon as I can throw my leg across a horse. Will two hundred francs serve you to reach Paris?"

"Give me one hundred. I am no beggar."

He took the letter and the bank note, shook hands, and went away as abruptly as he came. The man was a murderer, with probably more than one life to account for; and yet he carried his crimes with a certain dignity, and had, at all events, that grand manner which comes from the habit of facing life fearlessly with the odds against.

Lory sat up and watched him. He rang the bell.

"See that man off the premises," he said to the servant, "and then beg Mademoiselle Lange to be good enough to return here."

Denise kept him waiting a long time, and then came with reluctant steps. The mention of Corsica seemed to have changed her humour. She sat down, nevertheless, in the chair, placed there by Fate.

"You sent for me," she said, rather curtly.

"Because I could not come myself," he answered. "I did not want you to see that man. Or rather, I did not want him to see you. He is not one of your people - quite the contrary."

And de Vasselot laughed with significance.

"One of yours?" she suggested.

"So it appears, though I was not aware of the honour. He described you as 'that woman.'"

Denise laughed lightly, and threw back her head.

"He may describe me as he likes. Did he bring you news?"

And Denise turned away as she spoke, with that air of indifference which so often covers a keen desire for information, if it is a woman who seeks it.

"Yes," answered Lory, turning, as she turned, to look at her. He looked at her whenever opportunity offered. The cheek half turned from him was a little sunburnt, the colour of a peach that has ripened in the open under a Southern sun, for Denise loved the air. Perhaps he had only spoken the truth when he said that her absence made him tired. There are many in the world who have to fight against that weariness all their lives. At last, as if with an effort, Denise turned, and met his glance for a moment.

"Bad news," she said; "I can see that."

"Yes. It is bad enough."

"Of your estates?" inquired Denise.

"No. I never cared for the estate; I do not care for it now."

"Then it is of ... some one?"

Lory did not answer at once.

"I shall have to go back to Corsica," he said at length, "as soon as I can move - in a few days."

Denise glanced at him with angry eyes.

"I was told that story," she said, "but did not believe it."

De Vasselot turned and looked at her, but could not see her averted face. His eyes were suddenly fierce. He was a fighter - of a fighting stock - and he instantly perceived that he was called upon at this moment to fight for the happiness of his whole life. He put out his hand and deliberately took hold of the skirt of her dress. She should not run away at all events. He twisted the soft material round his half-disabled fingers.

"What story?" he asked quietly.

Denise's eyes flashed, and then suddenly grew gentle. She did not quite know whether she was furious or afraid.

"That there was some one in the Château de Vasselot to whom - whom you loved."

"It is you that I love, mademoiselle," he answered sharply, with a ring in his voice, which came as a surprise to both of them, and which she never forgot all her life. "No. Do not go. You are pulling on my injured arm and I shall not let go."

Denise sat still, silent and at bay.

"Then who was in the château?" she asked at last.

"I cannot tell you."

"If it is as you say - about me - and - I ask you not to go to Corsica?"

"I must go."

"Why?" asked Denise, with a dangerous quiet in her voice.

"I cannot tell you."

"Then you expect a great deal."

De Vasselot slowly untwined his fingers and drew in his arm.

"True," he said reflectively. "I must ask nothing or too much. I asked more than you can give, mademoiselle."

A faint smile flickered across Denise's eyes. Who was he, to say how much a woman can give? She was free to go now, but did not move.

"With Corsica and - " she paused and glanced at his helpless attitude in the long chair, - "and the war, your life is surely sufficiently occupied as it is," she said coldly.

"But these evil times will pass. The war will cease, and then one may think of being happy. So long as there is war, I must of course fight - fight - fight, while there is a France to fight for."

Denise laughed.

"That is your scheme of life?" she asked bitterly.

"Yes, mademoiselle."

She rose and turned angrily away.

"Then it is France you care for - if it is no one in Corsica. France - nothing and nobody - but France."

And she left him.

CHAPTER XXII.

IN THE MACQUIS

"Before man made us citizens, great Nature made us men."

The Abbé Susini had no money, but he was a charitable man in a hasty and impulsive way. Even the very poor may be charitable: they can think kindly of the rich. It was not the rich of whom the abbé had a friendly thought, but the foolish and the stubborn. For this fiery little priest knew more of the unwritten history of the macquis than any in Corsica - infinitely more than those whose business it was.

It is the custom at Ajaccio, and in a smaller way at Bastia, to ignore the darker side of Corsican politics, and the French officials are content with the endeavour to get through their term of office with a whole skin. It is not, as in other islands of the Mediterranean, the gospel of "mañana" which holds good here, but rather the gospel of "So I found it - it will last my time." So, from the préfet to the humblest gendarme, they come, they serve, and they go back rejoicing to France. They strike when absolutely forced to do so, but they commit the most fatal of all administrative errors - they strike gently.

The faults are not all on one side; for the islanders are at once turbulent and sullen. There are many who "keep the country," as the local saying is, and wander year after year in the mountain fastnesses, far above road or pathway, beyond the feeble reach of the law, rather than pay a trifling fine or bend their pride to face a week's imprisonment.

In the macquis, as in better society, there are grades of evil. Some are hiding from their own pride, others are evading a lifelong sentence, while many know that if the gendarme sees them he will shoot at sight - running, standing, sleeping, as a keeper kills vermin. Only a few months ago, on a road over which many tourists must have travelled, a young man of twenty-three was "destroyed" (the official term) by the gendarmes who wanted him for eleven murders. It is commonly asserted that these bandits are not dangerous, that they have no grievance against travellers. A starving man has a grievance against the whole world, and a condemned fratricide is not likely to pick and choose his next victim if tempted by a little money and the chance of escape therewith from the island.

It is, moreover, usual for a man to take to the macquis the moment that he finds himself involved in some trouble, or, it may be, merely under suspicion. From his retreat in the mountains he enters into negotiations with his lawyer, with the local magistrate, with his witnesses, even with the police. He distrusts justice itself, and only gives himself up or faces the tribunal when he has made sure of acquittal or such a sentence as his pride may swallow. Which details of justice as understood in a province of France at the beginning of the century may be read at the Assize terms in those great newspapers, *Le Petit Bastiais* or *Le Paoli Pascal*, by any who have a halfpenny to spend on literature.

It would appear easy enough to exterminate the bandits as one would exterminate wolves or other large game; but in such a country as Corsica, almost devoid of roads, thinly populated, heavily wooded, the expense would be greater than the administration is prepared to incur. It would mean putting an army into the field, prepared and equipped for a long campaign which might ultimately reach the dignity of a civil war. The bandits are not worth it. The whole country is not worth exploiting. Corsica is a small open wound on the great back of France, carefully concealed and only tended spasmodically from time to time at such periods as the health of the whole frame is sufficiently good to permit of serious attention being given to so small a sore. And such times, as the wondering world knows, are few and far between in the history of France.

The law-abiding natives, or such natives as the law has not found out, regard the denizens of the macquis with a tender pity not unmixed with respect. As often as not the bandit is a man with a real grievance, and the poor have a soft place in their hearts for a man with a grievance. And all Corsicans are poor. So all are for the bandits, and every man's hand is secretly or openly against the gendarme. Even in enmity, there is a certain sense of honour among these naïve people. A man will shoot his foe in the back, but he will not betray him to the gendarme. Among a primitive people a man commands respect who has had the courage to take the law into his own hands. Amidst a subject population, he who rebels is not without honour.

It was among these and such as these that the Abbé

Susini sought from time to time his lost sheep. He took a certain pleasure in donning the peasant clothes that his father had worn, and in going to the mountains as his forefathers had doubtless done before him. For every man worthy of the name has lurking in his being a remnant of the barbarian which makes him revolt occasionally against the life of the city and the crowded struggle of the streets, which sends him out to the waste places of the world where God's air is at all events untainted, where he may return to the primitive way of living, to kill and gather with his own hands that which must satisfy his own hunger.

The abbé had never known a very highly refined state of civilization. The barbarian was not buried very deep. To him the voice of the wind through the trees, the roar of the river, the fine, free air of the mountains had a charm which he could not put into words. He hungered for them as the exile hungers for the sight of his own home. The air of houses choked him, as sooner or later it seems to choke sailors and wanderers who have known what it is to be in the open all night, sleeping or waking beneath the stars, not by accident as an adventure, but by habit. Then the abbé would disappear for days together from Olmeta, and vanish into that mystic, silent, prowling world of the macquis. The sights he saw there, the men he met there, were among those things which the villagers said the abbé knew, but of which he never spoke.

During the stirring events of August and September the priest at Olmeta, and Colonel Gilbert at Bastia, watched each, in his individual way, the effect of the news upon a very sensitive populace. The abbé stood on the high-road one night within a stone's throw of Perucca, and, looking down into the great valley, watched the flickering flames consume all that remained of the old Château de Vasselot. Colonel Gilbert, in his little rooms in the bastion at Bastia, knew almost as soon that the château was burning, and only evinced his usual easy-going surprise. The colonel always seemed to be wondering that any should have the energy to do active wrong; for virtue is more often passive, and therefore less trouble.

The abbé was puzzled.

"An empty house," he muttered, "does not set itself on fire. Who has done this? and why?"

For he knew every drift and current of feeling amid his turbulent flock, and the burning of the château of Vasselot seemed to serve no purpose, and to satisfy no revenge. There was some influence at work which the Abbé Susini did not understand.

He understood well enough that a hundred grievances - a hundred unsatisfied vengeances - had suddenly been awakened by the events of the last months. The grip of France was for a moment relaxed, and all Corsica arose from its sullen sleep, not in organized revolt, but in the desire to satisfy personal quarrels - to break in one way or another the law which had made itself so dreaded. The burning of the Château de Vasselot might be the result of some such feeling; but the abbé thought otherwise.

He went to Perucca, where all seemed quiet, though he did not actually ring the great bell and speak to the widow Andrei.

A few hours later, after nightfall, he set off on foot by

the road that leads to the Lancone Defile. But he did not turn to the left at the cross-roads. He went straight on instead, by the track which ultimately leads to Corte, in the middle of the island, and amidst the high mountains. This is one of the loneliest spots in all the lonely island, where men may wander for days and never see a human being. The macquis is thin here, and not considered a desirable residence. In fact, the mildest malefactor may have a whole mountain to himself without any demonstration of violence whatever.

This was not the abbé's destination. He was going farther, where the ordinary traveller would fare worse, and hurried along without looking to the left or right. A half-moon was peeping through an occasional rift in those heavy clouds which precede the autumn rains in these latitudes, and gather with such astonishing slowness and deliberation. It was not a dark night, and the air was still. The abbé had mounted considerably since leaving the cross-roads. His path now entered a valley between two mountains. On either side rose a sharp slope, broken, and rendered somewhat inaccessible by boulders, which had at one time been spilled down the mountain-side by some great upheaval, and now seemed poised in patient expectance of the next disturbance.

Suddenly the priest stopped, and stood rooted. A faint sound, inaudible to a townsman's ear, made him turn sharply to the right, and face the broken ground. A stone no bigger than a hazel nut had been dislodged somewhere above him, and now rolled down to his feet. The dead silence of the mountains closed over him again. There was, of course, no one in sight.

"It is Susini of Olmeta," he said, speaking quietly, as if he were in a room.

There was a moment's pause, and then a man rose from behind a rock, and came silently on bare feet down to the pathway. His approach was heralded by a scent which would have roused any sporting dog to frenzy. This man was within measurable distance of the beasts of the forests. As he came into the moonlight it was perceivable that he was hatless, and that his tangled hair and beard were streaked with white. His face was apparently black, and so were his hands. He had obviously not washed himself for years.

"You here," said the abbé, recognizing one who had for years and years been spoken of as a sort of phantom, living in the summits - the life of an animal - alone.

The other nodded.

"Then you have heard that the gendarmes are being drafted into the army, and sent to France?"

The man nodded again. He had done so long without speech that he had no doubt come to recognize its uselessness in the majority of human happenings. The abbé felt in his pocket, and gave the man a packet of tobacco. The Corsicans, unlike nearly all other races of the Mediterranean, are smokers of wooden pipes.

"Thanks," said the man, in an odd, soft voice, speaking for the first time.

"I am going up into the mountains," said the abbé, slowly, knowing no doubt that men who have lived long with Nature are slow to understand words, "to seek an old man who has recently gone there. He is travelling with a man called Jean, who has the evil eye."

"The Count de Vasselot," said the outlaw, quietly. He touched his forehead with one finger and made a vague wandering gesture of the hand. "I have seen him. You go the wrong way. He is down there, near the entrance to the Lancone Defile with others."

He paused and looked round him with the slow and distant glance which any may perceive in the eyes of a caged wild beast.

"They are all down from the mountains," he said.

Even the Abbé Susini glanced uneasily over his shoulder. These still, stony valleys were peopled by the noiseless, predatory Ishmaels of the macquis. They were, it is true, not numerous at this time, but those who had escaped the clutch of the imperial law were necessarily the most cunning and desperate.

"Buon," he said, turning to retrace his steps. "I shall go down to the Lancone Defile. God be with you, my friend."

The man gave a queer laugh. He evidently thought that the abbé expected too much.

The abbé walked until midnight, and then being tired he found a quiet spot between two great rocks, and lying down slept there until morning. In the leather saddle-bag which formed his pillow he had bread and some meat, which he ate as he walked on towards the

Lancone Defile. Once, soon after daylight, he paused to listen, and the sound that had faintly reached him was repeated. It was the warning whistle of the steamer, the old *Persévérance*, entering Bastia harbour ten miles away. He was still in the shade of the great heights that lay between him and the Eastern coast, and hurried while the day was cool. Then the sun leapt up behind the hazy summits above Biguglia. The abbé looked at his huge silver watch. It was nearly eight o'clock. When he was near to the entrance of the defile he stood in the middle of the road and gave, in his high clear voice, the cry of the goat-herd calling his flock. He gave it twice, and then repeated it. If there were any in the macquis within a mile of him they could not fail to see him as he stood on the dusty road in the sunlight.

He was not disappointed. In a few minutes the closely-set arbutus bushes above the road were pushed aside and a boy came out - an evil-faced youth with a loose mouth.

"It is Jean of the Evil Eye who has sent me," he said glibly, with an eye on the abbé's hands in case there should be a knife. "He is up there with a broken leg. He has with him the old man."

"The old man?" repeated the abbé, interrogatively.

"Yes, he who is foolish."

"Show me the way," said Susini. "You need not look at my hands; I have nothing in them."

They climbed the steep slope that overhung the road, forcing their way through the thick brushwood, stumbling over the chaos of stones. Quite suddenly they came upon a group of men sitting round a smouldering fire where a tin coffee-pot stood amid the ashes. One man had his leg roughly tied up in sticks. It was Jean of the Evil Eye, who looked hard at the Abbé Susini, and then turning, indicated with a nod the Count de Vasselot who sat leaning against a tree. The count recognized Susini and nodded vaguely. His face, once bleached by long confinement, was burnt to a deep red; his eyes were quite irresponsible.

"He is worse," said Jean, without lowering his voice. "Sometimes I can only keep him here by force. He thinks the whole island is looking for him - he never sleeps."

Jean was interrupted by the evil-faced boy, who had risen, and was peering down towards the gates of the defile.

"There is a carriage on the road," he said.

They all listened. There were three other men whom the abbé knew by sight and reputation. One by one they rose to their feet and slowly cocked their old-fashioned single-barrelled guns.

"It is the carriage from Olmeta - must be going to Perucca," reported the boy.

And at the word Perucca, the count scrambled to his feet, only to be dragged back by Jean. The old man's eyes were alight with fear and hatred. He was grasping Jean's gun. The abbé rose and peered down through the bushes. Then he turned sharply and wrenched Jean's firearm from the count's hands.

"They are friends of mine," he said. "The man who shoots will be shot by me."

All turned and looked at him. They knew the abbé and the gun. And while they looked, Denise and Mademoiselle Brun drove past in safety.

CHAPTER XXIII.

AN UNDERSTANDING.

"Keep cool, and you command everybody."

When France realized that Napoleon III had fallen, she turned and rent his memory. No dog, it appears, may have his day, but some cur must needs yelp at his heels. Indeed (and this applies to literary fame as to emperors), it is a sure sign that a man is climbing high if the little dogs bark below.

And the little dogs and the curs remembered now the many slights cast upon them. France had been betrayed - was ruined. The twenty most prosperous years of her history were forgotten. There was a rush of patriots to Paris, and another rush of the chicken-hearted to the coast and the frontier.

The Baron de Mélide telegraphed to the baroness to quit Fréjus and go to Italy. And the baroness telegraphed a refusal to do so.

Lory de Vasselot fretted as much as one of his buoyant nature could fret under this forced inactivity. The sunshine, the beautiful surroundings, and the presence of friends, made him forget France at times, and think only of the present. And Denise absorbed his thoughts of the present and the future. She was a constant puzzle to him. There seemed to be two Denise Langes: one who was gay with that deep note of wisdom in her gaiety, which only French women compass, with odd touches of tenderness and little traits of almost maternal solicitude, which betrayed themselves at such moments as the wounded man attempted to do something which his crippled condition or his weakness prevented him from accomplishing. The other Denise was clear-eyed, logical, almost cold, who resented any mention of Corsica or of the war. Indeed, de Vasselot had seen her face harden at some laughing reference made by him to his approaching recovery. He was quick enough to perceive that she was endeavouring to shut out of her life all but the present, which was unusual; for most pin their faith on the future until they are quite old, and their future must necessarily be a phantom.

"I do not understand you, mademoiselle," he said, one day, on one of the rare occasions when she had allowed herself to be left alone with him. "You are brave, and yet you are a coward!"

And the resentment in her eyes took him by surprise. He did not know, perhaps, that the wisest men never see more than they are intended to see.

"Pray do not try," she answered. "The effort might delay your recovery and your return to the army."

She laughed, and presently left him. It is one thing to face the future, and another to sit quietly awaiting its approach. The majority of people spoil their lives by going out to meet the future, deliberately converting into a reality that which was only a dread. They call it knowing the worst.

The next morning Mademoiselle Brun, with a composed face and blinking eyes, mentioned casually to Lory that she and Denise were going back to Corsica.

"But why?" cried Lory; "but why, my dear demoiselle?"

"I do not know," answered Mademoiselle Brun, smoothing her gloves. "It will, at all events, show the world that we are not afraid."

De Vasselot looked at her non-committing face and held his peace. There was more in this than a man's philosophy might dream of.

"When do you go?" he asked after a pause.

"To-night, from Nice," was the answer.

And, as has been noted, Denise and mademoiselle arrived at Bastia in the early morning, and drove to the Casa Perucca, in the face of more than one rifle-barrel. Mademoiselle Brun never asked questions, and, if she knew why Denise had returned to Perucca so suddenly, she had not acquired the knowledge from the girl herself, but had, behind her beady eyes, put two and two together with that accuracy of which women have the monopoly. She meekly set to work to make the Casa Perucca comfortable, and took up her horti-cultural labours where she had dropped them.

"One misses the Château de Vasselot," she said one

morning, standing by the open window that gave so wide a view of the valley.

"Yes," answered Denise; and that was all.

Mademoiselle went into the garden with her leather gloves and a small basket. The odd thing about her gardening was, that it was on such a minute scale that the result was never visible to the ordinary eye. Denise had, it appeared, given up gardening. Mademoiselle Brun did not know how she occupied herself at this time. She seemed to do nothing, and preferred to do it alone. Returning to the house at midday, mademoiselle went into the drawing-room, and there found Denise and Colonel Gilbert seated at the table with some papers, and a map spread out before them.

Both looked up with a guilty air, and Denise flushed suddenly, while the colonel bit his lip. Immediately he recovered himself, and rising, shook hands with the new-comer.

"I heard that you had returned," he said, "and hastened to pay my respects."

"We were looking at the plans," added Denise, hurriedly. "I have agreed to sell Perucca to Colonel Gilbert - as you have always wished me to do."

"Yes; I have always wished you do it," returned Mademoiselle Brun, slowly. She was very cool and collected, and in that had the advantage over her companions. "Has the colonel the money in his pocket?" she asked with a dry smile. "Is it to be settled this afternoon?"

She glanced from one to the other. If love is blind, he certainly tampers with the sight of those who have had dealings with him. Denise was only thinking of Perucca. She had not perceived that Colonel Gilbert was honestly in love with her. But Mademoiselle Brun saw it. She was wondering - if this thing had come to Gilbert twenty years earlier - what manner of man it might have made of him. It was a good love. Mademoiselle saw that quite clearly. For a dishonest man may at any moment be tripped up by an honest passion. Which is one of those practical jokes of Fate that break men's hearts.

"You know as well as I do," said Colonel Gilbert, with more earnestness than he had ever shown, "that the sooner you and mademoiselle are out of the island the better."

"Bah!" laughed mademoiselle. "With you at Bastia to watch over us, mon colonel! Besides, we Peruccas are invincible just now. Have we not burnt down the Château de Vasselot?"

Gilbert winced. Mademoiselle wondered why.

"I want it settled as soon as possible," put in Denise, turning to the papers. "There is no need of delay."

"None," acquiesced mademoiselle. She wanted to sell Perucca and be done with it, and with the island. She was a woman of iron nerve, but the gloom and loneliness of Corsica had not left her at ease. There was a haunting air of disaster that seemed to brood over the whole land, with its miles and miles of untenanted mountains, its malarial plains, and deserted seaboard. "None," she repeated. "But such transactions are not to be carried through, in a woman's drawing-room, by two women and a soldier."

She looked from one to the other. She did not know why one wanted to buy and the other to sell. She only knew that her own inclination was to give them every assistance, and to give it even against her better judgment. It could only be, after all, the question of a little more or a little less profit, and she, who had never had any money, knew that the possession of it never makes a woman one whit the happier.

"Then," said the colonel with his easy laugh - for he was inimitable in the graceful art of yielding - "Then, let us appoint a day to sign the necessary agreements in the office of the notary at Bastia. I tell you frankly I want to get you out of the island."

The colonel stayed to lunch, and, whether by accident or intention, made a better impression than he had ever made before. He was intelligent, easy, full of information and *o rara avis!* proved himself to be a man without conceit. He never complained of his ill-fortune in life, but his individuality thrust the fact into every mind, that this was a man destined for distinction who had missed it. He seemed to be riding through life for a fall, and rode with his chin up, gay and *debonnaire*.

Mademoiselle Brun felt relieved by the thought that the end of Corsica, and this impossible Casa Perucca, was in sight. She was gay as a little grey mouse may be gay at some domestic festival. She sent the widow to the cellar, and the occasion was duly celebrated in a bottle of Mattei Perucca's old wine.

With coffee came the question of fixing a date for the

signature of the deed of sale at the notary's office at Bastia. And instantly the mouse skipped, as it were, into a retired corner of the conversation and crouched silent, watching with bright eyes.

"I should like it to be done soon," said the colonel, who, at the suggestion of his hostess, had lighted a cigarette. He seemed more himself with a cigarette between his fingers to contemplate with a dreamy eye, to turn and twist in reflective idleness. "You will understand that my future movements are uncertain if, as now seems possible, the war is not over."

"But surely it is over," put in Denise, quickly.

The colonel shrugged his shoulders.

"Who can tell? We are in the hands of a few journalists and lawyers, mademoiselle. If the men of words say 'Resist,' we others are ready. I have applied to be relieved of my command here, since they are going to fortify Paris. Shall we say next week?"

"To-day is Thursday - shall we say Monday?" replied Denise.

"Make it Wednesday," suggested Mademoiselle Brun from her silent corner.

And after some discussion Wednesday was finally selected. Mademoiselle Brun had no particular reason why it should be Wednesday, in preference to Monday, and, unlike most people in such circumstances, advanced none.

"We shall require witnesses," she said as the colonel

took his leave. "I shall be able to find two to testify to the signature of Denise."

The colonel had apparently forgotten this necessity. He thanked her and departed.

"And on Wednesday," he said, "I shall in reality have the money in my pocket."

During the afternoon mademoiselle announced her intention of walking to Olmeta. It would be advisable to secure the Abbé Susini as a witness, she said. He was a busy man, and a journey to Bastia would of necessity take up his whole day. Denise did not offer to accompany her, so she set out alone at a quick pace, learnt, no doubt, in the Rue des Saints Pères.

"They will not shoot at an old woman," she said, and never looked aside.

The priest's housekeeper received her coldly. Yes the abbé was at home, she said, holding the door ajar with scant hospitality. Mademoiselle pushed it open and went into the narrow passage. She had not too much respect for a priest, and none whatever for a priest's housekeeper, who kept a house so badly. She looked at the dirty floor, and with a subtle feminine irony, sought the mat which was lying in the road outside the house. She folded her hands at her waist, and still grasping her cheap cotton umbrella, waited to be announced.

The Abbé Susini received her in his little bare study, where a few newspapers, half a dozen ancient volumes of theology and a life of Napoleon the Great, represented literature. He bowed silently and drew forward his own horsehair armchair. Mademoiselle

Brun sat down, and crossed her hands upon the hilt of her umbrella like a soldier at rest under arms. She waited until the housekeeper had closed the door and shuffled away to her own quarters. Then she looked the resolute little abbé straight in the eyes.

"Let us understand each other," she said.

"Bon Dieu! upon what point, mademoiselle?"

Mademoiselle was still looking at him. She perceived that there were some points upon which the priest did not desire to be understood. She held up one finger in its neutral-coloured cotton glove, and shook it slowly from side to side.

"None of your theology," she said; "I come to you as a man - the only man I think in this island at present."

"At present?"

"Yes, the other is in France, recovering from his wounds."

"Ah!" said the abbé, glancing shrewdly into her face. "You also have perceived that he is a man - that. But there is our good Colonel Gilbert. You forget him."

"He would have made a good priest," said mademoiselle, bluntly, and the abbé laughed aloud.

"Ah! but you amuse me, mademoiselle. You amuse me enormously." And he leant back to laugh at his ease.

"Yes, I came on purpose to amuse you. I came to tell

you that Denise Lange has sold Perucca to Colonel Gilbert."

"Sacred name of - thunder," he muttered, the mirth wiped away from his face as if with a cloth. He sat bolt upright, glaring at her, his restless foot tapping on the floor.

"Ah, you women!" he ejaculated after a pause.

"Ah, you priests!" returned Mademoiselle Brun, composedly.

"And you did not stop it," he said, looking at her with undisguised contempt.

"I have no control. I used to have a little; now I have none."

She finished with a gesture, describing the action of a leaf blown before the wind.

"But I have put off the signing of the papers until Wednesday," she continued. "I have undertaken to provide two witnesses, yourself if you will consent, the other - I thought we might get the other from Fréjus between now and Wednesday. A boat from St. Florent to-night could surely, with this wind, reach St. Raphael to-morrow."

The abbé was looking at her with manifest approval.

"Clever," he said - "clever."

Mademoiselle Brun rose to go as abruptly as she had come.

"Personally," she said, "I shall be glad to be rid of Perucca for ever - but I fancied there are reasons."

"Yes," said the priest, slowly, "there are reasons."

"Oh! I ask no questions," she snapped out at him with her hand on the door. On the threshold she paused. "All the same," she said, "I do ask a question. Why does Colonel Gilbert want to buy?"

The priest threw up his hands in angry bewilderment.

"That is it!" he cried. "I wish I knew."

"Then find out," said mademoiselle, "between now and Wednesday."

And with a curt nod she left him.

CHAPTER XXIV.

CE QUE FEMME VEUT.

"All nature is but art, unknown to thee!
All chance, direction which thou canst not see."

It rained all night with a semi-tropical enthusiasm. The autumn rains are looked for in these latitudes at certain dates, and if by chance they fail, the whole winter will be disturbed and broken. With sunrise, however, the clouds broke on the western side of the island, and from the summit of the great Perucca rock the blue and distant sea was visible through the grey confusion of mist and cloud. The autumn had been a dry one, so the whole mountain-side was clothed in shades of red and brown, rising from the scarlet of the blackberry leaves to the deep amber of the bare rock, where all vegetation ceased. The distant peeps of the valley of Vasselot glowed blue and purple, the sea was a bright cobalt, and through the broken clouds the sun cast shafts of yellow gold and shimmering silver. The whole effect was dazzling, and such as dim Northern eyes can scarce imagine.

Mademoiselle Brun, who had just risen from the table where she and Denise had had their early breakfast of coffee and bread, was standing by the window that opened upon the verandah where old Mattel Perucca had passed so many hours of his life.

"One should build on this spot," she began, "a convalescent home for atheists."

She broke off, and staggered back. The room, the verandah, the whole world it seemed, was shaking and vibrating like a rickety steam-engine. For a moment the human senses were paralyzed by a deafening roar and rattle. Mademoiselle Brun turned to Denise, and for a time they clung to each other; and then Denise, whose strong young arms half lifted her companion from the ground, gained the open window. She held there for a moment, and then staggered across the verandah and down the steps, dragging mademoiselle with her.

There was no question of speech, of thought, of understanding. They merely stood, holding to each other, and watching the house. Then a sudden silence closed over the world, and all was still. Denise turned and looked down into the valley, smiling beneath them in its brilliant colouring. Her hand was at her throat as if she were choking. Mademoiselle, shaking in every limb, turned and sat down on a garden seat. Denise would not sit, but stood shaking and swaying like a reed in a mistral. And yet each in her way was as brave a woman as could be found even in their own country.

Mademoiselle Brun leant forward, and held her head between her two hands, while she stared at the ground between her feet. At last speech caine to her, but not her natural voice.

"I suppose," she said, passing her little shrivelled hand

across her eyes, "that it was an earthquake."

"No," said Denise. "Look!" And she pointed with a shaking finger down towards the river.

A great piece of the mountain-side, comprising half a dozen vine terraces, a few olive terraces, and a patch of pinewood, had fallen bodily down into the river-bed, leaving the slope a bare and scarified mass of rock and red soil. The little Guadelle river, a tributary of the Aliso, was completely dammed. Perucca was the poorer by the complete disappearance of one of its sunniest slopes, but the house stood unhurt.

"No more will fall," said Denise presently. "See; there is the bare rock."

Mademoiselle rose, and came slowly towards Denise. They were recovering from their terror now. For at all events, the cause of it lay before them, and lacked the dread uncertainty of an earthquake. Mademoiselle gave an odd laugh.

"It is the boundary-line between Perucca and Vasselot," she said, "that has fallen into the valley."

Denise was thinking the same thought, and made no answer. The footpath from the château up to the Casa by which Gilbert had come on the day of Mattei Perucca's death, by which he had also ridden to the château one day, was completely obliterated. Where it had crept along the face of the slope, there now rose a bare red rock. There was no longer a short cut from the one house to the other. It made Perucca all the more inaccessible.

"Curious," whispered Mademoiselle Brun to herself, as she turned towards the house. She went indoors to get a hat, for the autumn sun was now glaring down upon them.

When she came out again, Denise was sitting looking thoughtfully down into the valley where had once stood the old château, now gone, to which had led this pathway, now wiped off the face of the earth.

"There is assuredly," she said, without looking round, "a curse upon this country."

Which Seneca had thought eighteen hundred years before, and which the history of the islands steadily confirms.

Mademoiselle was drawing on her gloves, and carried her umbrella.

"I am going down the pathway to look at it all," she said.

There was nothing to be done. When Nature takes things into her own hands, men can only stand by and look. Denise was perhaps more shaken than the smaller, tougher woman. She made no attempt to accompany mademoiselle, but sat in the shade of a mimosa tree, and watched her descend into the valley, now appearing, now hidden, in the brushwood.

Mademoiselle Brun made her way to the spot where the pathway was suddenly cut short by the avalanche of rock and rubble and soil. It happened to be the exact spot where Colonel Gilbert's heavy horse had stumbled months before, where the footpath crossed the bed of a small mountain torrent. A few loosened stones had come bowling down the slope, set free by the landslip. These had fallen on to the pathway, and there shattered themselves into a thousand pieces. Mademoiselle stood among the *débris*. She looked down in order to make sure of her foothold, and something caught her eye. She knelt down eagerly, and then, looking up, glanced round surreptitiously like a thief. She could not see the Casa Perucca. She was alone on this solitary mountain-side. Slowly she collected the *débris* of the broken rock, which was mixed with a red powdery soil.

"Ciel!" she whispered, "Ciel! what fools we have all been!"

She rose from her knees with one clasped handful of rubble. Slowly and thoughtfully she climbed the hill again. On the terrace, where she arrived hot and tired, the widow Andrei met her. The woman had been to the village on an errand, and had returned during made-moiselle's absence.

"The Abbé Susini awaits you in the library," she said. "He asked for you and not for mademoiselle, who has gone to her own garden."

Mademoiselle hurried into the library. The arrival of the abbé at this moment seemed providential, though the explanation of it was simple enough.

"I came," he said, looking at her keenly, "on a fool's errand. I came to ask whether the ladies were afraid."

Mademoiselle gave a chilly smile.

"The ladies were not afraid, Monsieur l'Abbé," she

said. "They were terrified - since you ask."

She went to a side-table and brought a newspaper; for even in her excitement she was scrupulously tidy. She laid it on the table in front of the abbé, rather awkwardly with her left hand, and then, holding her right over the newspaper, she suddenly opened it, and let fall a little heap of stones and soil. Some of the stones had a singular rounded appearance.

The abbé treated her movements with the kindly interest offered at the shrine of childhood or imbecility. It was evident that he supposed that the landslip had unhinged Mademoiselle Brun's reason.

"What is that?" he asked soothingly, contemplating the mineral trophy.

"I think," answered mademoiselle, "that it is the explanation."

"The explanation of what, if one may inquire?"

"Of your precious colonel," said mademoiselle. "That is gold, Monsieur L'Abbé. I have seen similar dirt in a museum in Paris." She took up one of the pebbles. "Scrape it with your knife," she said, handing it to him.

The abbé obeyed her, and volunteered on his own account to bite it. He handed it back to her with the marks of his teeth on it, and one side of it scraped clean showing pure gold. Then he walked pensively to the window, where he stood with his back turned to her in deep thought for some minutes. At length he turned on his heel and looked at her.

"It began," he said, holding up one finger and shaking it slowly from side to side, which seemed to indicate that his hearer must be silent for a while, "long ago. I see it now."

"Part of it," corrected mademoiselle, inexorably.

"He must have discovered it two years ago when he first surveyed this country for the proposed railway. I see now why that man from St. Florent shot Pietro Andrei on the high-road. Pietro Andrei was in the way, and a little subtle revival of a forgotten vendetta secured his removal. I see now whence came the anonymous letter intended to frighten Mattei Perucca away from here. It frightened him into the next world."

"And I see now," interrupted the refractory listener, "why Denise received an offer for the estate before she had become possessed of it, and an offer of marriage before we had been here a month. But he tripped and fell then," she concluded grimly.

"And all for money," said the abbé, contemptuously.

"Wait," said mademoiselle - "wait till you have yourself been tempted. So many fall. It must be greater than we think, that temptation. You and I perhaps have never had it."

"No," replied the abbé, simply. "There has never been more than a sou in my poor-box at the church. I see now," continued Susini, "who has been stirring up this old strife between the Peruccas and the Vasselots - offering, as he was, to buy from one and the other alternately. This *dirt*, mademoiselle, must lie on both estates."

"It lies between the two."

The priest was deep in thought, rubbing his stubbly chin with two fingers.

"I see so much now," he said at length, "which I never understood before."

He turned towards the window, and looked down at the rocky slope with a new interest.

"There must be a great quantity of it," he said reflectively. "He has walked over so many obstacles to get to it, with his pleasant laugh."

"He has walked over his own heart," said mademoiselle, persistently contemplating the question from the woman's point of view.

The priest moved impatiently.

"I was thinking of men's lives," he said. Then he turned and faced her with a sudden gleam in his eye. "There is one thing yet unexplained - the burning of the Château de Vasselot. An empty house does not ignite itself. Explain me that."

Mademoiselle shrugged her shoulders.

"That still remains to be explained," she said. "In the mean time we must act."

"I know that - I know that," he cried. "I have acted! I am acting! De Vasselot arrives in Corsica to-morrow night. A letter from him crossed the message I sent to him by a special boat from St. Florent last night."

"What brings him here?"

The abbé turned and looked at her with scorn.

"Bah!" he cried. "You know as well as I. It is the eyes of Mademoiselle Denise."

He took his hat and went towards the door.

"On Wednesday morning, if you do not see me before, at the office of the notary, in the Boulevard du Palais at Bastia," he said. "Where there will be a pretty salad for Mister the Colonel, prepared for him by a woman and a priest - eh! Both your witnesses shall be there, mademoiselle - both."

He broke off with a laugh and an upward jerk of the head.

"Ah! but he is a pretty scoundrel, your colonel."

"He is not my colonel," returned Mademoiselle Brun. "Besides, even he has his good points. He is brave, and he is capable of an honest affection."

The priest gave a scornful laugh.

"Ah! you women," he cried. "You think that excuses everything. You do not know that if it is worth anything it should make a man better instead of worse. Otherwise it is not worth a snap of my finger - your honest affection."

And he came back into the room on purpose to snap his finger, in his rude way, quite close to Mademoiselle Brun's parchment face.

CHAPTER XXV.

ON THE GREAT ROAD.

"Look in my face; my name is Might-Have-Been.
I am also called No More, Too Late, Farewell,"

"This," said the captain of the Jane, the Baron de Mélide's yacht, "is the bay of St. Florent. We anchor a little further in."

"Yes," answered Lory, who stood on the bridge beside the sailor, "I know it. I am glad to see it again - to smell the smell of Corsica again."

"Monsieur le Comte is attached to his native country?" suggested the captain, consulting the chart which he held folded in his hand.

De Vasselot was looking through a pair of marine glasses across the hills to where the Perucca rock jutted out of the mountain side.

"No; I hate it. But I am glad to come back," he said.

"Monsieur will be welcomed by his people. It is a great power, the voice of the people." For the captain was a Republican.

"It is the bleating of sheep, mon capitaine," returned de Vasselot, with a laugh.

They stood side by side in silence while the steamer crept steadily forward into the shallow bay. Already a boat had left the town wall, and was sailing out leisurely on the evening breeze towards them. It came alongside. De Vasselot gave some last instructions to the captain, said farewell, and left the ship. It was a soldier's breeze, and the boat ran free. In a few minutes de Vasselot stepped ashore. The abbé was waiting for him at the steps. It was almost dark, but de Vasselot could see the priest's black eyes flashing with some new excitement. De Vasselot held out his hand, but Susini made a movement, of which the new-comer recognized the significance in his quick way. He took a step forward, and they embraced after the manner of the French.

"Voilà!" said the abbé, "we are friends at last."

"I have always known that you were mine," answered Lory.

"Good. And now I have bad news for you. A friend's privilege, Monsieur le Comte."

"Ah," said Lory, looking sharply at him.

"Your father. I have found him and lost him again. I found him where I knew he would be, in the macquis, living the life that they live there, with perfect tranquillity. Jean was with him. By some means or other Jean got wind of a proposed investigation of the château. The Peruccas people have been stirred up lately; but that is a long story which I cannot tell you now. At all events, they quitted the château a few hours before the house was mysteriously burnt down. To-day I received a message from Jean. Your father left their camp before daybreak to-day. All night he had been restless. He was in a panic that the Peruccas are seeking him. He is no longer responsible, mon ami; his mind is gone. From his muttered talk of the last few days, they conclude that he is making his way south to Bonifacio, in order to cross the straits from there to Sardinia. He is on foot, alone, and deranged. There is my news."

"And Jean?" asked de Vasselot, curtly; for he was quick in decision and in action.

"Jean has but half recovered from an accident. The small bone of his leg was broken by a fall. He is following on the back of an old horse which cannot trot, the only one he could procure. I have ready for you a good horse. You have but to follow the track over the mountains due south - you know the stars, you, who are a cavalry officer - until you join the Corte road at Ponte Alle Leccia, then there is but the one road to Bocognano. If you overtake your poor father, you have but to detain him until Jean comes up. You may trust Jean to bring him safely back to the yacht here as arranged. But you must be at Bastia at the Hotel Clément at ten o'clock on Wednesday morning. That is absolutely necessary. You understand - life or death, you must be there. I and a woman, who is clever enough, are mixing a salad for some one at Bastia on Wednesday morning, and it is you who are the vinegar."

"Where is the horse?" asked Lory.

"It is a few paces away. Come, I will show you."

"Ah!" cried Lory, whose voice had a ring of excitement in it that always came when action was imminent. "But I cannot go at that pace. It is not only Jean who has but one leg. Your arm - thank you. Now we can go."

And he limped by the side of Susini through the dark alleys of St. Florent. The horse was waiting for them beneath an archway which de Vasselot remembered. It was the entry to the stable where he had left his horse on the occasion of his first arrival in Corsica.

"Aha!" he said, with a sort of glee as he settled himself in the saddle. "It is good to be across a horse again. Pity you are a priest; you might come with me. It will be a fine night for a ride. What a pity you are a priest! You were not meant for one, you know."

"I am as the good God made me, and a little worse," returned Susini. "That is your road."

And so they parted. Lory rode on, happy in that he was called upon to act without too much thought. For those who think most, laugh least. De Vasselot's life had been empty enough until the outbreak of the war, and now it was full to overflowing. And though France had fallen, and he himself, it would appear, must be a pauper; though his father must inevitably be a living sorrow, which one who tasted it has told us is worse than a dead one; though Denise would have nothing to say to him, - yet he was happier than he had ever been. He was wise enough not to sift his happiness. He had never spoken of it to others. It is wise not to confide one's happiness to another; he may pull it to pieces in his endeavour to find out how it is made.

The onlooker may only guess at the inner parts of another's life; but at times one may catch a glimpse of the light that another sees. And it is, therefore, to be safely presumed that Lory de Vasselot found a certain happiness in the unswerving execution of his duty. Not only as a soldier, but as a man, he rejoiced in a strict sense of duty, which, in sober earnest, is one of the best gifts that a man may possess. He had not inherited it from father or mother. He had not acquired it at St. Cyr. He had merely received it at second-hand from Mademoiselle Brun, at third-hand from that fat old General Lange who fell at Solferino. For the schoolgirl in the Rue du Cherche-Midi was quite right when she had pounced upon Mademoiselle Brun's secret, which, however, lay safely dead and buried on that battlefield. And Mademoiselle Brun had taught, had shaped Henri de Mélide; and Henri de Mélide had always been Lory de Vasselot's best friend. So the thin silver thread of good had been woven through the web of more lives than the little woman ever dreamt. Who shall say what good or what evil the meanest of us may thus accomplish?

De Vasselot never thought of these things. He was content to go straight ahead without looking down those side paths into which so many immature thinkers stray. He had fought at Sedan, had thrown his life with no niggard hand into the balance. When wounded he had cunningly escaped the attentions of the official field hospitals. He might easily have sent in his name to Prussian head-quarters as that of a wounded officer begging to be released on *parole*. But he cherished the idea of living to fight another day. Denise, with word and glance, and, more potent still, with silence, had tempted him a hundred times to abandon the idea of further service to France. "She does not understand," he concluded; and he threw Denise into the balance. She made it clear to him that he must choose between her and France. Without hesitation he threw his happiness into the balance. For this Corsican - this dapper sportsman of the Bois de Boulogne and Longchamps - was, after all, that creation of which the world has need to be most proud - a man.

Duty had been his guiding light, though he himself would have laughed the gayest denial to such an accusation. Duty had brought him to Corsica. And - for there is no human happiness that is not spiced by duty - he had the hope of seeing Denise.

He rode up the valley of the Guadelle blithely enough, despite the fact that his leg pained him and his left arm ached abominably. Of course, he would find his father - he knew that; and the peace and quiet of some rural home in France would restore the wandering reason. And all was for the best in the best possible world! For Lory was a Frenchman, and into the French nature there has assuredly filtered some of the light of that sunny land.

At more than one turn of the road he looked up towards Perucca. Once he saw a light in one of the windows of the old house. Slowly he climbed to the level of the tableland; and Denise, sitting at the open window, heard the sound of his horse's feet, and wondered who might be abroad at that hour. He glanced at the ruined chapel that towers above the Château de Vasselot on its rocky promontory, and peered curiously down into the black valley, where the charred remains of his ancestral home are to be found to this day. Murato was asleep - a silent group of stone-roofed houses, one of which, however, had seen the birth of a man notorious enough in his day - Fieschi, the would-be assassin of Louis Philippe. Every village in this island has, it would seem, the odour of blood.

The road now mounted steadily, and presently led through the rocky defile where Susini had turned back on a similar errand scarce a week earlier. The rider now emerged into the open, and made his careful way along the face of a mountain. The chill air bespoke a great altitude, which was confirmed by that waiting, throbbing silence which is of the summits. Far down on the right, across rolling ranges of lower hills, a steady pin-point of light twinkled like a star. It was the lighthouse of Punta-Revellata, by Calvi, twenty miles away.

The night was clear and dark. A few clouds lay on the horizon to the south, and all the dome of heaven was a glittering field of stars. De Vasselot's horse was small and wiry - part Arab, part mountain pony - and attended to his own affairs with the careful and surprising intelligence possessed by horses, mules, and donkeys that are born and bred to mountain roads. After Murato the track had descended sharply, only to mount again to the heights dividing the watersheds of the Bevinco and the Golo. And now de Vasselot could hear the Golo roaring in its rocky bed in the valley below. He knew that he was safe now, for he had merely to follow the river till it led him to the high-road at Ponte Alle Leccia. The country here was more fertile, and the track led through the thickest macquis. The subtle scent of flowering bushes filled the air with a cool, soft flavour, almost to be tasted on the lips, of arbutus, myrtle, cistus, oleander, tamarisk, and a score of flowering heaths. The silence here was broken incessantly by the stirring of the birds, which swarm in these berry-bearing coppices.

The track crossed the narrow, flat valley, where, a hundred years earlier, had been fought the last great fight that finally subjugated Corsica to France. Here de Vasselot passed through some patches of cultivated ground - rare enough in this fertile land - noted the shadowy shape of a couple of houses, and suddenly found himself on the high-road. He had spared his horse hitherto, but now urged the willing beast to a better pace. This took the form of an uneven, fatiguing trot, which, however, made good account of the kilometres, and de Vasselot noted mechanically the recurrence of the little square stones every five or six minutes.

It was during that darkest hour which precedes the dawn that he skirted the old capital, Corte, straggling up the hillside to the towering citadel standing out grey and solemn against its background of great mountains. The rider could now see dimly a snow-clad height here and there. Halfway between Corte and Vivario, where the road climbs through bare heights, he paused, and then hurried on again. He had heard in this desert stillness the beat of a horse's feet on the road in front of him. He was not mistaken, for when he drew up to listen a second time there was no sound. The rider had stopped, and was waiting for him. The outline of his form could be seen against the starry sky at a turn in the road further up the mountain-side.

"Is that you, Jean?" cried Lory.

"Yes," answered the voice of the man who rarely spoke.

The two horses exchanged a low, gurgled greeting.

"Are we on the right road? What is the next village?" asked Lory.

"The next is a town - Vivario. We are on the right road. At Vivario turn to the right, where the road divides. He is going that way, through Bocognano and Bastelica to Sartene and Bonifacio. I have heard of him many times, from one and the other."

From one and the other! De Vasselot half turned in his saddle to glance back at the road over which he had travelled. He had seen and heard no one all through the night.

"He procured a horse at Corte last evening," continued Jean. "It seems a good one. What is yours?"

"I have not seen mine," answered de Vasselot; "I can only feel him. But I think there are thirty kilometres in him yet." As he spoke he had his hand in his pocket. "Here," he said. "Take some money. Get a better horse at Vivario and follow me. It will be daylight in an hour. Tell me again the names of the places on the road."

"Vivario, Bocognano, Bastelica, Cauro, Sartene, Bonifacio," repeated Jean, like a lesson.

"Vivario, Bocognano, Bastelica, Cauro, Sartene," muttered de Vasselot, as he rode on.

He was in the great forest of Vizzavona when the day broke, and he saw through the giant pines the rosy tints of sunrise on the summit of Monte D'Oro, from whence at dawn may be seen the coast-line of Italy and France and, like dots upon a map, all the islets of the sea. Still he met no one - had seen no living being but Jean since quitting St. Florent at the other extremity of the island.

It was freezingly cold at the summit of the pass where the road traverses a cleft in the mountain-range, and de Vasselot felt that weariness which comes to men, however strong, just before the dawn ends a sleepless night. The horse, as he had told Jean, was still fresh enough, and gained new energy as the air grew lighter. The mountain town of Bocognano lies below the road, and the scent of burning pinewood told that the peasants were astir. Here de Vasselot quitted the highway, and took a side-road to Bastelica. As he came round the slope of Monte Mezzo, the sun climbed up into the open sky, and flooded the broad valley of the Prunelli with light. De Vasselot had been crossing watersheds all night, climbing out of one valley only to descend into another, crossing river after river with a monotony only varied by the various dangers of the bridges. The valley of the Prunelli seemed no different from others until he looked across it, and perceived his road mounting on the opposite slope. A single horseman was riding southward at a good pace. It was his father at last.

CHAPTER XXVI.

THE END OF THE JOURNEY.

"La journée sera dure,
Mais elle se passera."

At the sight of the horseman on the road in front of him, those instincts of the chase which must inevitably be found in all manly hearts, were suddenly aroused, and Lory surprised his willing horse by using the spurs, of which the animal had hitherto been happily ignorant.

At the same time he made a mistake. He gave an eager shout, quite forgetting that the count had never seen him in uniform, and would inevitably perceive the glint of his accoutrements in the sunlight. The instinct of the macquis was doubtless strong upon the fugitive, There are certain habits of thought acquired in a brief period of outlawry, which years of respectability can never efface. The count, who had lived in secrecy more than half his life, took fright at the sight of a sword, and down the quiet valley of the Prunelli father and son galloped one after the other - a wild and uncanny chase.

With the cunning of the hunted, the count left the road

by the first opening he saw - a path leading into a pine-wood; but over this rough ground the trained soldier was equal to the native-born. The track only led to the open road again at a higher level, and de Vasselot had gained on his father when they emerged from the wood.

Lory had called to his father once or twice, reassuring him, but without effect. The old count sat low in his saddle and urged his horse with a mechanical jerk of the heels. Thus they passed through the village of Bastelica - a place with an evil name. It was early still, and but few were astir, for the peasants of the South are idle. In Corsica, moreover, the sight of a flying man always sends others into hiding. No man wishes to see him, though all sympathies are with him, and the pursuer is avoided as if he bore the plague.

In Bastelica there were none but closed doors and windows. A few children playing in the road instinctively ran to their homes, where their mothers drew them hurriedly indoors. The Bastelicans would have nought to do with the law or the law-breaker. It was the sullen indifference of the crushed, but the unconquered.

Down into the valley, across another river - the southern branch of the Prunelli - and up again. Cauro was above them - a straggling village with one large square house and a little church - Cauro, the stepping-stone between civilization and those wild districts about Sartene where the law has never yet penetrated. Lory de Vasselot had gained a little on the downward incline. He could now see that his father's clothes were mud-stained and torn, that his long white hair was ill-kempt. But the pursuer's horse was tired; for de

Vasselot had been unable to relieve him of his burden all through the night. Lame and disabled, he could not mount or dismount without assistance. On the upward slope, where the road climbs through a rocky gorge, the fugitive gained ground. Out on the open road again, within sight of Cauro, the count's horse showed signs of distress, but gained visibly. The count was unsteady in the saddle, riding heedlessly. In an instant de Vasselot saw the danger. His father was dropping with fatigue, and might at any moment fall from the saddle.

"Stop," he cried, "or I will shoot your horse!"

The count took no notice. Perhaps he did not hear. The road now mounted in a zigzag. The fugitive was already at the angle. In a few moments he would be back again at a higher level. Lory knew he could never overtake the fresher horse. There was but one chance - the chance perhaps of two shots as his father passed along the road above him. Should the gendarmes of Cauro, where there is a strong station, see this fugitive, so evidently from the macquis, with all the signs of outlawry upon him, they would fire upon him without hesitation. Also he might at any moment fall from the saddle and be dragged by the stirrup.

De Vasselot drew across the road to the outer edge of it, from whence he could command a better view of the upper slope. The count came on at a steady trot. He looked down with eyes that had no reason in them and yet no fear. He saw the barrel of the revolver, polished by long use in an inner pocket, and looked fearlessly into it. Lory fired and missed. His father threw back his head and laughed. His white hair fluttered in the wind. There was time for another shot. Lory took a longer aim, remembering to fire low, and horse and rider suddenly dropped behind the low wall of the upper road. De Vasselot rode on.

"It was the horse - it must have been the horse," he said to himself, with misgiving in his heart. He turned the corner at a gallop. On the road in front, the horse was struggling to rise, but the count lay quite still in the dust. Lory dismounted as well as he could. Mechanically he tied the two horses together, then turned towards his father. With his uninjured hand he took the old man by the shoulder and raised him. The dishevelled white head fell to one side with a jerk that was unmistakable. The count was dead. And Lory de Vasselot found himself face to face with that question which so many have with them all through life: the question whether at a certain point in the crooked road of life he took the wrong or right turning.

Death itself had no particular terror for de Vasselot. It was his trade, and it is easier to become familiar with death than with suffering. He dragged his father to the side of the road where a great chestnut tree cast a shadow still, though its leaves were falling. Then he looked round him. There was no one in sight. He knew, moreover, that he was in a country where the report of firearms repels rather than attracts attention. It occurred to him at that moment that his father's horse had risen to its feet - a fact which had suggested nothing to his mind when he had tied the two bridles together. He examined the animal carefully. There was no blood upon it; no wound. The dust was rubbed away from the knees. The horse had crossed its legs and fallen as it started at the second report of his pistol.

Lory turned and stooped over his father. Here again, was no blood - only the evidence of a broken neck.

Still, though indirectly, Lory de Vasselot had killed his father. It was well for him that he was a soldier - taught by experience to give their true value to the strange chances of life and death. Moreover, he was a, Frenchman - gay in life and reckless of its end.

He sat down by the side of the road and remembered the Abbé Susini's words: "Life or death, you must be at Bastia on Wednesday morning."

Mechanically, he drew his watch from within his tunic, which was white with dust. The watch had run down. And when Jean arrived a few minutes later, he found Lory de Vasselot sitting in the shade of the great chestnut tree, by the side of his dead father, sleepily winding up his watch.

"I fired at the horse to lame it - it crossed its legs and fell, throwing him against the wall," he said, shortly.

Jean lifted his master, noted the swinging head, and laid him gently down again.

"Heaven soon takes those who are useless," he said.

Then he slipped his hand within the old man's jacket. The inner pockets were stuffed full of papers, which Jean carefully withdrew. Some were tied together with pink tape, long since faded to a dull grey. He made one packet of them all and handed it to Lory.

"It was for those that they burnt the château," he said; "but we have outwitted them."

De Vasselot turned the clumsy parcel in his hand.

"What is it?" he asked.

"It is the papers of Vasselot and Perucca - your title-deeds."

Lory laid the papers on the bank beside him.

"In your pocket," corrected Jean, gruffly. "That is the place for them."

And while Lory was securing the packet inside his tunic, the unusually silent man spoke again.

"It is Fate who has handed them to you," he said.

"Then you think that Fate has time to think of the affairs of the Vasselots?"

"I believe it, monsieur le comte."

They fell to talking of the past, and of the count. Then de Vasselot told his companion that he must be in Bastia in less than twenty-four hours, and Jean, whose gloomy face was drawn and pinched by past hardships, and a present desire for sleep, was alert in a moment.

"When the abbé says it, it is important," he said.

"But it is easily done," protested de Vasselot, who like many men of action had a certain contempt for those crises in life which are but matters of words. Which is a mistake; for as the world progresses it grows more verbose, and for one moment of action, there are in men's lives to-day a million words.

"It is to be done," answered Jean, "but not easily. You

must ride to Porto Vecchio and there find a man called Casabianda. You will find him on the quay or in the Café Amis. Tell him your name, and that you must be at Bastia by daybreak. He has a good boat."

Lory rose to his feet. There was a light in his tired eyes, and he sighed as he passed his hand across them, for the thought of further action was like wine to him.

"But I must sleep, Jean, I must sleep," he said, lightly.

"You can do that in Casablanda's boat." Answered Jean, who was already changing de Vasselot's good saddle to the back of his own fresher horse.

Jean had to lift his master into the saddle, which office the wiry Susini had performed for him at St. Florent fourteen hours earlier. There is a good inn at Cauro where de Vasselot procured a cup of coffee and some bread without dismounting. Jean had given him a list of names, and the route to Porto Vecchio was not a difficult one, though it led through a deserted country. By midday, de Vasselot caught sight of the Eastern sea; by three o'clock he saw the great gulf of Porto Vecchio, and before sunset he rode, half-asleep, into the ancient town with its crumbling walls and ill-paved streets. He had ridden in safety through one of the waste places of this province of France - a canton wherein a few years ago a well-known bandit had forbidden the postal service, and that postal service was not - and he knew enough to be aware that the mysterious messengers of the macquis had cleared the way before him. But de Vasselot only fully realized the magic of his own name when he at length found the man, Casabianda - a scoundrel whose personal appearance must assuredly have condemned him without further evidence in any court of justice except a Corsican court - who bowed before him as before a king, and laid violent hands upon his wife and daughter a few minutes later because the domestic linen chest failed to rise to the height of a clean table cloth.

The hospitality of Casabianda outlasted the sun. He had the virtues of his primitive race, and that appreciation of a guest which urges the entertainer to give not only the best that he has, but the best that he can borrow or steal.

"There is no breeze," said this Porto Vecchian, jovially; "it will come with the night. In waiting, this is wine of Balagna."

And he drank perdition to the Peruccas.

With nightfall they set sail; the great lateen swinging lazily under the pressure of those light airs that flit to and fro over the islands at evening and sunrise. All the arts of civilization have as yet failed to approach the easiest of all modes of progression and conveyance – sailing on a light breeze. For here is speed without friction, passage through the air without opposition, for it is the air that urges. Afloat, Casabianda was a silent man. His seafaring was of a surreptitious nature, perhaps. For companion, he had one with no roof to his mouth, whose speech was incomprehensible - an excellent thing in law-breakers.

De Vasselot was soon asleep, and slept all through that quiet night. He awoke to find the dawn spreading its pearly light over the sea. The great plain of Biguglia lay to the left under a soft blanket of mist, as deadly they say, as any African miasma, above which the distant mountains raised summits already tinged with rose. Ahead and close at hand, the old town of Bastia jutted out into the sea, the bluff Genoese bastion concealing the harbour from view. De Vasselot had never been to Bastia, which Casabianda described as a great and bewildering city, where the unwary might soon lose himself. The man of incomprehensible speech was, therefore, sent ashore to conduct Lory to the Hotel Clément. Casabianda, himself, would not land. The place reeked, he said, of the gendarmerie, and was offensive to his nostrils.

Clément had not opened his hospitable door. The street door, of course, always stood open, and the donkey that lived in the entrance-hall was astir. Lory dismissed his guide, and after ringing a bell which tinkled rather disappointingly just within the door, sat down patiently on the stairs to wait. At length the ancient chambermaid (who is no servant, but just a woman, in the strictly domestic sense of that fashionable word) reluctantly opened the door. French and Italian were alike incomprehensible to this lady, and de Vasselot was still explaining with much volubility, and a wealth of gesture, that the man he sought wore a tonsure, when Clément himself, affable and supremely indifferent to the scantiness of his own attire, appeared.

"Take the gentleman to number eleven," he commanded; "the Abbé Susini expects him."

The last statement appeared to be made with that breadth of veracity which is the special privilege of hotel-keepers all the world over; for the abbé was asleep when Lory entered his apartment. He awoke, however, with a characteristic haste, and his first conscious movement was suggestive of a readiness to defend himself against attack.

"Ah!" he cried, with a laugh, "it is you. You see me asleep."

"Asleep, but ready," answered de Vasselot, with a laugh. He liked a quick man.

Without speaking, he unbuttoned his tunic and threw his bundle of papers on the abbé's counterpane.

"Voilà!" he said. "I suppose that is what you want for your salad."

"It is what Jean and I have been trying to get these three months," answered the priest.

He sat up in bed, and from that difficult position, did the honours of his apartment with an unassailable dignity.

"Sit down," he said, "and I will tell you a very long story. Not that chair - those are my clothes, my best soutane for this occasion - the other. That is well."

CHAPTER XXVII.

THE ABBÉ'S SALAD.

"He either fears his fate too much,
Or his deserts are small,
That dares not put it to the touch
To gain or lose it all."

"And mademoiselle's witnesses?" inquired the notary, when he had accommodated the ladies with chairs.

"Will arrive at ten o'clock," answered Mademoiselle Brun, with a glance at the notary's clock.

It was three minutes to ten. The notary was a young man, with smooth hair brushed straight back from a high forehead. He was one of those men who look clever, which, in some respects, is better than being clever. For a man who really has brains usually perceives his own limitations, while he who looks clever, and is not, has that boundless faith in himself which serves to carry men very far in a world which is too lazy to get up and kick impertinence as it passes.

The room had that atmosphere of mixed stuffiness and cigarette smoke which the traveller may sample in any French post-office. It is also the official air of a court of justice or a public bureau of any sort in France. There was a blank space on the wall, where a portrait of the emperor had lately hung. The notary would fill it by-and-by with a president or a king, or any face of any man who was for the moment in authority. Behind him, on the wall, was suspended a photograph of an elderly lady - his mother. It established confidence in the hearts of female clients, and reminded persons with daughters that this rising lawyer had as yet no wife.

The notary's bow to Mademoiselle Brun when she was seated was condescending, which betrayed the small fact that he was not so clever as he looked. To Denise he endeavoured to convey in one graceful inclination from the waist the deep regard of a legal adviser, struggling nobly to keep in bounds the overwhelming admiration of a man of heart and (out of office hours) of spirit. Gilbert, who had already exchanged greetings with the ladies, was leaning against the window, playing idly with the blind-cord. The notary's office was on the third floor. The colonel could not, therefore, see the pavement without leaning out, and the window was shut. Mademoiselle Brun noted this as she sat with crossed hands. She also remembered that the Hotel Clément was on the same side of the Boulevard du Palais as the house in which she found herself.

The notary had intended to be affable, but he dimly perceived that Denise was what he tersely called in his own mind *grande dame*, and was wise enough to busy himself with his papers in silence. He also suspected that Colonel Gilbert was a friend of these ladies, but he did not care to take advantage of his privilege in the presence of a fourth person, which left an unpleasant flavour on the palate of the smooth-haired lawyer. He glanced involuntarily at the blank space on the wall, and thought of the Republic.

"I have prepared a deed of sale," he said, in a formal voice, "which is as binding on both sides as if the full purchase-money had been exchanged for the title-deeds. All that will remain to be done after the present signature will be the usual legal formalities between notaries. Mademoiselle has but to sign here." And he indicated a blank space on the document.

Mademoiselle Brun was looking at the timepiece on the notary's wall. The town clocks were striking the hour. A knock at the door made the notary turn, with his quill pen still indicating the space for Denise's signature. It was the dingy clerk who sat in a sort of cage in the outer office. After opening the door he stood aside, and Susini came in with glittering eyes and a defiant chin. There was a pause, and Lory de Vasselot limped into the room after him. He was smiling and pleasant as he always was; even, his friends said, on the battlefield.

He looked at Denise, met her eyes for a moment and turned to bow with grave politeness to Gilbert. It was, oddly enough, the colonel who brought forward a chair for the wounded man.

"Sit down," he said curtly.

"These are my witnesses, Monsieur le Notaire," said Mademoiselle Brun.

The abbé was rubbing his thin, brown hands together, and contemplating the notary's table as a greedy man might contemplate a laden board. The notary himself was looking from one to the other. There was something in the atmosphere which he did not understand. It was, perhaps, the presence in the room of a cleverer head than his own, and he did not know upon whose shoulders to locate it. Denise, whose nature was frank and straightforward, was looking at Lory - looking him reflectively up and down - as a mother might look at a son of whose health she refrains from asking. Mademoiselle was gazing at the blank space on the wall, and the colonel was looking at mademoiselle with an odd smile.

He was standing in the embrasure of the window, and at this moment glanced at his watch. The notary looked at him inquiringly; for his attitude seemed to indicate that he expected some one else. And at this moment the music of a military band burst upon their ears. The colonel looked over his shoulder down into the street. He had his watch in his hand. De Vasselot rose instantly and went to the window. He stood beside the colonel, and those in the notary's office could see that they were talking quickly and gravely together, though the music drowned their voices. Behind them, on the notary's table, lay their differences; in front lay that which bound them together with the strongest ties between man and man - their honour and the honour of France. The music died away, followed by the diminishing sound of steady feet. All in the room were silent for a few moments, until the two soldiers turned from the window and came towards the table.

Then the notary spoke: -

"Mademoiselle has but to sign here," he repeated.

He indicated the exact spot, dipped the pen in the ink, and handed it to Denise. She took the pen and half turned towards Lory, as if she knew that he would be the next to speak and wished him to understand once and for all that he would speak in vain.

"Mademoiselle cannot sign there," he said.

Denise dipped the pen into the ink again, but she did not sign.

"Why not?" she asked without looking round, her hand still resting on the paper.

"Because," answered Lory, addressing her directly, "Perucca is not yours to sell. It is mine."

Denise turned and looked straight at Colonel Gilbert. She had never been quite sure of him. He had never appeared to her to be quite in earnest. His face showed no surprise now. He had known this all along, and did not even take the trouble to feign astonishment. The notary gave a polite, incredulous, legal laugh.

"That is an old story, Monsieur le Comte."

At which point Susini so far forgot himself as to make use of a rude local method of showing contempt in pretending to spit upon the notary's floor.

"It is as old as you please," answered Lory, half turning towards Gilbert, who in his turn made a gesture in the direction of the notary, as if to say that the lawyer had received his instructions and knew how to act.

"Of course," said the notary in a judicial voice, "we are aware that the conveyance of the Perucca estate by the late Count de Vasselot to the late Mattei Perucca lacked formality; many conveyances in Corsica lacked formality in the beginning of the century. In many cases possession is the only title-deed. We can point to a possession lasting over many years, which carries the more weight from the fact that the late count and his neighbour Monsieur Perucca were notoriously on bad terms. If the count had been able, he would no doubt have evicted from Perucca a neighbour so unsympathetic."

"You seem," said de Vasselot, quickly, "to be prepared for my objection."

The notary spread out his hands in a gesture that conveyed assent.

"And if I had not come?"

"I regret to say, Monsieur le Comte, that your presence here bears little upon the transaction in hand. You are only a witness. Mademoiselle will no doubt complete the document now."

And the notary again handed Denise a pen.

"Hardly upon a title-deed which consists of possession only."

"Pardon me, but you have even less," said the notary. "If I may remind you of it, you have probably no title-deeds to Vasselot itself since the burning of the château."

"There you are wrong," answered Lory, quietly. And the abbé snapped both fingers and thumbs in a double-barrelled *feu de joie.*

"The count may have possessed title-deeds before his death, thirty years ago," said the notary, with that polite patience in argument which the certain winner alone can compass.

Then the colonel's quiet voice broke into the conversation. His mannerwas politely indifferent, and seemed to plead for peace at any cost.

"I should much like to be done with these formalities," he said - "if I may be allowed to suggest a little promptitude. The troops are moving, as you have heard. In an hour's time I sail for Marseilles with these men. Let us finish with the signatures."

"Let us, on the contrary, delay signing until the war is over," suggested Lory.

"You cannot bring your father to life again, monsieur, and you cannot manufacture title-deeds. Your father, the notary tells us, has been dead thirty years, and the Château de Vasselot has been burnt with all the papers in it. You have no case at all."

Lory was unbuttoning his tunic, awkwardly with one hand.

"But the notary is wrong," he said. "The Château de Vasselot was burnt, it is true, but here are the title-deeds. My father did not die thirty years ago, but yesterday morning, in my arms."

Gilbert smiled gently. His innate politeness obviously forbade him to laugh at this absurd story.

"Then where has he been all these years?" he inquired

with a good-humoured patience.

"In the Château de Vasselot."

There was a dead silence for a moment, broken at length by a movement on the part of Mademoiselle Brun. In her abrupt way she struck herself on the forehead as a fool.

"Yes," testified Susini, brusquely, "that is where he has been."

Denise remembered ever afterwards, that Lory did not look at her at this moment of his complete justification. It was now, and only for a moment, that Colonel Gilbert lost his steady imperturbability. From the time that Lory de Vasselot entered the room he had known that he had inevitably failed. From that instant the only question in his mind had been that of how much his enemies knew. It could not be chance that brought de Vasselot, and the Abbé Susini, and Mademoiselle Brun together to meet him at that time. He had been out-manoeuvred by some one of the three, and he shrewdly suspected by whom. There was nothing to do but face it - and he faced it with a calm audacity. He simply ignored mademoiselle's blinking glance. He met de Vasselot's quick eyes without fear, and smiled coolly in the abbé's fiery face. But when Denise turned and looked at him with direct and honest eyes, his own wavered, and for a brief instant he saw himself as Denise saw him - the bitterest moment of his life. The esteem of the many is nothing compared to the esteem of one.

In a moment he recovered himself and turned towards Lory with his lazy smile.

"Even to a romance there must be some motive," he said. "One naturally wonders why your father should allow his enemy to keep possession of a house and estate which were not his, and why he himself should remain concealed in the Château de Vasselot."

"That is the affair of my father. There was that between him and Mattei Perucca, which neither you nor I, monsieur, have any business to investigate. There are the title-deeds. You have a certain right to look at them. You are therefore at liberty to satisfy yourself that you cannot buy the Perucca estate from Mademoiselle Lange, because it does not belong to Mademoiselle Lange, and never has belonged to her! A fact of which you may have been aware."

"You seem to know much."

"I know more than you suspect," answered de Vasselot. "I know, for instance, your reason for desiring to buy land on the western slope of Monte Torre."

"Ah?"

By way of reply, de Vasselot laid upon the table in front of Colonel Gilbert, the nugget no larger than a pigeon's egg, that Mademoiselle Brun had found in the *débris* of the landslip. The colonel looked at it, and gave a short laugh. He was too indolent a man to feel an acute curiosity. But there were many questions he would have liked to ask at that moment. He knew that de Vasselot was only the spokesman of another who deliberately remained in the background. Lory had not found the gold, he had not pieced together with the patience of a clocksmith the wheels within wheels that

Colonel Gilbert had constructed through the careful years. The whole story had been handed to him whom it most concerned, complete in itself like a barrister's brief, and de Vasselot was not setting it forth with much skill, but bluntly, simply and generously like a soldier.

"Surely I have said enough," were his next words, and it is possible that the colonel and Mademoiselle Brun alone understood the full meaning of the words.

"Yes, monsieur," said Gilbert at length, "I think you have."

And he moved towards the door in an odd, sidelong way. He had taken only three steps, when he swung round on his heel with a sharp exclamation. The Abbé Susini, with blazing eyes - half mad with rage - had flown at him like a terrier.

"Ah!" said the colonel, catching him by the two wrists, and holding him at arm's length with steady northern nerve and muscle. "I know you Corsicans too well to turn my back to one."

He threw the abbé back, so that the little man fell heavily against the table; Susini recovered himself with the litheness of a wild animal, but when he flew at the closed door again it was Denise who stood in front of it.

CHAPTER XXVIII.

GOLD.

"I do believe yourself against yourself,
And will henceforward rather die than doubt."

All eyes were now turned on the notary, who was hurriedly looking through the papers thrown down before him by Lory.

"They have passed through my hands before, when I was a youth, in connection with a boundary dispute," he said, as if to explain his apparent hastiness. "They are all here - they are correct, monsieur."

He was a very quick man, and folding the papers as he spoke, he tied them together with the faded pink tape which had been fingered by three generations of Vasselots. He laid the packet on the table close to Lory's hand. Then he glanced at Denise and fell into thought, arranging in his mind that which he had to say to her.

"It is one of those cases, mademoiselle," he said at length, "common enough in Corsica, where a verbal agreement has never been confirmed in writing. Men who have been friends, become enemies so easily in

Henry Seton Merriman

this country. I cannot tell you upon what terms Mattei Perucca lived in the Casa. No one can tell you that. All that we know is that we have no title-deeds - and that monsieur has them. The Casa may be yours, but you cannot prove it. Such a case tried in a law court in Corsica would go in favour of the litigant who possessed the greater number of friends in the locality. It would go in your favour if it could be tried here. But it would need to go to France. And there we could only look for justice, and justice is on the side of monsieur."

He apologized, as it were, for justice, of which he made himself the representative in that room. Then he turned towards de Vasselot.

"Monsieur is well within his rights - " he said, significantly, " - if he insist on them."

"I insist on them," replied Lory, who was proud of Denise's pride.

And Denise laughed.

The notary turned and looked curiously at her.

"Mademoiselle is able to be amused."

"I was thinking of the Rue du Cherche-Midi in Paris," she said, and the explanation left the lawyer more puzzled than before. She took up her gloves and drew them on.

"Then I am rendered penniless, monsieur?" she asked the notary.

"By me," answered Lory. And even the notary was

silent. It is hard to silence a man who lives by his tongue. But there were here, it seemed, understandings and misunderstandings which the lawyer failed to comprehend.

The Abbé Susini had crossed the room and was whispering something hurriedly to Mademoiselle Brun, who acquiesced curtly and rather angrily. She had the air of the man at the wheel, to whom one must not speak. For she was endeavouring rather nervously to steer two high-sailed vessels through those shoals and quicksands that must be passed by all who set out in quest of love.

Then the abbé turned impulsively to Lory.

"Mademoiselle must be told about the gold - she must be told," he said.

"I had forgotten the gold," answered Lory, quite truthfully.

"You have forgotten everything, except the eyes of mademoiselle," the abbé muttered to himself as he went back to his place near the window. De Vasselot took up the packet of papers and began to untie the tape awkwardly with his one able hand. He was so slow that Mademoiselle Brun leant forward and assisted him. Denise bit her lip and pushed a chair towards him with her foot. He sat down and unfolded a map coloured and drawn in queer angles. This he laid upon the table, and, by a gesture, called Mademoiselle Brun and Denise to look at it. The abbé took a pencil from the notary's table, and after studying the map for a moment he drew a careful circle in the centre of it, embracing portions of the various colours and of the two estates described respectively as Perucca and Vasselot.

"That," he said to Lory, "is the probable radius of it so far as the expert could tell me on his examination of the ground yesterday."

Lory turned to Denise.

"You must think us all mad - at our games of cross-purposes," he said. "It appears that there is gold in the two estates - and gold has accounted for most human madnesses. Where the abbé has drawn this line there lies the gold - beyond the dreams of avarice, mademoiselle. And Colonel Gilbert was the only man who knew it. So you understand Gilbert, at all events."

"You did not know it when I asked your advice in Paris?"

"I learnt it two hours ago from the Abbé Susini; so I hastened here to claim the whole of it," answered Lory, with a laugh.

But Denise was grave.

"But you knew that Perucca was never mine," she persisted.

"Yes, I knew that, but then Perucca was valueless. So soon as I knew its value, I reclaimed it."

"I warn Monsieur de Vasselot that such frankness is imprudent; he may regret it," put in the notary with a solemn face. And Denise gave him a glance of withring pity. The poor man, it seemed, was quite at sea.

"Thank you," laughed de Vasselot. "I only judge myself as the world will judge me. You were very rich, mademoiselle, and I have made you very poor."

Denise glanced at him, and said nothing. And de Vasselot's breath came rather quickly.

"But the Casa Perucca is at your disposal so long as you may choose to live there," he continued. "My father is to be buried at Olmeta to-morrow, but I cannot even remain to attend the funeral. So I need not assure you that I do not want the Casa Perucca for myself."

"Where are you going?" asked Denise, bluntly.

"Back to France. I have heard news that makes it necessary for me to return. Gambetta has escaped from Paris in a balloon, and is organizing affairs at Tours. We may yet make a defence."

"You?" said Mademoiselle Brun. Into the one word she threw, or attempted to throw, a world of contempt, as she looked him up and down, with his arm in a sling, and his wounded leg bent awkwardly to one side; but her eyes glittered. This was a man after her own heart.

"One has one's head left, mademoiselle," answered Lory. Then he turned to the window, and held up one hand. "Listen!" he added.

It was the music of a second regiment marching down the Boulevard du Palais, towards the port, and, as it approached, it was rendered almost inaudible by the shouts of the men themselves, and of the crowd that cheered them. De Vasselot went to the window and opened it, his face twitching, and his eyes shining with excitement.

"Listen to them," he said. "Listen to them. Ah! but it is good to hear them."

Instinctively the others followed him, and stood grouped in the open window, looking down into the street. The band was now passing, clanging out the Marseillaise, and the fickle people cheered the new tricolour, as it fluttered in the wind. Some one looked up, and perceived de Vasselot's uniform.

"Come, mon capitaine," he cried; "you are coming with us?"

Lory laughed, and shouted back - Yes - I am coming."

"See," cried a sergeant, who was gathering recruits as he went - "see! there is one who has fought, and is going to fight again! Vive la France, mes enfants! Who comes? Who comes?"

And the soldiers, looking up, gave a cheer for the wounded man who was to lead them. They passed on, followed by a troup of young men and boys, half of whom ultimately stepped on board the steamer at the last moment, and went across the sea to fight for France.

De Vasselot turned away from the window, and went towards the table, where the papers lay in confusion. The abbé took them up, and began to arrange them in order.

"And the estate and the gold?" he said; "who manages

that, since you are going to fight?"

"You," replied de Vasselot, "since you cannot fight. There is no one but you in Corsica who can manage it. There is none but you to understand these people."

"All the world knows who manages half of Corsica," put in Mademoiselle Brun, looking fiercely at the abbé. But the abbé only stamped his foot impatiently.

"Woman's gossip," he muttered, as he shook the papers together. "Yes; I will manage your estate if you like. And if there is gold in the land, I will tear it out. And there is gold. The amiable colonel is not the man to have made a mistake on that point. I shall like the work. It will be an occupation. It will serve to fill one's life."

"Your life is not empty," said mademoiselle.

The abbé turned and looked at her, his glittering eyes meeting her twinkling glance.

"It is a priest's life," he said. "Come," he added, turning to the lawyer - "come, Mr. the Notary, into your other room, and write me out a form of authority for the Count de Vasselot to sign. We have had enough of verbal agreements on this estate."

And, taking the notary by the arm, he went to the door. On the threshold he turned, and looked at Mademoiselle Brun.

"A priest's life," he said, "or an old woman's. It is the same thing."

And Lory was left alone with mademoiselle and Denise. The window was still open, and from the port the sound of the military music reached their ears faintly. Mademoiselle rose, and went to the window, where she stood looking out. Her eyes were dim as she looked across the sordid street, but her lips were firm, and the hands that rested on the window-sill quite steady. She had played consistently a strong and careful game. Was she going to win or lose? She held that, next to being a soldier, it is good to be a soldier's wife and the mother of fighting men. And when she thought of the Rue du Cherche-Midi, she was not able to be amused, as the notary had said of Denise.

There was a short silence in the notary's office. De Vasselot was fingering the hilt of his long cavalry sword reflectively. After a moment he glanced across at Denise. He was placed as it were between her and the sword. And it was to the sword that he gave his allegiance.

"You see," he said, in a low voice, "I must go."

"Yes, you must go," she answered. She held her lip for a moment between her teeth. Then she looked steadily at him. "Go!" she said.

He rose from his chair and looked towards Mademoiselle Bran's back. At the rattle of his scabbard against the chair, mademoiselle turned.

"There is a horse waiting in the street below," she said - "the great horse that Colonel Gilbert rides. It is waiting for you, I suppose."

"I suppose so," said Lory, who went to the window and

looked curiously down. Gilbert was certainly an odd man. He had left in anger, and had left his horse for Lory to ride. He waited a moment, and then held out his hand to Mademoiselle Brun. All three seemed to move and speak under a sort of oppression. It was one of those moments that impress themselves indelibly on the memory - a moment when words are suddenly useless - when the memory of an attitude and of a silence remains all through life.

"Good-bye, mademoiselle," said Lory, with a sudden cheerfulness; "we shall meet in France next time."

Mademoiselle Brun held out her shrinking little hand.

"Yes, in France," she answered.

To Denise, Lory said nothing. He merely shook hands with her. Then he walked towards the door, haltingly. He used his sword like a walking stick, with his one able hand. Denise had to open the door for him. He was on the threshold, when Mademoiselle Brun stopped him.

"Monsieur de Vasselot," she said, "when the soldiers went past, you and Colonel Gilbert spoke together hurriedly; I saw you. You are not going to fight - you two?"

"Yes, mademoiselle, we are going to fight - the Prussians. We are friends while we have a common enemy. When there is no enemy - who knows? He has received a great appointment in France, and has offered me a post under him. And I have accepted it."

CHAPTER XXIX.

A BALANCED ACCOUNT.

"Let the end try the man."

Bad news, it is said, travels fast. But in France good news travels faster, and it is the evil tidings that lag behind. It is part of a Frenchman's happy nature to believe that which he wishes to be true. And although the news travelled rapidly, that Gambetta - that spirit of an unquenchable hope - had escaped from Paris with full power to conduct the war from Tours, the notification that the army of de la Motterouge had melted away before the advance of von der Tann, did not reach Lory de Vasselot until he passed to the north of Marseilles with his handful of men.

That a general, so stricken in years as de la Motterouge, should have been chosen for the command of the first army of the Loire, spoke eloquently enough of the straits in which France found herself at this time. For this was the only army of the Government of National Defence, the *debris* of Sedan, the hope of France. General de la Motterouge had fought in the Crimea: "Peu de feu et beaucoup de bayonette" had been his maxim then. But the Crimea was fifteen years earlier, and de la Motterouge was now an old man. Before the superior numbers and the perfectly drilled and equipped army of von der Tann, what could he do but retreat?

Thus, on their arrival in France, Colonel Gilbert and Lory de Vasselot were greeted with the news that Orleans had fallen into the hands of the enemy. It was the same story of incompetence pitted against perfect organization - order and discipline meeting and vanquishing ill-considered bravery. All the world knows now that France should have capitulated after Sedan. But the world knows also that Paris need never have fallen, could France only have produced one mediocre military genius in this her moment of need. The capital was indeed surrounded, cut off from all the world; but the surrounding line was so thin that good generalship from within could have pierced it, and there was an eager army of brave men waiting to join issue from the Loire.

It was to this army of the Loire that Colonel Gilbert and de Vasselot were accredited. And it was an amateur army. It came from every part of France, and in its dress it ran to the picturesque. Franctireurs de Cannes rubbed shoulders with Mobiles from the far northern departments. Spahis and Zouaves from Africa bivouacked with fair-haired men whose native tongue was German. There were soldiers who had followed the drum all their lives, and there were soldiers who did not know how to load their chassepots. There were veteran non-commissioned officers hurriedly drilling embryo priests; and young gentlemen from St. Cyr trying to form in line grey-headed peasants who wore sabots. There were fancy soldiers and picturesque fighters, who joined a regiment because its costume appealed to their conception of patriotism. And if a man prefers to fight for his country in the sombrero and cloak of a comic-opera brigand, what boots it so long as he fights well? It must be remembered, moreover, that it is quite as painful to die under a sombrero as under a plainer covering. A man who wears such clothes sees the picturesque side of life, and may therefore hold existence as dear as more practical persons who take little heed of their appearance. For when the time came these gentlemen fought well enough, and ruined their picturesque get-up with their own blood. And if they shouted very loud in the café, they shouted, Heaven knows, as loud on the battle-field, when they faced those hated, deadly, steady Bavarians, and died shouting.

Of such material was the army of the Loire; and when Chanzy came to them from North Africa - that Punjaub of this stricken India from whence the strong men came when they were wanted - when Chanzy came to lead them, they commanded the respect of all the world. For these were men fighting a losing fight, without hope of victory, for the honour of France. They fought with a deadly valour against superior numbers behind entrenchments; they endeavoured to turn the Germans out of insignificant villages after allowing them time to fortify the position. They fought in the open against an invisible enemy superior in numbers, superior in artillery, and here and there they gained a pitiful little hard-earned advantage.

De Vasselot, still unable to go to the front, was put to train these men in a little quiet town on the Loire, where he lodged with a shoemaker, and worked harder than any man in that sunny place had ever worked before. It was his business to gather together such men as could sit a horse, and teach them to be cavalry soldiers. But first of all he taught them that the horse was an animal possessing possibilities far beyond their most optimistic conception of that sagacious but foolish quadruped. He taught them a hundred tricks of heel and wrist, by which a man may convey to a horse that which he wishes him to do. He made the horse and the man understand each other, and when they did this he sent them to the front.

In the meantime France fed herself upon false news and magnified small successes into great victories. Gambetta made many eloquent speeches, and issued fiery manifestoes to the soldiers; but speeches and manifestoes do not win battles. Paris hoped all things of the army of the Loire, and the army of the Loire expected a successful sortie from Paris. And those men of iron, Bismarck, Moltke, and the emperor, sat at Versailles and waited. While they waited the winter came.

De Vasselot, who had daily attempted to use his wounded limbs, at length found himself fit for active service, and got permission to join the army. Gilbert was no longer a colonel. He was a general now, and commanded a division which had already made its mark upon that man of misfortune - von der Tann, a great soldier with no luck.

One frosty morning de Vasselot rode out of the little town upon the Loire at the head of a handful of his newly trained men. He was going to take up his appointment: for he held the command of the whole of the cavalry of General Gilbert's division. These were days of quick promotion, of comet-like reputations and of great careers cut short. De Vasselot had written to Jane de Mélide the previous night, telling her of his movements in the immediate future, of his promotion, of his hopes. One hope which he did not mention was that Denise might be at Fréjus, and would see the letter. Indeed, it was written to Denise, though it was addressed to the Baronne de Mélide.

Then he went blithely enough out to fight. For he was quite a simple person, as many soldiers and many horse-lovers are. He was also that which is vaguely called a sportsman, and was ready to take a legitimate risk not only cheerfully, but with joy.

"It is my only chance of making her care for me," he said to himself. He may have been right or wrong. There is a wisdom which is the exclusive possession of the simple. And Lory may have known that it is wiser to store up in a woman's mind memories that will bear honour and respect in the future, than to make appeal to her vanity in the present. For the love that is won by vanity is itself vanity.

He said he was fighting for France, but it was also for Denise that he fought. France and Denise had got inextricably mixed in his mind, and both spelt honour. His only method of making Denise love him was to make himself worthy of her - an odd, old-fashioned theory of action, and the only one that enables two people to love each other all their lives.

In this spirit he joined the army of the Loire before his wounds had healed. He did not know that Denise loved him already, that she had with a woman's instinct divined in him the spirit, quite apart from the opportunity, to do great things. And most men have to content themselves with being loved for this spirit and not for the performance which, somehow, is so seldom accomplished.

And that which kept them apart was for their further happiness; it was even for the happiness of Denise in case Lory never came back to her. For the majority of people get what they want before they have learnt to desire. It is only the lives of the few which are taken in hand and so fashioned that there is a waiting and an attainment at last.

Lory and Denise were exploring roads which few are called upon to tread - dark roads with mud and stones and many turnings, and each has a separate road to tread and must find the way alone. But if Fate is kind they may meet at the end without having gone astray, or, which is rarer, without being spattered by the mud. For those mud-stains will never rub off and never be forgotten. Which is a hard saying, but a true one.

Lory had left Denise without any explanation of these things. He had never thought of sparing her by the simple method of neglecting his obvious duty. In his mind she was the best of God's creations - a woman strong to endure. That was sufficient for him; and he turned his attention to his horses and his men. He never saw the background to his own life. It is usually the onlooker who sees that, just as a critic sees more in a picture than the painter ever put there.

Lory hardly knew of these questions himself. He only half thought of them, and Denise, far away in Provence, thought the other half. Which is love.

Lory took part in the fighting after Orleans and risked his life freely, as he ever did when opportunity offered. He was more than an officer, he was a leader. And it is better to show the way than to point it out. Although his orders came from General Gilbert, he had never met his commanding officer since quitting the little sunny town on the Loire where he had recovered from his wounds. It was only after Chateaudun and after the Coulmiers that they met, and it was only in a small affair after all, the attempted recapture of a village taken and hurriedly fortified by the Germans. It was a night-attack. The army of the Loire was rather fond of night-fighting; for the night equalizes matters between discipline and mere bravery. Also, if your troops are bad, they may as well be beaten in the dark as in the daylight. The survivors come away with a better heart. Also, discipline is robbed of half its strength by the absence of daylight.

Cavalry, it is known, are no good at night; for horses are nervous and will whinny to friend or foe when silence is imperative. And yet Lory received orders to take part in this night-attack. Stranger things than that were ordered and carried out in the campaign on the Loire. All the rules of warfare were outraged, and those warriors who win and lose battles on paper cannot explain many battles that were lost and won during that winter.

There was a moon, and the ground was thinly covered with snow. It was horribly cold when the men turned out and silently rode to the spot indicated in the orders. These were quite clear, and they meant death. De Vasselot had practically to lead a forlorn hope. A fellow-officer laughed when the instructions were read to him.

"The general must be an enemy of yours," he said. And the thought had not occurred to Lory before.

"No," he replied, "he is a sportsman."

"It is poor sport for us," muttered the officer, riding away.

But Lory was right. For when the moment came and he was waiting with his troopers behind a farm building, a scout rode in to say that reinforcements were coming. As these rode across the open in the moonlight, it was apparent that they were not numerous; for cavalry was scarce since Eeichshofen. They were led by a man on a big horse, who was comfortably muffled up in a great fur-coat.

"De Vasselot," he said in a pleasant voice, as Lory went forward to meet him. "De Vasselot, I have brought a few more to help you. We must make a great splash on this side, while the real attack is on the other. We must show them the way - you and I." And Gilbert laughed quietly.

It was not the moment for greetings. Lory gave a few hurried orders in a low voice, and the new-comers fell into line. They were scarcely in place when the signal was given. A moment later they were galloping across the open towards the village - a sight to lift any heart above the thought of death.

Then the fire opened - a flash of flame like fork-lightning running along the ground - a crashing volley which mowed the assailants like a scythe. Lory and Gilbert were both down, side by side. Lory, active as a cat, was on his legs in a moment and leapt away from the flying heels of his wounded horse. A second volley blazed into the night, and Lory dropped a second time. He moved a little, and cursed his luck. With difficulty he raised himself on his elbow.

"Gilbert," he said, "Gilbert."

He dragged himself towards the general, who was lying on his back.

"Gilbert," he said, with his mouth close to the other's ear, "we should have been friends, you know, all the same, but the luck was against us. It is not for one to judge the other. Do you hear? Do you hear?"

Gilbert lay quite still, staring at the moon with his easy, contemplative smile. His right arm was raised and his great sabre held aloft to show the way, as he had promised, now pointed silently to heaven.

Lory raised himself again, the blood running down his sleeve over his right hand.

"Gilbert," he repeated, "do you understand?" Then he fell unconscious across the general's breast.

CHAPTER XXX.

THE BEGINNING AND THE END.

"I gave - no matter what I gave - I win."

The careful student will find in the back numbers of the *Deutsche Rundschau*, that excellent family magazine, the experiences of a German military doctor with the army of General von der Tann. The story is one touched by that deep and occasionally maudlin spirit of sentimentality which finds a home in hearts that beat for the Fatherland. Its most thrilling page is the description of the finding, by the narrator, of the body of a general officer during a sharp night engagement, across which body was lying a wounded cavalry colonel, who had evidently devoted himself to the defence of his comrade in arms.

The reminiscent doctor makes good use of such compound words as "brother-love" and "though-superior-in-rank-yet-comrade-in-arms-and-companions- in-death-affectionate," which linguistic facility enables the German writer to build up as he progresses in his narration words of a phenomenal calibre, and bowl the reader over, so to speak, at a long range. He finishes by mentioning that the general was named Gilbert, a man of colossal engineering skill, while the wounded officer was the Count Lory de Vasselot, grandson of one of Napoleon's most dashing cavalry leaders. The doctor finishes right there, as the Americans say, and quite forgets to note the fact that he himself picked up de Vasselot under a spitting cross-fire, carried him into his own field hospital and there tended him. Which omission proves that to find a brave and kind heart it is not necessary to consider what outer uniform may cover, or guttural tongue distinguish, the inner man.

Lory was shot in two places again, and the doctors who attended him laughed when they saw the old wounds hardly yet healed. He would be lame for years, they said, perhaps for life. He had a bullet in his right shoulder and another had shattered his ankle. Neither was dangerous, but his fighting days were done, at all events for this campaign.

"You will not fight against us again," said the doctor, with a smile on his broad Saxon features, and in execrable French, which was not improved by the scissors that he held between his lips.

"Not in this war, perhaps," answered the patient, hopefully.

Again the tide of war moved on; and, daily, the cold increased. But its chill was nothing to that cold, slow death of hope that numbed all France. For it became momentarily more apparent that those at the head of affairs were incompetent - that the man upon whom hope had been placed was nothing but a talker, a man of words, an orator, a wind-bag. France, who has usually led the way in the world's progress, had entered upon that period of words - that Age of Talk - in which she still labours, and which must inevitably be the ruin of all her greatness.

For two weeks Lory lay in the improvised German field hospital in that remote village, and made the astounding progress towards recovery which is the happy privilege of the light-hearted. It is said among soldiers that a foe is no longer a foe when he is down, and de Vasselot found himself among friends.

The German doctor wrote a letter for him.

"It will be good practice for my French," said the artless Teuton, quite frankly. And the letter was sent, but never reached its destination. Lory could learn no news, however. In war there are, not two, but three sides to a question. Each combatant has one, and Truth has the third, which she often locks up for ever in her quiet breast.

At last, one morning quite early, a horseman dismounted at the door of the house in the village street, where the hospital flag hung lazily in the still, frosty air "It is a civilian," said an attendant, in astonishment, so rare was the sight of a plain coat at this time. There followed a conversation in muffled voices in the entrance hall; not a French conversation in many tones of voice - but a quiet Teutonic talk as between Germans and Englishmen. Then the door opened, and a man came into the room, removing a fur coat as he came. He was a tall, impassive man, well dressed, wearing a tweed suit and a single eye-glass. He might have been an Englishman. He was, however, the Baron de Mélide, and his manner had that repose which belongs to the new aristocracy of France and to the shreds that remain, here and there, of the old.

"Left my ambulance to subordinates," he explained as he shook Lory's hand. "Humanity is an excellent quality, but one's friends come first. It has taken me some time to find you. Have procured your parole for you. You are quite useless, they say," - the baron eyed Lory with a calm and experienced glance as he spoke - "so they release you on parole. They are not generous, but they have an enormous common sense."

The doctor, who understood French, laughed good-naturedly, and the baron twisted his waxed moustache and looked slightly uncomfortable. He was conscious of having said the wrong thing as usual.

And all the while de Vasselot was talking and laughing, and commenting on his friend's appearance and clothes, and goodness of heart - all in a breath, as was his manner. Also he found time to ask a hundred questions which the stupid would take at least a week to answer, but his answer to each would be the right one.

It was during the great cold of the early days of January, that the baron and Lory turned their backs on that bitter valley of the Loire. They had a cross-journey to Lyons, and there joined a main line train, in which they fell asleep to awake in the brilliant sunshine, amid the cool grey-greens, the bare rocks and dark cypresses of the south. After Marseilles the journey became tedious again.

"Heavens!" cried Lory, impatiently, "what a delay! Why need they stop at this little station at all?"

The baron made no reply just then. The train travelled five miles while he stared thoughtfully at the grey hills.

It was six months since he had seen the vivacious lady who was supposed by this one-eyed world to rule him.

"After all," he said at length, "Fréjus is a little station."

For the baron was a philosopher.

When at last they reached the quiet tree-grown station, where even to this day so few trains stop, and so insignificant a business is transacted, they found the Baroness de Mélide on the platform awaiting them. She was in black, as were all Frenchwomen at this time. She gave an odd little laugh at the sight of her husband, and immediately held her lip between her teeth, as if she were afraid that her laugh might change to something else.

"Ah!" she said, "how hungry you both look - and yet you must have lunched at Toulon."

She looked curiously from one drawn face to the other as the baron helped Lory to descend.

"Hungry," she repeated with a reflective nod. "Perhaps your precious France does not satisfy."

And as she led the way to the carriage there was a gleam, almost fierce, of triumph in her eyes.

The arrival at the château was uneventful. Mademoiselle Brun said no word at all; but stood a little aside with folded hands and watched. Denise, young and slim in her black dress, shook hands and said that she was afraid the travellers must be tired after their long journey.

"Why should Denise think that I was tired?" the baron inquired later, as he was opening his letters in the study.

"Mon ami," replied the baroness, "she did not think you were tired, and did not care whether you were or not."

Lory had the same room assigned to him that opened on to the verandah where heliotrope and roses and Bougainvilliers contended for the mastery. Outside his windows were placed the same table and long chair, and beside the last the other chair where Denise had sat - which had been placed there by Fate. The butler was, it appeared, a man of few ideas. He had arranged everything as before.

After his early coffee Lory went to the verandah and lay down by that empty chair. It was a brilliant morning, with a light keen air which has not its equal all the world over. The sun was powerful enough to draw the scent from the pinewoods, and the sea-breeze swept it up towards the mountains. Lory waited alone in the verandah all the morning. After luncheon the baron assisted him back to his long chair, and all the party came there and drank coffee. Coffee was one of Mademoiselle Brun's solaces in life. "It makes existence bearable," she said - "if it is hot enough." But she finished her cup quickly and went away. The baron was full of business. He received a score of letters during the day. At any moment the preliminaries of peace might now be signe d. He had not even time for a cigarette. The baroness sat for some minutes looking at Lory, endeavouring to make him meet her shrewd eyes; but he was looking out over the plain of Les Arcs. Denise had not sat down, but was standing rather restlessly at the edge of the verandah near the heliotrope which clambered up the supports. She had picked a piece of the delicate flower and was idly smelling it.

At last the baroness rose and walked away without any explanation at all. After a few minutes, which passed slowly in silence, Denise turned and came slowly towards Lory. The chair had never been occupied. She sat down and looked away from him. Her face, still delicately sunburnt, was flushed. Then she turned, and her eyes as they met his were stricken with fear.

"I did not understand," she said. And she must have been referring to their conversation in that same spot months before. She was either profoundly ignorant of the world or profoundly indifferent to it. She ought, of course, to have made some safe remark about the weather. She ought to have distrusted Lory. But he seemed to know her meaning without any difficulty.

"I think a great many people never understand, mademoiselle."

"It has taken me a long time - nearly four months," said Denise, reflectively. "But I understood quite suddenly at Bastia - when the soldiers passed the notary's office. I understood then what life is and what it is meant to be."

Lory looked up at her for a moment,

"That is because you are nearer heaven than I am," he said.

"But it was you who taught me, not heaven," said

Denise. "You said - well, you remember what you said, perhaps - and then immediately after you denied me the first thing I asked you. You knew what was right, and I did not. You have always known what was right, and have always done it. I see that now as I look back. So I have learnt my lesson, you see." She concluded with a grave smile. Life is full of gravity, but love is the gravest part of it.

"Not from me," persisted Lory.

"Yes, from you. Suppose you had done what I asked you. Suppose you had not gone to the war again, what would have become of our lives?"

"Perhaps," suggested Lory, "we have both to learn from each other. Perhaps it is a long lesson and will take all our lives. I think we are only beginning it. And perhaps I opened the book when I told you that I loved you, here in the verandah!"

Denise turned and looked at him with a smile full of pity, and touched with that contempt which women sometimes bestow upon men for understanding so little of life.

"Mon Dieu!" she said, "I loved you long before that."

The sun was setting behind the distant Esterelles - those low and lonesome mountains clad from foot to summit in pine - when Mademoiselle Brun came out into the garden. She had to pass across the verandah, and instinctively turned to look towards that end of it where de Vasselot had come a second time to lie in the sun and heal his wounds - a man who had fought a good fight.

Denise was holding out a spray of heliotrope towards Lory and he had taken, not the flower, but her hand: and thus without a word and unconsciously they told their whole story to mademoiselle.

The little old woman walked on without showing that she had seen and understood. She was not an expansive person.

She sat down at the corner of the lowest terrace and with blinking eyes stared across the great plain of Les Arcs, where north and south meet, where the palm tree and the pine grow side by side, towards the Esterelles and the setting sun. The sky was clear, but for a few little puffs of cloud low down towards the west, like a flock of sheep ready to go home, waiting for the gate to open.

Mademoiselle's thin lips were moving as if she were whispering to the God whom she served with such a remarkable paucity of words. It may have been that she was muttering a sort of grim *Nunc Dimittis* - she who had seen so many wars. "Now lettest Thou Thy servant depart in peace."

www.ingramcontent.com/pod-product-compliance
Lightning Source LLC
Chambersburg PA
CBHW021308250626
47155CB00002B/442